Praise for Liza Palmer's
first novel,
Conversations with the Fat Girl

"Kudos to Liza Palmer."

—*People*

"Engaging and poignant and heartbreakingly real . . . a winning conversation."

—Jennifer Weiner, bestselling author of *Good in Bed,*
In Her Shoes, and *Little Earthquakes*

"The descriptions of Olivia's catty pals are priceless."

—*Entertainment Weekly*

"Smart, funny, and heartbreakingly honest . . . This is one conversation I never wanted to end!"

—Johanna Edwards, author of
The Next Big Thing

"Will connect with women everywhere . . . Palmer's quick wit keeps you laughing."

—*Pasadena Star News*

"Reflective yet riotous, sardonic yet compassionate . . . An accomplished and wonderful debut."

—Amanda Stern, author of *The Long Haul*

more . . .

Also by Liza Palmer

Conversations with the Fat Girl

seeing me naked

Liza Palmer

NEW YORK   BOSTON

5 Spot
Hachette Book Group USA
237 Park Avenue
New York, NY 10017

Visit our Web site at www.5-spot.com.

5 Spot is an imprint of Grand Central Publishing. The 5 Spot name and logo is a trademark of Hachette Book Group USA, Inc.

Printed in the United States of America

First Edition: January 2008
10 9 8 7 6 5 4 3 2 1

Library of Congress Cataloging-in-Publication Data

Palmer, Liza.
   Seeing me naked / Liza Palmer.—1st ed.
     p. cm.
   ISBN-13: 978-0-446-69837-5
   ISBN-10: 0-446-69837-7
  1. Self-actualization (Psychology)—Fiction.   2. Women cooks—Fiction.
I. Title.
   PS3616.A343S44 2008
   813'.6—dc22

                      2007014142

For Grammy and Jack

acknowledgments

In my first book's acknowledgments, I recounted my habit of taking time right as I was falling asleep to give thanks, with held breath, for the people in my life. This habit continues to this day. But with age comes a certain seriousness in those seconds, a seriousness that knows how lucky I am and how families and people like the ones in my life just don't come along that often. Words, my stock-in-trade, can't seem to ever harness my absolute adoration for the people who follow.

- As with all things in my life, all good stems from my mom.
- For Don—the shoes have been filled, and they're yours forever.
- For Alex—cups of coffee and early-morning trips to the airport; our yin-and-yang everything seems to only bring us closer.
- For Joe—your success is a testament to the strong man you are. The girlies are lucky to have a dad like you.
- For Zoë and Bonnie—you melt me with your beauty, make me laugh with your luscious quirks (I now say

"easy peasy, lemon squeezie" with regularity). My love of you two has actually messed me up a little. I honestly didn't know I could love like this, that love could be this big.

- For Kim Resendiz (or, as one particular business refers to her, Keen Resendig)—you've made me feel a part of something, and not just the *New York Times* crossword. Your strength is riveting, and I hope to someday come as close as I can to it.

- For Tito, Nico, Ely, Rodrigo, Diego, David, Xavier, Nadine, Antoine, Denise, Kwon, Michael, Bill Gallagher, and Lynn and Rich Silton—you make me walk in this world a little taller, a little less freaked out, and thankful that I belong to such a majestic tribe.

- For Christy Fletcher—I constantly marvel at how it was that I happened upon you—oh, wait, I was querying agents desperately. Okay, let's rephrase: I constantly marvel at how it was that you happened upon me (better). You took a chance on a kid from the wrong side of the tracks, and by "tracks," I mean outside of Brooklyn and not named Jonathan.

- For Amy Einhorn—Without your all-important checkmarks, how would I ever know how funny I am? I've now taken to just checkmarking everything, particularly my own witty one-liners. I'll make a sign of a checkmark in the air, accompanied by a little sound effect (a chh-chh of sorts). So, thank you for turning me into a slightly Tourette-ish, highly dependent person who now uses bizarre sound effects, *as well as* an abundance of ellipses and dashes—just because I can. But not in books, you know, because you'll just take 'em out. Chh-chh. ← You're dying to edit that last line, huh?

- For Emily Griffin—Poor, poor Emily. No one . . . *no one* . . . wants the task of looking at one of my first drafts, let alone wading through it and making some sense out of it. Emily, with Wellies and a machete, somehow made my first drafts into something rather lovely and gave hope to a nation that this dog just might hunt after all.

- For Melissa and Kate—thank you for fielding my e-mails regarding anything from tax questions to urgent directions to your office as I'm in a cab somewhere in Manhattan and . . . well, no need to relive it, you poor dears.

- For Araminta, Sara, Isobel, Emma and Alison—I'm already planning my next trip to the UK. This time I might be able to do more as a tourist than eat biscuits in the Harrods café . . . not that there's anything wrong with that.

- For Liza Wachter and the RWSH agency—thank you for all that you've done, especially letting me have the ultimate joy of saying, "Hi, Liza, this is Liza." It's the little things.

- For Elly, Kim, Frances Jalet-Miller, Beth Thomas, Dorothea Halliday, Bill Tierney, and everyone at Grand Central Publishing and Hodder who has been integral to putting this book into some kind of order. Thank you so much.

- For Megan Crane—in this solitary, writerly life, it's nice to have someone to talk to about all this crazy shit, and doing so driving up the coast of California with a cup of coffee, fighting about the iPod and laughing hysterically, sure isn't a bad way to do it.

- For Levi Nuñez—the people I've mentioned above have no idea how much they are indebted to you. Your ability to talk sense to me about my writing, and not face the full wrath of my ego, is miraculous. It's like a gift or something. Like a Dr. Dolittle kind of thing—soothing ravenous, shockingly arrogant animals with a combination of Mexican food and the pleasure of knowing that I was going to be able to give as good as I got with your work. Too bad your stuff is as good as it is . . . I haven't quite gotten the level of merciless delight I was hoping I would.

- For Karen Rawers and Bastide—thank you for giving me a backstage pass to your world. It was so phenomenally important, I can't begin to thank you. Well, I can begin, but I think it's the ending that's a little tricky.

- For Lyn Nierva—the bestest Web site Diva of all time, and not a bad tour guide, either . . . Them ribs are a-calling! You, Cathy, and I have got to hit up Billy Bob's stat!

- Thank you to Henry Glowa; Norm Freed; Larry, Ricca, Matthew, and Adam Wolff; David Green; Kerri and Erik Einertson; Carrie Cogbill; Kathie Bradley; Delia Camp; Emily, Steve, and Lucy Marrin-Allison; Paz, Philip, and Jacob Stark; Michelle Rowen; Peter Riherd; Dick, Ann, and Sarah Gillette; the Spa Book Club; Sharon Milan; Brandon Dunn; Amanda Herrington; Marilyn Marino; Tasha Brown; and as always, Poet.

- Now, let's see if I can get through typing this without losing my shit. What's filling my heart most these days is the love, and immense loss, of my grandfather Captain John Dryden Kuser—Jack, to me. He wouldn't let me, or any of his grandkids, call him anything but Jack. He passed away March 8, and I just . . . well, I miss him. Thank you to the Carmelite sisters at Santa Teresita who made his final days so beautiful.

chapter one

The crowd simmers down as the bookstore owner approaches the podium.

"I'm very excited to have such an amazing crowd here tonight for one of L.A.'s prodigal sons. I'm extremely pleased to welcome you to a very special night of literature—a night we hope will be a beacon in these, the darkest of days in publishing. This debut novel is a far cry from the paint-by-numbers, just-add-water types of books that are overtaking our bookshelves and best-seller lists. At just thirty-two years of age, this writer commands the publishing industry to sit up and take notice. Real literature is back with the publication of *The Ballad of Rick Danko*, by Rascal Page!" I visualize a dazzling shower of pyrotechnics from behind the man as he builds to a climax. A girl in the middle of the bookstore lets out a tiny yelp. Rascal sighs.

I try to push away the insistent drone of my workweek. It keeps bumping up against my consciousness, like a seemingly bottomless hamper of dirty clothes. The perfection of the restaurant is never that far away. Never finished. I can never just sit. But tonight I take a deep breath and try to relax into my brother's big night with happiness and a splash, a *hint,* really, of my usual knotted stomach.

I give Rascal a sympathetic smile as the obsequious, cloying introduction drones on. We're both waiting for the mention of *him*. Dad. I peek out into the crowd. Mom is beaming. Her long legs are crossed at the ankles and slanted to one side—nothing out of place. The only untidy thing about her is the overwhelming pride she's feeling right now for her firstborn. Rascal smiles at her. She snaps a picture of him.

"So, without further ado, let me present the heir apparent! Scion of one of the giants of twentieth-century American literature! The successor to the throne!" Rascal and I flinch in unison at each sentence. The man continues with a flourish, "Raskolnikov Page!" The crowd goes wild. Mom winces every time someone calls Rascal Raskolnikov. She lost a bet to Dad for the right to name their first son, and believe it or not, *Rascal* turned out to be the lesser of two evils. Rascal walks up to the podium and looks out into the crowd. I see his eyes fix on someone. I crane my neck to look past the stacks of books.

A wave of recognition rolls through the audience. He leans casually against one of the bookcases at the back of the store. Mom looks over her shoulder, gives him a small wave, and quickly turns her attention back to Rascal. I watch the people as they slowly realize whom they're standing next to.

Ben Page. My dad.

The kind of cultural icon that doesn't exist anymore. I remember for my best friend, Laurie's, eleventh birthday, her parents took us to Disneyland. Later that year, when my eleventh birthday rolled around, Laurie asked what I was doing to celebrate. I said I was going to New York to watch my father receive his second Pulitzer Prize.

Rascal clears his throat and takes a long drink from the bottle of water set out for him on the podium.

"Thank you for coming out tonight. I'm going to start by

reading a passage from the novel, and then I'll take some questions before we call it a night," Rascal says as people in the audience shift and contort in their chairs. Who will they look at? It's an embarrassment of riches. Rascal's pale skin contrasts with his mop of dark brown curls. His features are delicate: pinkish lips, gentle blue eyes. His build is slight, with thin, long fingers, and his shoulders look as if a wire hanger is poking through his threadbare sweater. People always tell us we could be twins, much to Dad's chagrin. We both got Mom's patrician genes. We were built for an aristocratic existence. Neither one of us inherited Dad's workhorse build, that olive skin, the coarse hair, or his almost black eyes—which, as he grows older, are beginning to turn to sunlit amber and, in the innermost circles, the lightest of blues.

Rascal begins reading.

My body relaxes as my brother's voice fills the room. The audience is drawn in and can barely keep up. His prose is hot and fast, like a come-on to a one-night stand. He reads only the opening chapter, and even live, it won't be enough for them. The crowd applauds as Rascal closes the book and looks up.

"Okay. Any questions?" Rascal takes a drink of his water. Several anxious hands shoot into the air. He points to a twenty-something young man in the third row who has more product in his hair than I do, and I believe he's wearing a *velvet* blazer.

"I just want to say that, first off, you are like a god, man," the guy oozes. The crowd titters. Rascal forces a smile. I can see him look toward the back of the room at Dad. Is my brother embarrassed? I glance quickly at Dad. He's rubbing his eyes like he has a headache. Ahhh—the unwashed masses and their inconvenient adoration of our family. I've always wondered why Dad was so bothered by people whose only sin was simply enjoying and connecting with his work. I've never made a big

fuss to Dad about his writing, even though his brilliance awes
me—humbles me. I was afraid it would open up an unwelcome dialogue about what exactly I was doing with my life and,
more importantly, what am *I* doing to change the world? I've
found the best and safest method in dealing with my father is
to keep a safe distance and watch the fireworks from a remote
mountaintop.

"I just want to know if, like—you know, coming from the
family you did helped you get published. I mean, it probably
didn't hurt having Page as your last name, right?" The guy looks
eagerly around at the crowd for validation. Everyone in the
room has silently asked this question in his or her mind. But
now they all act horrified that this guy had the nerve to ask
it, especially as the first question. Rascal is unimpressed. He's
used to it—the constant comparisons to Dad in every area of
his life.

"Let's see." Rascal draws it out like a pitcher's windup before
hurling a hundred-mile-an-hour fastball. He continues, "My
father is perhaps the greatest writer of his generation, and I roll
up and say I've written this manuscript that I think is pretty
good. Now, any other writer, on his best day, doesn't get constantly measured against my father. But in every single review
of my book, I'm compared, head to head, with him. So, yeah, I
probably moved right to the top of the slush pile in my agent's
office. But after that, I'm kinda fucked, huh?" The crowd laughs
nervously. Everyone checks to see if Dad is laughing. His face
is expressionless and focused. The same look is mirrored in
Rascal as he points to a woman in the front row who's raised
her hand. I've spent so many years trying to free myself from
these great shadows. The hitch is, I'm equal parts repulsed and
enticed by them.

"Who are your influences, Raskolnikov? Who inspired you

to—I mean, besides the obvious, of course—who inspired you to write?" The woman sneaks a coquettish look back at Dad.

"Ma'am, my own mother doesn't call me Raskolnikov," Rascal corrects with the slightest of edges to his voice. Mom tenses. In turn, Rascal flashes a conciliatory smile to the woman. The bookstore owner who introduced him shifts in his chair. Rascal continues speaking. "I went through the usual list of rebellious-guy literature—Burroughs, Thompson, Bukowski, Rollins, just like every other zit-faced kid with a constant hard-on. I found Milan Kundera because one of his covers had a naked lady on it. A lot of Richard Ford. I went through a whole Pynchon thing. Hope that answers your question, ma'am . . ." Rascal trails off. Mom is wincing. She didn't bargain for "constant hard-on" talk. I'm unfazed by it. My brother and I are the truest blend of our two parents: We'll tell you to fuck off but then apologize profusely, call you "ma'am" or "sir," and follow that up with some kind of card and/or flower arrangement.

"And your father?" the woman blurts. The entire room gasps.

"I don't know . . . Dad? Who are your influences?" Rascal casually takes a drink from his water bottle as the entire room shifts in their chairs to get an official look at the great Ben Page. The woman tries to correct the misunderstanding. She tries to spit out that what she meant to ask was whether Rascal was influenced by his father, not who inspired Ben to write. "It's a misunderstanding," she yells. Rascal slowly sips. Dad doesn't move from his languid, leaning position—his arms crossed across his wide chest, his black hair swooping effortlessly over his eyes. His lower lip is forever contorted into a relaxed curl that, when not cradling his beloved pipe, looks like an ominous snarl. How many times have I seen this look? I take a long breath. Finished batting the woman around like a trapped mouse, Rascal has offered the woman up for sacrifice. Dad goes in for the kill.

"Come to the party, Lady. I named my own kid Raskolnikov. You do the math." Dad's voice is smooth as he finishes with a benign smile. Rascal is nodding and laughing to himself. The crowd goes wild. Rascal looks up from the podium. There is the sweetest moment between them. Nothing like the evisceration of an overzealous fan to bring father and son together.

Our family: bonding through blood sport.

chapter two

While my father is a literary god, and his son is hailed as the second coming, the only place people read my name is on a menu—and that's only if they read the asterisk: *pastry chef, Elisabeth Page. I am a pastry chef. And while that might lead one to conjure up visions of chocolate éclairs and cheesecake, I like to think that my creations are a bit less run-of-the-mill.

I didn't learn to cook at anyone's side. I didn't stand on a child-sized chair and watch the enchantment of a dash of this and a smidgen of that. When I was a kid, we used to go to a little hole-in-the-wall French restaurant on special occasions. The owner would roll out this massive dessert cart at the end of each meal. He wouldn't even look at Mom and Dad. He'd just turn to Rascal and me and tell us to choose whatever we wanted. When the check came, our desserts were never included in the bill. I thought this man was as close to magic as there was. He made us all feel so enveloped, so loved. My dream was born then.

One day I asked Mom if I could make my own lunches. I'd come down to the kitchen the night before and stare into the pantry, with its endless possibilities. I loved the snapshot I'd get as I closed the lid over the lunch I'd composed—something that was finished and flawless. The next day at school I'd serve my creations to my friends—little measured offerings of love and acceptance. Envelopment. I knew, even at that young age, that making these beautiful gems every day allowed me to bring comfort and show my love for someone. I could communicate anything I was feeling through food and never have to muddy my hands in the mess of emotion.

I applied to the Culinary Institute after only one week at Columbia University. I was accepted for the following year and giddily told Columbia I wouldn't be coming back for my sophomore year. I got confused phone calls from my mom, my dad, my academic adviser, and my high school guidance counselor. Rascal finally called two weeks later to ask if he could crash on my couch for a few weeks while he got his head together. Some things never change.

I decided to go into pastry when a visiting chef used the phrase "to taste" in reference to the amount of salt required for the complicated soufflé he was making. It was my second week at culinary school.

"Is it a tablespoon? Teaspoon? Quarter of a tablespoon?" I asked, pencil at the ready. I noticed that the other students were becoming uncomfortable. Well, I thought, a little discomfort now at my expense will certainly pay off when our soufflés don't taste like a fucking salt lick during exams.

"Chef Page, cooking is about taste—it's not an exact science. That's really the beauty of it, don't you think?" He smiled smugly, certain he'd just given me the nugget of brilliance that would fuel my entire culinary career. I immediately made plans to go into another branch of the culinary arts that didn't condone such reckless abandon.

Chef Canet recruited me as head pastry chef for Beverly after he tasted my creations at a tiny *bouchon* in Lyon, France, where I apprenticed after graduating from the institute. In France, "apprentice" meant I was lucky to do anything in the kitchen during the day and extremely fortunate to scour copper pots with lemon and salt late into the night. My culinary instruction consisted of hurried moments when I was herded into the tiniest of kitchens and shouted at in French to slice this, garnish that, or clean that up. I'd never felt so invigorated or alive. I was paid next to nothing. I slept in a closet-sized room in the pastry chef's house when I wasn't working and saw very little of Lyon outside of that closet and the kitchen of the *bouchon*. After close to two years as a kitchen slave, I was allowed to assist the pastry chef on rare occasions. I learned French as quickly as I could, and kept my head down and my hands busy.

Always the trendsetter, Chef Canet opened his first restaurant in Los Angeles. He felt there was an untapped clientele just waiting for him there. That, and his ex-wives and lovers pretty much littered the streets of New York, Las Vegas, and France. L.A. would be a clean slate for him. For me, it meant going home.

I back into the restaurant, balancing the flat of peaches I purchased on the way in this morning at the local farmer's market, along with another embarrassingly complicated coffee drink containing far too much espresso. My BlackBerry is pressed against my ear as I try to listen to Mom's message. This could take days.

"Elisabeth? Where are you? Well, give me a call back. It was lovely seeing you the other week at the reading, sweetie. I'm so glad you could make it. We've arrived at the Montecito house. I need to know when we can expect you. Will you be joining us for lunch or dinner, darling? Sweetheart, pick up. Okay, well . . . be sure to call so I can have Iris set a place for you. Your brother is already here. He's brought a girl. This one's name is Sarah or something. Samantha. Doesn't matter, I suppose—we won't have to remember it for long. Dear, are you there? Okay, well, see you soon, darling." Mom still believes I have one of those old-timey answering machines somehow hooked up to my BlackBerry and that I can listen to it like a speakerphone.

I beep the BlackBerry off and refocus. Saturday night at Beverly, one of the hottest restaurants in Los Angeles. A night of satisfying the bland yet pompous palates of out-of-towners, playing host to birthday or anniversary dinners, and trying not to upset any already awkward first dates. What this means for me: Everyone wants dessert. When the locals come into the restaurant during the week, they don't usually order dessert. This is L.A., after all.

"Chef Page, come here. Now." Chef Canet doesn't look up— his demands are always heeded, his words always heard. I hurry over to him, still trying to balance the flat of peaches, my coffee, and the BlackBerry. When he's not on a book tour or in a photo shoot or on a morning news show—this breaks down to about once a month—Chef Canet swans into the kitchen, announcing that he must improve the quality of the food in his restaurant. This announcement always leads to a night of displaced chefs, melodramatic (and spectacularly explosive) faux firings, and an amped-up tension that rivals the front lines of battle. Tonight Chef has taken over the fish specialist's station. He is slicing the feature with the precision of a Beverly Hills plastic surgeon. He has never ventured over to the pastry corner—not his thing, he says.

"Put that down," Chef says. I set the flat of peaches in the walk-in refrigerator. I throw my purse, phone, and coffee down at my station and nod a quick hello to Samuel, my first assistant. He is buttoned up tight in his chef's jacket. His coffee-colored skin matches his tight curls perfectly. Julie, my second assistant, whizzes past me on her way to the employee lockers. She nods hello, and I can smell the sharp after-waft of the patchouli oil she insists on slathering on every morning. Julie is far enough away from Chef Canet that her signature scent is allowed. Truth be told, Chef Canet could use a signature scent besides the one he seems so fond of: all-night bender and poor dental hygiene. Nonetheless, I've trained myself to exhale as Julie passes.

"Yes, Chef?" I straighten my chef's jacket as I approach him. Physically, he has a softness that's quite misleading. At first glance he seems young, wide-eyed, naive, even. But upon closer inspection, his stark blue eyes are bloodshot and his bitten-down fingernails are raw and scraggly. His lean six-foot frame never betrays his love of food; the two heart attacks he's had in his thirty-seven years weren't due to overconsumption of food. Overconsumption of something, but not food.

"We will do salmon tonight. I could not pass it up, yes? It was fresh. What do you have, then, for the dessert feature?" The beautiful cadence of his French accent makes his request sound almost melodic. Saturdays we usually do a veal feature. But no problem. I can understand not being able to pass up the fresh salmon.

"I could do an almond cake with some of the mission figs from yesterday," I think out loud.

"Good. Now go," he says from behind his greasy strands of dark hair, never taking his eyes off the luscious fish. Pleasant-ries are the first victim in a streamlined kitchen.

"Thank you, Chef," I say, quickly retreating to my corner of the kitchen. Ten thousand thoughts are blurring together in my brain. The presence of Chef Canet in the kitchen tonight has thrown me off my game. I've been formulating this peach feature for weeks, and now I have to all but scrap it. Balancing taste profiles is an art. Peach and salmon together are a bit too Bobby Flay for my taste. I haven't packed for my trip up north to Montecito. I'm not even sure I even want to go up north first thing in the morning. I make an executive decision to do the almond and fig cake and keep the peach feature as well. The fallout from this decision and the stress that it will cause will help me avoid thinking about tomorrow. A silver lining, if you will. I breathe deeply and welcome the calm that will come once I get my hands deep in a dessert.

George, the sommelier, catches up with me and asks if I could try the wine he's chosen to pair with the peach feature. As we approach, Julie immediately straightens up, then whips her long strawberry-blond hair wildly over her head in a bizarre heavy-metal video move straight out of 1986.

"*Bonjour,* George, *comment ça va?*" Julie spouts her newly acquired Berlitz French like a freshman psychology major telling everyone they're "projecting." I'm not quite sure why Julie feels the need to speak French to the very American George. It just doesn't pack the same punch as if French were his native language. Trifles, I'm sure. I toy with the idea of speaking Latin to shake things up a bit for the old girl. Not much of a plan when all I'd be able to say would be *e pluribus unum* and *carpe diem.*

"Not bad, Julie. Chef Page? The wine?" George says in perfect English as he presents me with a pristine glass containing just the correct amount of wine. I announce that another dessert feature has been added. Samuel and Julie take note of the changes and scurry away in search of the items needed for one more dish than was expected. George writes down the new feature as he anxiously awaits the verdict on his wine, obviously realizing he has yet another pairing to figure out.

I swirl the wine around and give it a delicate sip. Julie is back and prepping the bread pudding, a mainstay of our menu. She has put her hair back into a ponytail and has tucked it under a gingham handkerchief. Samuel returns and switches on the large mixer, beginning our almond cake. I've never seen him show this kind of enthusiasm or flair anywhere else. Samuel's passion for life is funneled into each and every dessert he makes. I swish the wine. It needs something.

"It's a little . . . No. Julie? Grab me . . . No, those . . . the peaches. I just took them from the . . . No, fresh from the walk-in." Julie starts and stops with each one of my demands. Her obnoxious air of being the perpetual hall monitor and resident toady is almost as bad as the patchouli oil. "Stop. I'll just do it myself," I say, not looking up.

While this is going on, Samuel, unbidden, goes back to the walk-in and brings a succulent ripe peach to our station. He quickly washes and slices the peach and sets it in front of me.

"There, Chef." He wipes his knife, swipes off the cutting board with a cloth, and resumes his attentions to the almond cake. Julie stands there with her mouth slightly open, her eyes narrowed. A kitchen at this level is always highly competitive. Julie just lost that round to Samuel, and she knows it. She will do one of two things—try to best him later on tonight or sabotage something of his in the very near future. Samuel better gird his loins. But if I know Samuel, he's already donned an athletic supporter.

◆

I stagger home to my apartment around two in the morning. The phone is ringing as I fumble for my keys. I'm officially exhausted and still have to pack for the two days I'll be spending at my parents' Montecito house.

At this hour, my first thought is that someone (read: Rascal) is dead and the faceless caller would like me to come down to the station to identify the body. But then I remember that there *is* one other person who calls this late. I finally get the door unlocked and walk over to my desk where the phone is. I knock over an empty water bottle and somehow manage to turn on my printer as I scramble for the phone in the dark. "Hello?"

"Do you know what the answer to any question you ask me is going to be from now on? It's ingenious, really."

If I didn't know it was Will, the voice on the other end would be disturbing. Will's full name is William Dryden Houghton III. As a child, he tried to convince the other kids at school that his middle name was actually Dragon—William *Dragon* Houghton III. But since the gymnasium was dedicated to the first William Dryden Houghton, the game was up before it began.

Will's vowels are drawn out, and the deep layers in that velvety smooth voice are just sufficient to paint the picture of the man behind this late-night phone call. The last time I saw him, his yellow-y blond hair was cut short, as it usually is. The blue of his eyes is comparable to a painter's appreciation of the color, true and bright, unlike the dull versions one usually finds in real life. The All-American Boy.

"Take some penicillin and call me in the morning?" I say, my shoulders loosening up. Our witty banter is a studied match that always borders on a bad Tom Stoppard play. I walk over to the lamp at the foot of my bed and turn it on. I run my finger along the stark white shade. I'll have to dust tomorrow before my run.

"Twelve beers," Will says. I walk over to the kitchen, bend down, and locate the feather duster under the sink. I can't help myself.

"As in . . ." I tuck the cordless phone into the nook between my shoulder and jaw. I quickly dust the lamp shade. Better now than later. "Why, Will Houghton, how have you passed the time between connecting flights?"

Will pauses and, with perfect comic timing, intones, "Twelve beers." I can hear the announcement of a plane departing in the background as I put the feather duster back under the kitchen sink.

"Where are you?" I walk into the bathroom and flip on the light, catching sight of my reflection. Dark circles under my eyes. My hair is up in some attempt at a ponytail. I can still smell the kitchen on me.

"Twelve beers," Will answers.

"Funny," I dismiss.

"I'm at JFK, on a layover from Heathrow. It's fucking freezing here." As usual, I have no idea where Will was or where he's going. He could be on his way to the farthest corners of the earth or my apartment, I never know. He continues, "But I'll be home in time to drive up for your parents' thing." My breath catches. His mom, Anne, has a house minutes from my parents' place. This trip just got a lot more interesting.

"How did you even know about that?" I ask. The autumn chill has crept into my apartment. I love every warm blankety moment of it.

"Twelve beers." Will is very pleased with himself. I hear him exhale.

"You're smoking again?" I ask, quickly taking off my chef's whites and putting them into the washer. I found this great European stacked washer/dryer that takes up no space at all. I pull my running gear out of the dryer and set it out on the chair for tomorrow morning.

"Smoking *still*. I'm smoking *still*."

"Didn't you try to quit? Why did you take it up again?" Actually, I can't remember ever seeing Will without a cigarette. At twelve years old, he stole Marlboro Reds from the tennis pro's gym bag. Will has since graduated to the far more elite

Gauloises brand, pronouncing that Marlboro Reds are for fake cowboys and strippers. I guess stealing cigarettes from your mother's lover might be construed as rebellious. But for Will, it was another attempt to get some kind of attention other than the long depositions, meetings with lawyers, and hearings to decide custody of a child whom each parent seemed to want only because the other one did.

"Twelve beers," he says again. This little game is becoming tiresome.

"You know, I have a question for you," I ask.

"Oh yeah?" Will bites.

"You want to know what makes someone wholly unfunny?" I ask.

"Twelve beers?" Will answers.

"Pretty much."

"Come by my parents' place tomorrow before you go to your parents'. We'll . . . talk," Will invites.

"Talk, huh?" I ask. Will Houghton was my first. First everything. First everywhere. I haven't had good "talk" in much, *much* too long.

Will is silent. "Noonish? You still know the code, right?" he finally asks.

"Yes," I answer. His birthday: 131. I hear another announcement of a departing plane.

"That's me. See you tomorrow—oh, I mean today," he signs off.

"See you then," I say. My stomach lurches as I turn on the shower.

chapter three

B y the time I was twenty-four, my liver was shot, and I had lost three toes to gangrene."

So begins my father's debut novel, *The Coward*. He smoked like a chimney, looked like a matinee idol, and had his choice of any woman.

He chose Ballard Foster. My mother. The sole heir to the Foster Family Fortune—a running joke in our family. Not the fortune, mind you, but the alliteration of the phrase. It was always said with lisps, in the voice of Daffy Duck and with saltine crackers stuffed to capacity in tiny, ornery mouths: Fausta Famiwee Fortoon, à la Barbara Walters—so it was a bit surreal when Barbara Walters actually did a show on my dad and said our name just like that. We even tried the obligatory "say it ten times fast" rule, much to the displeasure of the overseers of the Foster Family Fortune.

Instead of marrying someone from her social set, my mom married a nobody whom she met at one of her charity functions. He was a young naval aviator stationed in San Diego, and she was a debutante on summer break from Stanford University. Or, from the point of view of the Foster relatives, she was a mark, and he was a gold digger. They were married in a tiny chapel at the naval station with Will's mom, Anne, as the maid of honor. She was the only friend who stood by Mom while she made "the biggest mistake of her life."

Ben Page. The biggest mistake of Mom's life.

He flew helicopters in the war and, at twenty-three, was shot down over North Vietnam. After being released from a North Vietnamese POW camp, he was sent home for good. It was while recuperating at Balboa Naval Hospital that he wrote *The Coward,* the novel that began a career that has spanned thirty years, eleven books, four movie adaptations, two Pulitzers, and a partridge in a pear tree.

The Coward came out in 1971, at a time when the country was deeply divided and changing. Dad's book was a wrenching first-person account of the horrors and utter waste of war. He and his book were an integral part of the growing antiwar movement, and he became the poster boy for disillusionment and dissent. He appeared on late-night talk shows more often than Truman Capote had, and when it came to getting an intellectual sound bite for the nightly news, he was more sought after than Norman Mailer. Dad rented a run-down cottage in Laurel Canyon for his workspace, got stoned with a veritable *Who's Who* list of pop culture, lazed around the pool with Warren Beatty and Jack Nicholson, and hung out backstage at *The Last Waltz* with Lawrence Ferlinghetti and Neil Young.

As she came of age, Mom took the helm of the Foster Family Foundation. My grandmother Elisabeth died from a fall off a horse when Mom was in her teens. When my grandfather died shortly thereafter, he left Mom the entire Foster Family Fortune. In his will, he stipulated that Mom was to be raised by her aunt, my great-aunt Brooke—or rather, Mom was to spend the school year at boarding school, summer in Montecito with her extended family, and keep a room at Aunt Brooke's house in Pasadena.

Despite the pain and trauma that both my parents had experienced up until then, neither one gave up hope that someday they could be part of a family. They also knew that neither would give up a hold on independence. It's odd they never quite put together that desiring a family while craving independence is a bit of a contradiction, to say the least.

My bags are packed and waiting for me by the door. Two hours up the 101 Freeway, and I'll be staying at my parents' summer home again. Driving through the same two enormous rock columns and up the tree-lined drive. Sitting at the long dining table in the same seat I've been assigned my entire life. And sleeping in the same tiny twin bed.

I take off my running gear and put it in the washer. I can still feel the breakfast I ate at Joan's on Third flipping in my stomach. Joan's is the official end point of my morning run. Each morning, after a cleansing three-mile route through my West Los Angeles neighborhood, I sit and read the *L.A. Times* over an Americano and a bowl of yogurt and granola. Despite my run, my stomach has been churning all morning. I chalk it up to parental stress on the horizon. I grab the box of Pepto-Bismol chewables next to the sink and pop two pink pills, chewing and washing them down with a swig from the bottle of Pellegrino in the refrigerator. I pocket two more tablets for the road and pour the entire contents of my Bialetti stovetop espresso maker into a travel mug. No sugar. No milk. Straight.

I walk out of my small galley kitchen and into the front room. I chose this apartment for its proximity to the restaurant. I've grown fonder of it over the years because of its great style, hardwood floors, and abundance of natural light. I open the French doors. They overlook the communal courtyard and burbling fountain. I sip my coffee and breathe in the morning air. Another day.

After an hour on the 101 Freeway, I look over at my passenger seat. My BlackBerry sits next to the iPod that's connected to the car stereo. The iPod is sitting next to a bottle of water, which is propped up next to the laptop. I have an electronic entourage. The red dot that indicates unread e-mail on my BlackBerry has been flashing the entire time. The ringer is set on silent, but I can see that I've already missed six calls. It's a tossup whether the calls are from Mom or Chef Canet or some combination of both. Just because the restaurant is closed on Sundays and Mondays doesn't mean that I won't hear from Chef.

I turn up the sound on my stereo and roll down my window. I'm driving through the picture-perfect section of the 101 between Ventura County and Montecito. Ocean on one side, mountains on the other. I breathe in deeply and change into the slow lane.

The town of Montecito nestles cozily between the Pacific Ocean and the Santa Ynez Mountains, just south of Santa Barbara. It's said to be one of the wealthiest communities in the nation, filled to bursting with huge estates hidden behind massive gated walls. Some of these estates were built a long time ago by the robber barons of a bygone era, like my grandfather. Others have been added more recently by a bevy of celebrities, show business people, and the modern-day robber barons of finance and technology. The Montecito old-timers discreetly turn up their noses at the new arrivals' displays of wealth: fancy new cars, ridiculous baubles, and bling. You can always tell the old money. They don't have to try that hard. The old Mercedes, the Chanel suit, and a foundation named after your family. This is where I spent my idyllic summers as a kid.

I drive slowly down Montecito's main street, Coast Village Road, past small elegant shops, nurseries, and bistros. Montecito has a slightly rustic yet decidedly upscale look; wooden street signs with white lettering mark the winding roads. I have forgotten all things Los Angeles and embrace the hundred-mile expanse between me and the pressure and stress of Beverly. I turn my car toward Will's mom's house. I tap the numbers into the small touchpad at the main entrance: 1 . . . 3 . . . 1.

The huge gate swings open, and I drive between the large rock columns. I twist open the lid of my water and drink. My stomach is in knots. I have no idea what the next few hours will hold. I pull up next to Will's 1988 Jeep Grand Wagoneer. It's parked in front of the six-car garage. The ugly oxidized maroon paint is only slightly uglier than the faux-wood siding. This is Will's Montecito car—a car that reeks of old money. When he's in L.A., Will prefers the luxury of the brand new black Porsche Cayman his mom bought him for his birthday. Even though we're grown up now, I still look at Will and see the eight-year-old hellion who called his mom "stupid fuck-it" at a black-tie charity event; the same boy who always seemed to finagle an invitation to dinner at our house so he didn't have to eat with the housekeeper. My family, with all of our flaws, is the only family Will has ever known. Mom always welcomed Will and has remained loyal to Anne, reminding everyone how faithful Anne was during the first years of Mom's marriage to "the biggest mistake of her life." I know she's brokenhearted at the parenting choices, or lack thereof, that Anne has made over the years, and the harm those choices have done to Will, yet she still holds out hope for both of them.

I park my Audi wagon next to the Jeep and scoop all of my electronics into my purse. I zip the purse closed, sling it across my chest, and get out, beeping my car locked from habit. Just who's going to scale the six-foot wall of the Houghton manse and steal my car? I guess L.A. isn't so far out of my mind after all. I almost beep the car unlocked out of embarrassment.

I smooth my camel cashmere sweater down over the silk camisole I'm wearing with my tweed pants. I'm wearing black Chuck Taylors for the drive, with a pair of kitten heels stashed in the car, just so Mom won't faint at the sight of me. I start to knock on the back kitchen door and then quickly lower my hand. I look around. I try the latch on the door and find that it's unlocked. I look around again.

"Are you being followed?" Will asks. He's sitting at the large kitchen table with the entire *L.A. Times* spread out in front of him. A half-full French press sits next to a mug of steaming coffee. An ashtray and a pack of Gauloises are almost hidden by the dissected newspaper.

"What?" I turn around and slowly close the door behind me. In that millisecond, I try to gather myself. He looks amazing. No shirt. Pajama bottoms. Bare feet. His yellow brush of hair is slightly grown out and a bit ruffled. He's clean-shaven and smells of his morning shower. Dad likes to say that Will is a true example of a man—strong, bold, and intrepid. It doesn't help that Rascal is usually off somewhere with a wineglass dangling from his long fingers, wearing some kind of scarf and talking about his feelings.

Standing in front of Will now is like turning a key and entering a place that exists only in my mind. Bred to constantly raise the bar higher, I can't stop checking for imperfections in my life. Everything must be weighed and measured. Everything is up for criticism. Everything could be better. Being here means everything doesn't have to be perfect . . . for a while.

How did I allow myself to go without him for so long? How long *has* it been? The last time I was with someone was Will, and that was a year ago, right before he embedded in Iraq for a story he was writing for *Vanity Fair.* Will went to Israel immediately after Iraq. Until last night's phone call, I thought he was still in Lebanon on a story for *Esquire*. I've long since given up the job-related flings and late-night flirtations of my twenties. My momentary flush of sweet oblivion is inevitably negated by the realization that nothing could survive my brutal schedule or an unannounced visit by Will. I'll drop everything for just one night with him. It's been like this for years. But here we are, after knowing each other all our lives, always picking up right where we left off yet always starting right back at square one.

I feel my shoulders lower away from my ears. I breathe in as I set my keys and purse on the long soapstone counter.

"Do your parents know you're in town yet?" Will says, folding up a portion of the paper as he stands.

"Why are you still talking?" I say, pulling him in for a long-overdue kiss.

Will pulls at my now-inconvenient cashmere sweater. The world falls away. As it always has. My sweater comes up and off. The camisole is being manhandled within an inch of its life. I'm pushing his pajama bottoms farther and farther down.

The kitchen floor is cold on my back, though I can feel my face flushed with heat. Will smiles and laughs in between kisses. I say something about calling Mom and letting her know I might be a little late. The funny thing is we've been here before, on this actual kitchen floor. So many times we've been unable to make it past the first few steps without falling into each other. I reach for my pants pocket and pull out the fun-size box of condoms I bought at a gas station on the 101. Will lifts himself up and reaches underneath the *L.A. Times* for his own strip of condoms and smiles.

There's no place like home. There's no place like home. There's no place like home.

chapter four

"Hi, Mom!" I announce into my BlackBerry as I beep my car unlocked. My hair is still wet from my hour-long shower with Will. He trails behind me, trying to light a cigarette.

"Darling, why didn't you call? Did you get any of my messages?" Mom asks. I'm waving off Will and his cigarette, mouthing frantically, "Not in my car . . . not in my car . . . no smoking . . . no smoking." Will lights the cigarette and blows smoke out through his nose. He opens the door and climbs in.

"I just stopped by to get Will so we could drive over together," I say, climbing into the car and immediately rolling down all the windows. My body aches—the wonderful, wonderful ache of Will.

"I'll have Iris make those appetizers he likes so much," Mom says. Iris and her husband, Robert, have worked for Mom and Dad for over twenty years. I let Mom know we'll be there within minutes and hang up.

"So, we're rocking the Genesis, huh?" Will says, cigarette hanging out of his mouth as he taps every button on my car stereo.

"Yeah, a little 'Follow You, Follow Me.' Great road song," I say.

"The lyrics are ass—Oy! It's the pedal on the right, Mary!" Will yells out the window at a giant boat of a Cadillac that's going about three miles an hour. The poor woman behind the wheel doesn't hear a thing. I laugh over the offensive Genesis song. Will taps the forward button and lands on a more suitable Nick Drake song. "I could have been a sailor . . . could have been a cook . . ." Will sits back in the passenger seat and rests his hand casually on my leg.

The eucalyptus- and fireplace-scented winds of Montecito drift in through the open windows. A single curl of Will's hair sticks to the nape of his neck. As I pull through the large rock columns that mark Mom and Dad's drive, I twirl the curl in my fingers. Will leans in to my twirling. Then we slam our doors and walk into the house past the parked cars.

"Whose is that?" Will asks, pointing to Dad's favorite new toy. This is the first I've seen it. God, it really is beautiful.

"Dad's," I say. "That's the car he's wanted since he was a teenager."

"What's so special about it?" Will says, running his finger down the side of the car.

"It's a 1966 427 Corvette. Marina blue. Four-speed. A hundred percent original. Side-pipe exhaust in the classic hard-top coupe," I parrot. Rascal and I have been hearing about this car our entire lives.

"How much did he have to pay for that?" Will asks.

I sigh. "About half a million dollars."

"Jesus, I knew they were popular, but—" he says. We walk past the Corvette, Mom's old Mercedes diesel wagon, a brand-new sleek BMW, and on into the house.

"Well, another guy wanted it at the Barrett-Jackson auction, and Dad doesn't like to lose," I say, walking up the front steps.

The house has gone through many decorating incarnations over the years. Mom is still developing her own style after growing up with all the heirlooms and antiques that she was never allowed to touch. So she practices on the Montecito house. She has a team of designers on speed dial. She went through a hideous nautical phase for a while. We're not allowed to mention it in front of company. She decorated the front of the house with life preservers and buoys with our last name emblazoned across them. After that, she did the whole shabby-chic thing. White everywhere. She transformed the gardens into a carbon copy of the English countryside. We were okay with it at the time. But one summer we all looked around and noticed that the shit just looked dirty and worn out. Vintage, my ass. That "aged" armoire was just plain old.

Last summer Mom redid the entire house again, this time in a modern/Asian style, filling it with sleek furniture in pale blues and chocolate browns, with persimmon accents. She's even had some work done outside, I see. She's had some paths installed leading to peaceful Zen gardens. I definitely like it.

"Darling!" Mom is wearing one of her beach-house outfits: a beautiful creamy-white cashmere sweater and a simple pair of black pencil pants. She's never had a problem defining her fashion sense. She looks radiant. She kisses my cheek and then rubs the lipstick off. Will steps forward, and Mom plants a kiss on his cheek. She rubs the lipstick off his cheek as he smiles and looks embarrassed.

"What are you doing with all this, William? They don't have barbers in Lebanon?" Mom smirks, tugging on his just slightly grown-out, yellow hair.

"No, Ballard. No barbers—just death and destruction," Will says as we walk into the foyer. Mom closes the door behind us. The strap of my suitcase is digging into my shoulder.

"Where is everyone?" I ask, in code. "Everyone" means Dad.

"He's in his study," Mom says.

"And Rascal?" I ask.

"He's in the guesthouse with that Sarah somebody. To look at him, you'd think there are no barbers in Santa Monica, either," Mom says as Robert reaches for my suitcase. Will puts his hands in his pockets and does that rocking thing he does, side to side, almost as if he's finding his sea legs on some invisible ship that only he has boarded. That's how I usually find him in crowds—rocking. I give Robert a hug, and he takes the bag from me.

"We're going to go say hi to Rascal, Mom," I say.

"Give your father a kiss before you go out there, Elisabeth," Mom adds.

"I'll be in the guesthouse," Will says, motioning in that direction. It's no coincidence that Will began smoking, just like Rascal, just like Dad. Will has looked up to Rascal like a god since we were all kids. His unofficial older brother.

"Be sure to knock, darling. You know how he is," Mom says to me. I catch up with Robert and climb the stairs to the tower.

The house has three stories. The entire ground floor is used mostly for entertaining, although Dad's study lurks moodily in one of the dark corners. Mom and Dad's master suite is on the second floor, along with several guest bedrooms, a media room, Mom's yoga studio, and numerous balconies. Iris and Robert stay in one of the two guest cottages in the back gardens. Rascal and I sleep on the third floor. Mom set up this space when we were little: two cubbies overlooking the library. During the nautical phase, she had two wooden plaques installed, one with CROW'S NEST—PORT SIDE for me and one with CROW'S NEST—STARBOARD SIDE for Rascal. The only way to get to these cubbies is by climbing a ladder.

My bed is made up with white, flowered sheets and a comforter, leftovers from the shabby-chic days. The nautical bell is still right by my bed. The burled wood is untouched. The third floor is where all of Mom's decorating mistakes go to die slow, painful deaths. Because Rascal is the elder child, he has earned the right to stay in one of the guest cottages while I am still relegated to the Crow's Nest. Despite lengthy conversations about other guest rooms—all of which are far more luxurious—my parents refuse to see the need for a change. The notion is simply never entertained. I've slept in the Crow's Nest my whole life, and apparently, I'll continue to do so until the day I die.

Robert sets my bag on the bed and awkwardly climbs out of the Crow's Nest. I sit down. I have to arch my neck forward so I don't bang my head on the sloping ceiling. My purse is still around my shoulder, and I'm gripping my BlackBerry. The room smells like lavender. I'm sure there are many sachets hidden about. Being home again brings up all of my reasons for deciding early on that I was going to find a career as far away from Dad's legacy as possible. I had thought working in a restaurant and becoming a chef would lessen the constant comparisons.

I pull my purse tight and carefully stand, bending and contorting to free myself from the ever shrinking confines of the Crow's Nest. Onward and downward—to see Dad.

chapter five

Dad?" I knock on the heavy wooden door, then stuff my hands in my pockets. I hear the creaking of the old office chair and the violent tapping of a typewriter. On and on. A pause. Tap. Tap. Tap. The music of my childhood. How many years of my life were spent waiting outside this door? After Rascal and I were disciplined by Mom, we'd be told to wait for Dad—he'd want a word with us, too. The hours would pass as we forgot what we were fighting about. We learned over the years to bring a deck of cards or Scrabble.

After several minutes, I hear the magical zip of the paper being pulled from the typewriter and my body straightens.

"Come on in," Dad yells.

I open the door and see my father behind his desk. His black hair is graying slightly, but it still manages to swoop just over his eyes, never falling into them, somehow floating above, effortlessly. He's wearing a dark sweater over a white T-shirt, faded Levi's, and loafers without socks. He's been wearing this same outfit for decades. He doesn't look up from his old type-writer as I close the door behind me. I sit down in one of the big leather club chairs in front of his desk and take in the room.

The slightest coating of dust glimmers from every sur-face as the sunlight shines through the windows. The smell of pipe smoke is embedded in the curtains and lush fabrics of the room. As always, the focus of the room remains a collection of items that Rascal and I have dubbed Dad's Shrine to Manhood: a black-and-white photo of the helicopters he used to fly in Vietnam, his dog tags, his Colt .45 sidearm, and the small handful of novels he has worn out over the years with reading, rereading, analyzing, dog-earing, highlighting, and annotating. These are the books that shaped the man who sits before me now. *Influenced* him, if you will. His Pulitzers are displayed unceremoniously as bookends on a sagging shelf of other people's masterpieces. The framed photos seem more like a time capsule than an accurate depiction of our family as it is now. Rascal and me as babies—I'm propped up in an ice cream bucket with a two-year-old Rascal giggling wildly at my predicament. A baby picture of Dad, sporting long hair and a baptismal gown. A formal picture of Dad in his navy uniform, the ominous snarl in full effect. A faded color picture of Mom posing on a jetty at the shore, looking more like a pinup girl than my mother.

"How are you, Bink?" he asks. I had a penchant for pacifiers, or "binkies," when I was a baby. So the nickname "Binky" still follows me around, though only Dad and Rascal still call me that. Thank God. Dad takes the piece of paper and lays it facedown in a neat pile on his desk. He walks over to me and gives me a kiss on top of my head, making a big thwack noise, as he always has. I can't help but smile.

"Doing good," I say.

"How's the *restaurant*?" Dad asks. He rests his body against the large oak desk, crossing one leg over the other and placing his arms across his chest.

"Doing good," I say.

"And they say you don't have a future in words," Dad stabs.

"There's hope for me yet, Pop," I parry.

"I saw they gave this year's James Beard Award to some guy in New York. Have you thought about relocating there so you could be taken more seriously?" Dad begins, forgoing the usual newspaper clipping as proof of his argument.

"That guy is a twenty-five-year-old wunderkind who's opening up another restaurant in the newest casino in Vegas," I say.

"Have *you* thought about going to Vegas?" Dad presses.

"You know I don't like to gamble," I try. Dad doesn't break a smile. The first bead of sweat drips down the side of my face.

"When am I going to see that restaurant you've been thinking about opening?" Dad stands and walks over to open the large window that looks out onto the grounds.

"I'm working my five-year plan," I say, hoping no one notices that my five-year plan has morphed into a bloated eleven-year plan. Dad looks as unimpressed as ever. His heroes change the world. My heroes just feed them.

"I'm serious here. You can't work in that kitchen forever," Dad says, turning away from the window. The sunlight hits his face and his almost-black eyes.

"Why don't we wait until dinner, get all liquored up, and then have ourselves a real party," I say, lifting myself from the chair. I have to get out of this interrogation room, where I'm forever depicted as a trapped baby in an ice cream bucket.

"I'm just asking the questions you should be asking yourself," Dad says. You mean the questions that wake me up in the middle of the night in a cold sweat? Yeah, they've crossed my mind. Dad stands in front of me. He still has that quiet power. He's gotten no less intimidating as I've gotten older.

"You know, Tolkien said that if more of us valued food and cheer and song above hoarded gold, it would be a merrier world," I say, turning for the door. That churning in my stomach is back.

"You've been working on that the whole way up here, right?" Dad says, linking my arm in his.

"Pretty much," I say.

"Well played," Dad allows.

"I saw the Corvette outside. Nice," I say, a wide smile stretching across my face.

"It'll work."

"You've only wanted it your whole life," I say. Dad shrugs and allows himself the smallest of smiles.

"Is Will here?" he asks, opening the door to his study.

"Yes," I say.

"He part of your five-year plan, too?" Dad asks.

"Who are you now, Mom?"

"Well, say hi to him for me, before Rascal starts putting lipstick on him or something," Dad says.

"Yes, I'll look into that," I say. Dad gives me a big bear hug and heads into the kitchen. In between the Spanish Inquisition and big thwacking kisses on the top of my head, Dad has insinuated that I'm going nowhere fast and that Rascal is an effeminate disappointment. Definitely a great start. Also, the Will question is coming up more and more of late. I wish I had an answer.

I bolt into the backyard in search of Will. Or Rascal. Or my dignity. Or my confidence. Or my independence. Or benchmarks I can reach before they change again.

I pull out my BlackBerry and scroll through the e-mails as I walk across the grass past Mom's massive rose garden. Even though it's late into September, it's been so warm that Mom hasn't pruned them yet. They are blooming and gorgeous. They smell incredible. I finally reach the small guest cottage. I turn the door handle as I read an e-mail from Chef Canet talking about a great little restaurant he jetted to in Taos this morning. He's signed the e-mail Christian. I type back that the restaurant sounds great.

"Always the height of efficiency, I see," Will says from one of the large chocolate-brown mohair chairs. I quickly slip the BlackBerry in my pocket.

"Takes one to know one."

"We were about to send in the ground troops, but we thought we'd get drunk first," Rascal says, emerging from the kitchen. He's carrying a newly opened bottle of white wine with four glasses dangling from his other hand. A smile cracks across my face. Rascal's dark, curly hair is as unkempt as usual. And in just the couple of weeks since I've seen him, he has grown a very noticeable—and apparently highly controversial—beard. His delicate, refined features are beginning to be obscured.

"Thanks for that," I say, taking a glass from Rascal as I perch on the arm of Will's chair. He rubs my back absently. My eyes fall on this Sarah Somebody Mom has been talking about.

"This is Avery," Rascal continues, introducing me to the New Girl. I've seen her before. Or I've seen fifty other girls who look just like her. The emaciated body that somehow manages to support a giant lollipop head. Her lustrous, chocolate hair flows past her tiny yet muscular upper arms and pools perfectly on her perky, and fully purchased, breasts. Avery smiles. I am nearly blinded by a full set of veneers.

"Have we met?" I ask, shaking her hand. Rascal hands Will a glass of wine.

"No, I don't think so." Avery has an odd expression on her face.

Rascal absentmindedly lights a cigarette: Pall Mall—the anti-Gauloises. Will pats his pockets for his own cigarettes as Rascal throws him his lighter.

"Have you come in to Beverly? You know the restaurant on—" I start.

Avery interrupts, "Beverly Boulevard? I've been in there, but I don't think we met there." Her tone is polite. Will throws the lighter back to Rascal. I let out a cough. Vacations with the folks are just the time to throw the threat of lung cancer right out the window.

"Oh," I answer, holding out my empty wineglass for Rascal. He stands and pours me a glass.

"Avery's one of them fancy movie stars," Rascal says, topping me off, the cigarette dangling from his mouth. Avery blushes and sputters, feigning embarrassment. Rascal hands her a wineglass and pours.

"Oh, would I have seen you in anything?" I ask, perching once again on Will's chair. He resumes rubbing my back. I take the most giant gulp of wine I can manage.

"Do you just want the bottle?" Rascal asks.

"Yeah, you can leave that right there," I answer. It's one of those conversations that no one else really hears. We speak between pauses. I'm not sure he even finished the question before I knew what he was going to say and had planned the proper sarcastic response. On the surface, Rascal's detached demeanor remains intact. He looks like he has the innate security of someone who has never had to worry about anything, least of all money. He wants to be taken seriously, yet he always falls into allowing himself to be a product. He's put his name on some embarrassing Hollywood screenplays so the resulting film will get more attention. He goes to every club opening on the promise of free booze and hot girls. Rascal has pretty much whored the family name for Jack Daniel's and pussy.

About two years ago, he vanished for nine months. He didn't tell anyone—not even me—where he'd be. He finally turned up in a broken-down log cabin just outside Missoula, Montana, with the finished manuscript for *The Ballad of Rick Danko*.

The novel debuted three weeks ago on the *New York Times* best-seller list. It's been there ever since. At first the book was a curiosity, the work of the "heir to the throne." And writing about a tragic character from the sixties, no less. But as the great reviews came in and word of mouth spread, the book began selling on its own merit.

Rascal asked me not to read it—not in manuscript form, not when I saw a galley sitting on his coffee table one afternoon, and not even when he called me over to his Santa Monica bungalow to pop open a bottle of champagne in honor of the first official copies of the book arriving at his door. But I couldn't help myself. I stole a copy from the bottom of a stack taunting me from a slightly opened box by the front door and read it that very day. When I finished it in the wee hours of the morning, I went back to Rascal's. The book was brilliant. We hugged and cried. Of course, the moment fizzled a bit when his latest lollipophead strolled out of the bedroom completely nude. But she saved us both from the awkward moment when I would have to answer the question of whether his book was better than *The Coward*. I still haven't answered the question, and Rascal has yet to ask it again. Comparing the two books is like comparing the two men. Dad is obviously the original. *The Coward* launched an entirely new literary subgenre. But *The Ballad of Rick Danko*, well, it has more heart—like Rascal.

"So, is she your girlfriend?" Avery asks Will, trying to change the subject. Rascal pours himself a hefty glass of wine and sets the bottle down on the small side table. I take another drink. Will's hand has stopped rubbing my back. Avery waits. As do I.

"Do adults still use the word 'girlfriend'?" Will asks. His voice is clear and smooth. Rascal sits on the couch opposite me and crosses his legs. He dangles the wineglass languidly over the side of the couch.

"Avery is an interesting name," I blurt. Will takes his hand off my back.

"It's actually not my real name. My agent thought it sounded more sophisticated," Avery says. The elephant stands boldly in the middle of the room.

"Than?" Will asks.

"Crystal," Avery admits. Rascal barks with laughter. The elephant begins to waddle out.

"Are you actually passing judgment on someone else's name?" I'm laughing a little too loudly. Rascal puts out his cigarette and gives me the finger.

"Where did you two meet?" Will asks.

"I'm in talks to star in the film adaptation of Rascal's novel," Avery announces.

"You're not starring in it, dear. The lead is a male. *Obviously*," Rascal corrects.

"They picked up the option?" I ask.

"Yeah, didn't I tell you?" Rascal says.

"That would explain the BMW," Will adds.

"That fucking car . . ." Rascal shakes his head as if he's disgusted with himself.

"Do Mom and Dad know?" I ask.

"I'm going to wait until I know more," Rascal says. Despite the handful of Oscars for the film adaptations of his books, Dad has never been happy with the movie versions of his novels.

The ripple effect means that, as a people, the Pages believe that nothing good comes out of Hollywood.

"To the bastardization of another great novel," I toast, standing and raising my glass. Everyone joins me.

"Hear, hear!" Will slams his glass into mine.

"Long live the bastards!" Rascal toasts while Avery tinks her glass into Rascal's but says nothing.

chapter six

Dinner is business as usual. Dad questions Will on his latest trip to hell; political theory is bandied about like a shuttlecock; and Will and I stifle giggles at Avery's complete cluelessness. When Dad asks the poor girl whether she voted last year, she says yes, she voted for *Crash* and was happy it took home Best Picture. Then she went on a long tirade about how she didn't even bother to see *Brokeback Mountain* because she heard it was slow and Heath Ledger was a mumbler—and mumbling is *not* acting, despite what everyone thinks.

Dad takes a long drink of his Scotch and gently asks Avery if she's in the movie business. She beams and "confesses" that she is. Mom asks her what movies she's been in, using the tone of voice she uses to speak to the kids at the local elementary school where she volunteers. Avery rattles off a list of movies none of us have seen, action/adventure stuff. She tells us a few of the plots and whispers conspiratorially that the movie she's working on now is so secret she shouldn't even be talking about it. No one presses her further.

"So, Dragon? How long were you in Lebanon?" Dad asks, sipping his Scotch.

"I just got back. I was in Israel before that. I'm just finishing that piece for *Esquire*. Then I had to fly to London for a story.

But that was for the *Washington Post*," Will explains, not missing a beat. Once again, we are forced to compare the two boys: Will, the world-traveling war correspondent who looks every bit the part, and Rascal, someone so burdened by his delicate beauty that his whole life has been about proving how bad he is despite the angelic visage.

"But I can tell *you* guys!" Avery interrupts.

"Excuse me?" I ask.

"Avery, just—" Rascal soothes.

"The movie! The super-secret movie! Do you guys wanna know about it?" Avery looks around the table. Will leans forward. Rascal downs the rest of his wine.

"Sure," Mom obliges. She couldn't be less interested. Her idea of entertainment is sitting in her garden with a good book and a cup of tea.

"It's not like we're ever going to see it," Dad says. Will clears his throat. Rascal glares at Dad. The look that passes between them isn't really anger. Just disappointment that once again the bar is inches from Rascal's fingertips.

"I'd love to know what it is," Mom says, trying to smooth over the moment. Avery smiles and excitedly tells us about the movie and how it's based on this video game and how the script stays really—and I'll quote her here—"true to the original work." Oh, God. Poor Avery. She's blissfully unaware of the hornet's nest she's swatted. Dad stares at her from the head of the table.

"Ben's had several books made into movies," Mom blurts preemptively, before Dad can say it less civilly. Rascal pours himself another glass of wine.

"*Oh?* Are you a producer?" Avery leans toward Dad, pulling her blouse farther down in front.

"No, sweetie." Dad gets up and pours himself another Scotch.

"Dad's a novelist," Rascal says, sitting back in his chair.

"Like you?" Avery questions. The entire table cringes in unison.

"He wrote *The Coward*," Will whispers so only Avery can hear.

She stares at Will, her eyes on fire. "I saw that in high school. It's based on a book? I didn't know he was still alive. He *wrote* that?" She's built quickly from a whisper to a near-shriek of horror. Will puts his finger over his mouth and tells her to shhhhhh. I allow the tiniest of smiles to crawl across my face. Will winks at me.

"Fuckers ruined it," Dad blurts, oblivious to Will and Avery's conversation.

"Oh?" Avery asks coyly, now completely aware of who Dad is. We don't come to her rescue. We don't have to. He's Ben Page. He gets to talk like this. His boorish behavior has gone unchecked for decades. Unchecked by society, unchecked by his publisher, and unchecked even by his own family. The surlier he is, the more profanity he spews, the more enthusiastically Avery will eat up every F-word.

"Put some bullshit Hollywood ending on it," Dad says. That was actually quite tame. I breathe a small sigh of relief. Will puts his arm around the back of my chair. Rascal sips his wine; his eyes are unfocused and elsewhere.

"You know, in all my years in the biz, I've learned that producers really have the project's best interests at heart," Avery oozes. There is a collective hunkering down at the table. We're all in the movie theater, and the lights have dimmed.

"What did you say?" Dad's voice is quiet and low. It always amazes me how many people offer themselves up for this battery. It's as if you open up the cage, believing you'll be the only one the wild animal doesn't bite.

"I just think that we're all on the same side here, trying to put out the best movie that we possibly can," Avery explains, not catching on at all.

Dad zeroes in. "It must be terrifying to have to worry about something as fleeting as your looks when it comes to your career. I mean, you gain five pounds and—" Dad snaps his fingers. Avery looks as though she's been shot. Dad continues, "That's it. Back to Podunk." Dad forks up a roasted potato and takes a bite.

"I was nominated for a Golden Globe last year when I played that poor retarded girl who sang the national anthem at the Super Bowl, and that was *not* about looks," Avery yells. I instinctively lean in to Will as we wait for the fireworks to stop. He curls his hand over my shoulder, steadying both of us. I sip my water. Rascal's face is expressionless. Avery is merely another offering to Dad, like the overzealous fan. They will share in her evisceration.

"*Just* a Golden Globe?" Dad sighs. Mom straightens her napkin on her lap. Dad cracks that patented award-winning smile. It still sends chills down my spine.

"Ben," Mom soothes.

"Do you honestly think that a bunch of Nancy boys with eight cell phones and manicured nails can make a better story out of something that's already perfect? You think they know better about that life? About what it feels like to look over the edge and not know whether or not you're going to come back this time? How alone that feels? How your entire life has been about this search for something that matters, something that means something, and how maybe it's easier to just end it all, just put yourself out of your misery?" Dad's voice gets louder with each word. We all know this monologue by heart. Rascal toyed with the idea of using it to get into acting school at one point.

"No, sir. I didn't know . . . I just . . ." Avery stutters.

"Of course you didn't know. You're not paid to think. You're paid to eye-fuck an entire audience, and when that ship sails, you'll go back to being nothing," Dad says, swirling the Scotch around in his glass and going for the jugular.

"I'm starting my own production company . . . I'm looking for projects on my own . . ." Avery is rambling wildly.

"You go ahead and do that. And when you find the first wrinkle you can't Botox away, *then* why don't you preach to me how empowered you feel," Dad says.

"How do you like the ahi?" Mom blurts to Rascal, trying valiantly to interrupt the flow of Dad's rant.

"Fuckers ruined it," Rascal answers. Dad barks out a laugh and beams at Rascal. Avery titters nervously and excuses herself to go to the bathroom. Will and I look at each other. We have the same unspoken conversation we've been having all of our lives across a series of dinners that have ended in fireworks. Ours are not unlike the expressions on the faces of two people who just survived a car accident. As the smoke billows from under the hood, you look to each other to see if you've made it through in one piece.

Mom finally sips her wine. All is back to normal. Whatever that is. Rascal looks down at his plate. Dad grabs the now-empty decanter and walks into the kitchen, past Iris and Robert. He never asks either of them to do anything for him. It's his one small act of rebellion against the Foster Family Fortune. Rascal watches Dad exit the room. It's as if we're all left to stomp out the glowing embers of the bonfire that Dad absent-mindedly started.

Dinner wears on. Avery has been in the bathroom for some time now, and Will jokes about sending in a search party. I joke that maybe we should send in a plumber and an eating-disorder specialist. Mom scolds me, saying that my joke is in poor taste. I'm tempted to make another joke about vomit being the true culprit of poor taste, but I hold my tongue.

"Weren't you going to make us that famous dessert of yours?" Mom says. She's getting a little tipsy. We've all been hitting the bottle a little hard to get through tonight's three-ring circus.

"I didn't know you wanted me to, Mom. But if you want, I can go plate up the berry crumble you have in the kitchen. Is it raspberry?" I ask.

"Mixed. It's mixed berry," Mom says, swaying slightly in her chair.

"Mom, that's enough," Rascal says, leaning across and sliding Mom's wineglass out of her reach. She hardly notices. Will is trying to blend in with the scenery as much as possible. It's a holdover from his childhood. The less of a problem he was, the longer he got to stay at our house. I imagine that's a hard habit to break. As are others.

I put my napkin on the table and walk toward the kitchen, in search of a mixed-berry crumble and sanctuary. I push open the door and find my father leaning in to an obviously smitten Avery. He has a twirl of her chocolate hair in his long fingers, and she's giggling quietly with her head tilted slightly down. I can't move. Avery pulls away from Dad and clears her throat. Dad looks at me over his shoulder and straightens up. The strand of Avery's flawlessly dyed hair falls from his fingers.

Flash.

This is one of those snapshots that will definitely land in the eternal slide show that runs in my mind. Specific scenes replayed and replayed right before I fall asleep or whenever my mind is idle. Good and bad events burned behind my eyes. This one will definitely live on forever in the pantheon.

"What's going on in here, Pop?" I keep my voice low, out of some horribly misplaced sense of protectiveness for my dad. Avery starts acting like she's trying to find something in one of the kitchen drawers. Way to commit to a scene, Avery. Working with props and everything.

"Ben was just—I mean, your dad—Well . . ." Avery has pulled a rubber spatula from a drawer. She's holding it up with a triumphant "aha" expression.

"We were just talking Hollywood stuff, Bink," Dad says.

"Then why aren't you throttling her?" I joke. Avery laughs nervously. I see a bit of spittle land on my dad's cheek.

I feel sick to my stomach. This is wrong on so many levels. So wrong. But . . . Rascal and I always used to talk. You don't hang out with fucking Warren Beatty and Jack Nicholson because you hold monogamy sacred. Dad was a legend in his time, and adding to his celebrity were stories of the long lines of women he'd seduced. I guess I thought all that was somehow in the past. Dad's pushing sixty now, no longer the kid from the wrong side of the tracks trying to conquer the world one doe-eyed starlet at a time. I thought it was ancient history. I certainly didn't think he would pull this shit in the goddamn kitchen with Mom just a few feet away. I also never realized that seeing it in person—as opposed to harboring vague suspicions or reading about it in yellowing magazine articles—would be this devastating.

"I'd better get back out there," Avery says, walking across the kitchen with the rubber spatula. At the kitchen door, she turns to me. "Can you, um, not mention this to your brother?" Her syrupy-sweet perfume wafts over me.

"You know, you really mustn't mumble, *Crystal*." I don't even bother to look at her. She slinks past me and out into the dining room. I hear the door open and close behind me.

Dad reaches up into the liquor cabinet and pulls out a bottle of Macallan Scotch, 1949. Must be some night—that vintage runs into the thousands. He takes out an old-fashioned glass from another cabinet. He pours. He drinks. He pours again and turns to walk out of the kitchen, leaving the empty decanter behind and choosing to just go with the bottle. I'm still standing in the doorway.

"Nothing happened, Bink," Dad says, his voice loose and grumbly. I close my eyes, and the copperplate of an image burns behind my eyelids. He's right; there was no kissing. It's not like she was straddling him or anything. But Jesus, it was far from nothing.

"I just came in to get the mixed-berry crumble," I explain. He's standing so close I can smell him. He still smells the same: like a forest with a hint of pipe smoke.

"Good thing it wasn't your brother. Would have landed in his next book for sure," Dad jokes. He ruffles my hair and pushes open the door.

chapter seven

I open the cabinet and take out six of Mom's dessert plates. The routine of the kitchen is the only thing that can calm me again. Iris comes into the kitchen, asking if she can help me with anything. No doubt I've taken too long. I would apologize or try to explain, but I don't think Hallmark makes a card for walking in on your father wooing your brother's lollipophead. Iris opens the big Sub-Zero refrigerator and pulls out a beautiful mixed-berry crumble. She sets it on the counter, and I begin plating the dessert.

"Thanks," I say, a little too intensely.

"It's good having you kids home," Iris says as she takes the first two plates into the dining room. Robert comes in and takes out two more plates. I take the last two. I back out of the kitchen and turn around just as Robert is setting the plates in front of Rascal and a very twitchy Avery. The plates I have are for Will and me. Iris and Robert are trained to serve in order of importance. Good to know where I stand.

"Are you working in *our* kitchen now?" Dad says, laughing, as I put a plate in front of Will. Are you still cheating on Mom? I want to scream. At almost sixty? With this useless piece of shit? I stare at Rascal. Does he know?

"Thanks," Will whispers, almost in my ear.

The image of Dad in the kitchen with Avery doing "nothing" is playing on a loop inside my head. Rascal hasn't looked at Avery since she sat back down. Does Mom know? Has she done the same math that Rascal and I have? Does she think it's all in the past as well, or is this something she just lives with? I take the napkin from my lap and lay it carefully beside my plate. I take a long drink of my wine and set the glass back on the table. Just sit. Stay quiet.

But I can't. "Excuse me." I push my chair back from the table and head for the deck outside the dining room. I hate myself for being so weak, so emotional. I knew this information. I knew Dad was a womanizer. But God—seeing it. Seeing him. Seeing *them*. Will stands and follows me out onto the deck. Mom takes this opportunity to ask if anyone wants the mixed-berry crumble à la mode. Rascal mumbles yes. Avery pushes the plate of calories as far away from her as possible, ensuring that her career will last for at least a few more moments.

"You okay?" Will asks.

"No," I whisper, plotting out the fastest route to the farthest mountaintop. Will puts his arm around me.

"Let's take a walk," he says. He tilts his head and looks right into my eyes.

"Can I stay with you tonight?" I ask, moving away enough so that Will's arm falls away. I catch a blur of Avery in the dining room. She's sitting back in her chair and signaling to Iris to take her untouched plate.

"Absolutely," Will says, pulling me back to him. I breathe in deeply, trying to calm my stomach.

"I walked in on my dad and *Avery*," I whisper. Will doesn't move. "I don't want to talk about it," I add.

"Okaaaay," he says. We're both rocking back and forth.

"Let's go back to my place." Rascal ambles out onto the deck, carrying a cup of coffee.

"Dad just said I look like Ted Neeley from *Jesus Christ Superstar*," Rascal announces.

"Not even close. You're more Paul McCartney, you know in that one photo, the one where he's got the baby in his coat," I say, trying to sound light and unaffected.

"*The* baby? I believe it's actually *his* child, Elisabeth," Rascal corrects.

"Well, yeah, I knew that," I say.

"That's a great shot," Will absently adds. An awkward silence falls.

"You let me know when you're ready to go," Will says to me. He smiles at Rascal and then walks back into the dining room. I straighten myself up.

"Bit overly dramatic, don't you think?" Rascal says, eyeing Will.

"So, how into Avery are you?" I say.

"Why? Are you soliciting new members for your book club?" Rascal toys.

"Will you be serious?" I plead.

"Oh, let me guess. Avery doesn't know who Dad is; Dad gets pissed. Avery excuses herself for the world's longest trip to the bathroom and is soon joined by the world-famous author, who has to prove how memorable and relevant he is. Jesus, Bink, I couldn't even write that into a novel. People would think it was too predictable." Rascal leans on the banister overlooking the grounds.

"It's not as if Avery is some big loss, for the love of God," I say.

"It's not about goddamn Avery," Rascal says, his voice a low growl.

"No, I guess it's not," I say, backing down. I decide not to ask

Rascal why every woman he "dates" has the IQ of a cotton swab, or point out that had he brought someone halfway intelligent, she probably would have acted quite differently in the kitchen. Maybe—maybe I just hope she would. I think about the fan in the bookstore, an offering. A trapped mouse. Another way Dad and Rascal compete.

"You better fucking believe it's not," Rascal says, straightening up.

"You've walked in on him before?" I ask, prodding a little.

"Yep," Rascal spits out. The statement hangs in the crisp air between us. Rascal looks over at me, and for a second, he lets me in on the pain he vigilantly keeps from everyone else. The weight of it smothers me. He continues, "And Avery and I just met, so, really one common denominator in this little equation." His head dips. There is a darkness to him right now that scares me. I break our eye contact and look into the dining room. Rascal slowly leans back over the banister. Once again he's a million miles away.

"Are you at least going to tell them your option was picked up for the book?" I ask, trying to get back on solid ground.

"Are you kidding? On the same day we were treated to the legendary 'bunch of Nancy boys with eight cell phones and manicured nails' monologue? No way." Rascal imitates Dad's voice to a T. He takes a slow sip of his coffee, not missing a beat.

"I can't believe her name is Crystal," I say quietly, finding a napkin on the teak patio table and wiping my nose. It's freezing out here.

"Are you going back to L.A.? Do you want to stay out in the guesthouse with me?" Rascal takes the napkin away from me and puts it in his now empty coffee mug.

"No, I'll be fine. I'm going to stay at Will's tonight. At least I won't have to sleep in the goddamn Crow's Nest."

"I thought sleepovers were only reserved for girlfriends—or don't adults use the word 'girlfriend' these days?" Rascal lets that hang in the air awhile. He continues, "Now, if you'll excuse me, I've got a gal named *Crystal* to break up with." He squeezes my shoulder as he walks past me. The briefest of jolts passes between us, connecting us in whatever this night has revealed. Best not to talk any more about it. We'd have to actually admit that Dad was . . . well, that Dad *is* the common denominator that connects us and everything that we question about ourselves.

I follow Rascal inside and sit down next to Will at the table. He lays his arm on the back of my chair as I settle in. Dad is eating his crumble. Apparently, he didn't want it à la mode. Avery keeps blathering on about the weather and how it's so much cooler up here than it is in Los Angeles.

"I'm going to stay at Will's tonight," I say as nonchalantly as possible. I nervously get back up to pour myself a cup of tea from the sideboard.

"Why wouldn't you stay here, for crissakes?" Dad says.

"Yes, darling, why not stay here? Breakfast is going to be early. Two seatings would be inconvenient for Iris and Robert," Mom says, slurring her words slightly.

"We've talked about this before. The Crow's Nest, Port Side, feels a little claustrophobic. That's all," I say. It's ideal weather for a cup of tea and the confrontation I should have had with my parents years ago.

"It's the same room you've stayed in your whole life, Elisabeth. All of a sudden it's claustrophobic? Aren't you being a tad dramatic?" Mom demands. Rascal pushes the now-melted ice cream and crumble around his plate. Will sets down his fork and seems startled by the loud sound it makes. Dad breaks the smallest of smiles.

"Come on, Ballard . . . Mr. Page. I'd like Elisabeth to come and stay with me. I'll have her back in time for breakfast, I promise." His voice is velvety, with just the right hint of self-conscious awkwardness. Mom smiles broadly as Will finishes. Avery smiles at Will and flutters her eyelashes.

Are you fucking kidding me?

I lean in to her trajectory and raise an eyebrow. She quickly looks away and grabs for her glass of water. Dad flicks his hand dismissively. Mom finally yields and sends Robert upstairs for my bag.

As we say our goodbyes in the foyer, I look around at all that defines me. The rubric for success in my family has always been about legacy—what imprint will you make on this world. I have tried to live by these standards all my life. Measuring success and love by the teaspoon, always falling short, the goal constantly out of reach. My five-year plan has become an unending road to nowhere, both professionally and personally. I snap out of my reverie and take my bag from Robert. Mom kisses me on both cheeks. Dad kisses me on top of my head. Rascal waves to me as he walks out to the guest cottage with Avery trailing closely behind. Will stands with his arm around my waist. In that moment I'm met with a slide show of my own future: a future plagued with the reality of living life in a reactionary, almost passive, state. What would happen if I veered off course and asked Will point-blank to join me on my adventure? An adventure that would start with a conversation we should have had years ago about what it is we're doing with each other. Is there an Emerald City at the end of this yellow brick road, or does it just keep spiraling to nowhere?

chapter eight

B ack at Will's house, I take a long soak in the tub and then settle in by the fire, swaddled in one of his bathrobes. He's upstairs tweaking his piece for *Esquire,* so I'm left alone with my little epiphanies. Of course Will loves me, I think, he doesn't have to be all junior-prom about it and show up at my door with a wrist corsage every time I need a hug. But would that be such a bad thing? Why am I afraid to ask? I've always defined love as something intangible that can't be harnessed or quantified. I thought if I demanded that it be real, something I can count on, I'd be dumbing it down somehow. Making it ordinary.

I fall asleep in the warmth and comfort of the large couch by the dwindling fire. When I wake the next morning, I'm wrapped in an elaborate arrangement of blankets and pillows, all smelling of Will. Someone's in the kitchen. I sit up and straighten out my back, trying to work out the kinks caused by sleeping on a couch all night. I stand and cinch Will's bathrobe closed. I walk into the kitchen, hoping for a cup of coffee and maybe a crack at The Conversation, ending in a rerun of yesterday's kitchen antics before I go out for my morning run.

"The height of efficiency, I see," I coo as I walk into the large sun-filled kitchen. A tiny woman turns around quickly and clutches at her heart.

"Oh God, I'm so sorry. I thought you were Will—I thought you were William," I stutter, starting to back out of the kitchen.

"Mr. Houghton is still sleeping. Coffee?" The woman tentatively holds a steaming mug of coffee out to me. I cinch the robe tighter, making sure not to flash the poor woman. I take it and thank her.

"It's a pleasure to meet you," the woman says, extending her hand to me.

"Oh, I'm sorry. I'm Elisabeth Page, an old friend of William's." I extend my free hand to the woman.

"I'm Marcia," she says. Anne Houghton goes through approximately thirty-seven thousand housekeepers per year. *Marcia* won't see Christmas.

"Nice to meet you, Marcia," I say, taking a sip of my coffee.

She smiles. "Are you leaving this afternoon with Mr. Houghton?"

"I'm sorry?" I grip the mug of coffee tightly.

"He's leaving this afternoon for Venezuela. I didn't know if you worked with him or . . ." She slowly trails off, realizing she shouldn't have volunteered anything. The look on my face is one of sheer horror. He's leaving? To motherfucking Venezuela?

"Oh, I . . . uh . . ." I put down the coffee mug and stand there for a minute. I don't know what to think. Why didn't he tell me?

"Is everything okay?" the woman asks, approaching me warily. Like animal control might approach a rabid pit bull with one of those poles that has a metal lasso at the end of it.

"You know what? Everything's fine. Just fine," I say. My eyes refocus, and I set my jaw. My voice is low and robotic. I feel ridiculous. Join me on the adventure? I doubt that analogy even works when one's companion has the nasty habit of never fucking standing still for longer than a few seconds.

I walk back out into the great room. I can't wait to get out of here. No, I can't wait to get Will's robe off and get out of here. I strip off the robe and hurl it at the couch. Right then Marcia comes out of the kitchen, carrying the coffee mug I left on the counter. She gasps, rightfully so. I let out a long sigh and reach for the mug of coffee. Great.

"Oh, that's right. I forgot that. You're so kind." I take the mug of coffee and try to act like I'm not completely naked. Marcia averts her eyes and stammers something about not wanting the coffee to get cold. I nod confidently and continue, "Delicious. Thank you, Marcia." I walk as decorously as I can upstairs to get my luggage out of Will's bedroom. I whip open his door. He's lying in the middle of his huge bed, wearing nothing but a pair of boxers, his yellow hair buried deeply in a mound of down pillows.

"So, Venezuela?" I snap as I walk over to my suitcase, which is open on the large wooden bench at the foot of Will's bed.

"What?" Will stirs and turns his head so he can see me. He cranes his neck all the way around. "Are you naked? Why are you naked?" A smile curls on his sleepy face. He starts to sit up.

"You know, we don't lie to each other, Will. You could have just told me," I say, finding a pair of panties and slipping them on. Will rubs his eyes and sits up in bed.

"Omission is not lying," Will says lazily, almost snickering to himself.

"Why not tell me that you're leaving again?" I say, fastening my bra in the back.

"I knew you'd be mad," Will says, attempting to soothe me.

"You're damn right I'm mad. How could you do this?" I ask. My voice gets louder with every question.

"How could *I* do this? Let's review, shall we? Who was it

who moved to New York right after high school without consulting anyone?" Will says. His eyes are wide open, and his voice is no longer sleepy.

"What?" I say, crossing my arms.

Will whips off his covers and sits on the side of the bed.

"Right. And then who was it who moved to fucking France for four years?" Will says, his voice cracking slightly.

"Was this before or after you went to India for a year in search of a higher consciousness and instead found that fucking— What was her name? Soleil Moon McHippie No Job?" I scream.

"At least she was better than that Jean-Claude I Have a Small Turd Under My Nose," Will responds.

"*He,* at least, was an amazing chef," I offer, defending a man I dropped like a hot potato when Will called from the train station in Lyon.

"You know, at least I'm trying here. I came to see you. I mean, what do *you* think is the shorter flight? London to Venezuela, or London to JFK to *Los Angeles* to Venezuela?" Will rests his arms on his knees in a move that appears casual, but his hands are in tight fists.

"Well, I'm not British Airways, so . . ." I want to hurt him. I can't believe we're back here again.

Will's eyes flare, and a forced smile breaks over his face. "No, no, I'm sorry, you're right. You're not British Airways. I flew all the way back to L.A. to see you, even if it was only for a couple of days," he says into his lap.

"It's always just a couple of days. I wanted . . . I don't know . . . I wanted . . ." I trail off. What I want is too hard to put into words. I want to grab Will, hold him down, and make him stay.

"You've never really wanted to be serious and commit, either.

Your five-year plan doesn't make any room for commitment. So climb down off your high horse," Will says, his tone final, no longer intimate. He stands.

"High horse? Some woman in your kitchen had to tell me you were leaving this afternoon. There's no high horse here. I just . . . I thought you might stay a little longer this time," I say, my voice breaking. Will stands right in front of me. My hand rests on his chest, physically holding him back from leaving. I'm going to risk asking for something. Risk letting him know that I need something from him, that maybe I'm a little stronger when he's here, a little happier.

"Elisabeth, I . . ." Will begins.

"I want you to *stay*," I whisper, looking him right in the eye. He knows me too well not to understand what I mean. He holds my gaze, his brain searching for an answer—something he can say so we don't start fighting again. My vigilantly calculated life is spilling out of its measuring cup at an alarming rate.

"Why? So I can come visit you at the restaurant?" he says, his voice defeated.

I don't have an answer. I don't. I just want to make this work.

"I want to try. I'm not saying it'll be perfect. I want you to stay. Don't go," I say. How can I get such giantness across to him and still sound safely indifferent? Oh, that's right.

I can't.

"Please?" I whisper.

Will breathes deeply, his eyes focusing on mine, pleading with me not to muddy our last hours together before he has to leave again.

"You know I love you. I just never said I'd be good at it," he says, taking my hand off his chest. He kisses me lightly on my palm as he walks past me and out into the hallway.

chapter nine

I spend the rest of the morning at my parents', eating a large breakfast and enduring a barrage of questions about why Will isn't with me. Work, I say. The only lull in the interrogation comes when Mom asks Rascal why Avery had to leave for Los Angeles so early. Work, he says. Dad has been in his study all morning. Work, he says. Always work.

"I want to get home," I say to Rascal as he walks me to my car after breakfast. I've already said goodbye to Mom and told her to pass along my farewells to Dad.

"You can stay with me," Rascal says.

"I know. I . . . just want to get home," I say, beeping my car unlocked.

"You'll call if you need anything," Rascal says.

"I will," I say. My voice is still scarily monotone. Rascal leans close and brings me in for a tight big-brother hug. No one hugs me like Rascal. He doesn't let me go, even past that polite moment when both huggers know the hug has reached its zenith. He holds tight. He knows to keep going. He knows there's more hug needed. I melt in to him, and he holds tighter.

"Aren't we a pair?" I ask quietly in his ear.

"That we are," Rascal absently agrees.

"We're consistent," I add.

"Yeah, we're *both* fucked up." Rascal laughs, finally letting go.

He opens the car door. The car still smells of smoke from the night before. I roll down all the windows, trying to clear any lingering cigarette odor. I climb in, and Rascal shuts the door behind me.

"Be good," he warns.

"I will," I assure him.

"I think I'm going to take a long drive after I say my good-byes," Rascal says through the open window. He kisses me on the cheek and gives it a long squeeze. I wince.

"House of Pies on Halloween, right?" I remind him.

"Wouldn't miss it," he says.

As I pull down the long driveway, I watch Rascal in the rear-view mirror, getting smaller and smaller. The last time he went on a "drive," he was gone for six months. He got a job as a rigger at some oil field in Texas and took up with a waitress at the local watering hole à la *Five Easy Pieces*. He couldn't just find a job at a coffeehouse somewhere—no, Rascal has to go and get as dirty as possible. The more oil on his face, the less he's a Foster/Page.

What is it we're all trying to prove?

The 101 is empty. My windows are open, and my mind is racing. Will. Dad. Mom. My BlackBerry rings from the passenger seat. I quickly snatch it up and check to see who it is. Part of me wants it be Will, calling before he gets on the plane. What if he doesn't come back this time? What if my last words to him were some bullshit about high horses? But it's Mom.

"Hello?" I say, closing my window and turning down the music.

"Hello, darling," she says.

"How are you?" I ask, trying to make conversation. I feel like a traitor. Does she know it's *still* going on—and right in her kitchen?

"About last night," Mom begins. My stomach lurches.

"Yes?"

"Your father was out of line. He realizes he shouldn't have used that kind of language in front of guests," Mom says.

"What are you talking about?" I ask. The ocean whizzes by me. I'm not getting a chance to soak it in as much as I'd like.

"When your father was talking about the film adaptation, darling. I'm sure he made everyone uncomfortable. You must apologize to William when you see him next. I've already asked Rascal to let Avery know that . . . your father didn't mean to *do* what he did," Mom says.

"What are we talking about here, Mom?" God, she *has* to know.

"Darling, don't be coy. We all know how your father can be," Mom says. I take a deep sigh.

"I'll pass the message on to Will," I say, doubting the Black-Berry can convey the proper level of disappointment.

"Now, remember, the Grace Center benefit is next Sunday night at the Ritz. I'm counting on you to be there for a silent-auction item. Your father and Rascal have both donated signed first editions." Mom has her business voice on now, maintaining the status quo—fund-raisers, silent auctions, gala balls, refusing to admit that her husband was in some dark corner with a girl under half his age.

"What?" I say. That's it?

"We're having a benefit for the Grace Center this coming Sunday, Elisabeth. Don't you remember? You said you could donate a private cooking series and a nice basket of goodies for the silent auction. I'll e-mail you the details. Are you still available? Rascal probably won't be able to make it. But he did say that he'd bid on all the silent-auction items to get the bidding started."

"That's fine. The cooking series, and I'll bring the basket of goodies with me," I say.

"Perfect. Now, drive safely, darling." I listen closely for any sign that she knows what's going on. Nothing. Just my own breathing and the muffled sound of the California coast zooming by outside my rolled-up window. We say goodbye, and I put the BlackBerry on the front seat.

Then I pick it back up, dial quickly, and wait.

"This is Will Houghton. You know what to do." The mechanized voice rambles on about pressing one or paging this person and asking me to leave my message at the tone. Who doesn't know this by now? Do we still have to be told to wait for the tone?

"Hey, hi . . . it's me. Please be safe and call me when you get back. Halloween is coming up. Maybe we can shoot for that." I hesitate and swallow hard. "Okay . . . see you when you get back." I beep the BlackBerry off, continue down the 101, and wonder why, after thirty years, I still can't tell Will I love him.

Maybe I'm not so good at this, either.

chapter ten

I was about nine years old when I realized Dad wasn't like other fathers. I was starting fourth grade, and we were all going to the annual back-to-school night at my school. The whole family loaded up in the Mercedes wagon that Mom still drives today. It was my first back-to-school night that Dad had attended. Long months alone with his masterpieces, moody revisions, and book tours had always kept him from attending in the past.

I stood proudly at my desk. I'd decorated it with an elaborately drawn nameplate and had displayed a construction paper book bound with green twine for my parents' perusal. I grinned as Mom excitedly turned each page. She asked a ton of questions about my motivation, and pointed out specific lines in my fantastic poetry about pets I dreamed of having and school buses I didn't ride, and told me they were all so thoughtful. She sat at that tiny desk, her Chanel jacket bunching up around the metal cross bar, her long legs curled under the tiniest of chairs. But when I looked for my dad, he wasn't there. He never even made it into the classroom. He'd been stopped at the door by my classmates' parents, fans whom he most willingly obliged by reminiscing about his glory days, drawing a larger and larger crowd.

◆

I open the door to my apartment, drop my keys into the designated bowl, roll my suitcase into the bedroom, and collapse on the couch. I stare longingly at the silver espresso maker on the stovetop. Maybe if I try to use a bit of mind control, I can will it to make me an Americano. My stomach is still churning. It's good to be home and even better to be away from my parents. But at the same time, I feel more alone now than ever.

My short time with Will is still wet on the canvas—my head on his chest, listening to the gurglings of his stomach and his smoky voice resonating in my ears. I don't know what's worse—going without these things for so long that the memory fades or being reminded how glorious it feels to be held by him and have his touch linger on my body, only to give it up once more.

Though it's the last thing I want to do, I drag myself off the couch and hop in the shower. The Silver Lake farmers' market is already in full swing. If I hurry, I can catch the tail end. It's a bit of a drive from my apartment, but I'll feel better if I get up, get out, and keep my mind busy. It doesn't help to sit here alone and think. Maybe I can find something autumnal for tomorrow's feature. As I drive through the streets of Los Angeles, I notice pumpkin patches sprouting up where only vacant lots once stood. The holiday season has officially begun. Those pumpkin patches will morph into Christmas-tree lots as the weeks pass. I realize that I'm going to have to endure yet another holiday season alone. I focus back on the road and toy with the idea of using a pumpkin in tomorrow's feature.

I smell the delicious tamales as I walk from the parking lot to the farmers' market, just south of Sunset Junction. Tents and tents of fresh fruits and vegetables line the street, while street musicians squeeze in between and play for whatever pocket change you might throw their way. As I mill around the market, munching on an apple and carrying a bag of fresh tamales, I hear my name being called in the distance. I turn and see Samuel's very pregnant wife, Margot, waddling toward me. Margot owns and operates *property* (all lowercase, thank you very much), a clothing boutique specializing in all things handmade. Samuel trails behind her, pulling a rolling cart that's filled to the brim with fresh fare. They must live in Silver Lake. Of course they do. In L.A., each neighborhood has its own, very specific style; its inhabitants stick to a strict dress code pursuant to the neighborhood's bylaws. It's a community shorthand. Silver Lake is a burgeoning hipster community stuck between Los Angeles proper and Pasadena. Its dilapidated streets are filled with newly renovated houses sporting paint colors that would make Diego Rivera proud, surrounded by vertical slatted fences. Silver Lake is one of the few areas in L.A. County where young families might find a starter home for under a million dollars. For a few more weeks, that is. I thought about renting there when I moved back from Lyon, but with the notorious L.A. traffic, it was too far away from the restaurant.

"Elisabeth! So good to see you," Margot says, squeezing my hand and smiling serenely. Stray blond ringlets brush her cheeks, but the bulk of her hair is caught up in two thick braids that trail down her back. She looks like a wandering milkmaid who belongs somewhere on the plains of Nebraska. She has gained little to no baby weight on her tiny frame. I compliment her on how great she looks, and she responds that a little kundalini yoga, eating macrobiotically, and a lot of good sex did the trick. I stop listening and am tempted to poke out my own eardrums with a nearby street performer's flaming torches. Despite everything, there's an air of pure calm floating above Margot.

She comes in for a hug; it appears the hand squeeze wasn't enough for her. Margot grew up on the Los Angeles touchy-feely aesthetic. The few times I've met her have bordered on the Sapphic. I laugh and nervously twitter through the awkward embrace. When Margot releases me, I greet Samuel with a tentative wave. He seems out of his element. His usual white chef's jacket has been replaced by a white T-shirt under a vintage-looking plaid shirt that's half tucked in. He's exchanged his checked chef's pants for low-slung tan corduroys with a large leather belt.

"I'm thinking about a pumpkin something for tomorrow. What do you think?" I say to Samuel. He looks slightly stricken and thinks a little too long about his answer. He's probably mulling over thousands of recipes.

"You could go left field and do a pumpkin flan, or go kitsch and do a roulade with a pumpkin puree," he announces at last.

Margot claps her hands together, tilts her head to the side, and beams at him. Samuel's entire face relaxes as he takes her in—her wide smile, the very glow of her. As a giant smile breaks across his face in reply, I realize I've never, not one time, seen Samuel smile. I feel like a voyeur. They've retreated to a world of their own for a few seconds. I snap back to reality. The flan isn't a bad idea.

"Maybe the flan with some kind of praline?" I say, realizing I'm completely uncomfortable around their easy intimacy. Samuel tears his gaze away from Margot and nods at me, accepting my praise. His beautiful smile quickly recedes. It wasn't for me; it was for Margot alone. I ache. Where Will touched me, I can feel my body already starting to frost over.

Margot breaks the awkward silence. "Oh, I wanted to thank you for your RSVP to my baby shower. It's right around the corner, isn't it? We're really looking forward to it," Margot says.

Mom has instilled many things in me over the years. One thing I'll never be able to do is let an invitation lie around without responding. I'm also the fastest gun in the West when it comes to thank-you cards. I've been known to send a thank-you card for a thank-you card. I still don't know why, exactly, I was invited to Margot's baby shower. Based on information gleaned from Samuel, which isn't much, I've decided that Margot was one of those free-love girls who invited her entire classroom to her birthday parties, only to have the kids gag in unison as her parents presented them with a gluten-free cake and asked them all to donate to a worthwhile charity in lieu of presents.

"You're welcome. It should be really fun," I say, lying through my teeth. The only thing worse than a baby shower is a baby shower for someone you hardly know. That's a lie as well. There's simply nothing worse than a baby shower. Period. Doesn't really matter whom it's for.

"What are you doing for the rest of the day, Elisabeth?" Margot asks, like Mom always did when she asked Will what he was doing for dinner, knowing full well there was nothing—no food or company—waiting for him at home. God, do I look that pathetic? Is Margot like a witch or something? A mind reader? Is she like a dog or bee, able to smell fear? Or am I just that transparent today?

"I'm not sure—maybe clean the house, do some laundry." Every Monday, when the restaurant is closed, I get myself ready for the hectic week ahead. I do a heavy cleaning of the apartment and launder all of my linens. I was going to buy a nice bouquet of fresh-cut flowers today. Coming to the farmers' market is like therapy for me.

"Might I tempt you to come along with us to look at a few houses?" Margot beams. Samuel looks horrified.

"Oh, well . . ." I stall. That sounds like the exact thing I *don't* want to do, Margot. I can't stomach the notion of hunting for a house on my own, let alone for someone else. Renting an apartment is ideal for me right now. Leaky faucet? Call the landlord. Creak in the floorboard? Call the landlord. Problem with the space? Give notice and find a new one. No lawn to mow, no garden to tend. An apartment is perfect in the very definition of its transitory nature.

"Chef, you don't— Please don't feel obligated. Margot's a bit spontaneous . . ." Samuel trails off. She nudges him slightly, and he softens, shooting the smallest of smiles her way. They're fucking adorable. They are the last people in the entire world I want to be around, especially today. I thought Samuel was a quiet rock of a man, steely and resolute. Now I find out that, only through love, a happy marriage and a baby on the way, and blahblahBLAH, he's a new man and all smiley and endearing and shit. I would rather drive back up to my parents' Montecito house and spend a wonderful afternoon reconciling my checkbook over a nice bottle of merlot while Will finalizes his travel arrangements.

"Oh, Samuel, please!" Margot leans against Samuel, putting her hand on his chest. Get. Me. Out. Of. Here. I came here for a safe harbor, not to be reminded of what it is that I'm missing.

"The first house we're scheduled to see is right in Silver Lake—what do you think?" Margot presses. I'm twitchy and nervous. I never should have left my apartment.

"I'll have all of the pumpkins in the car, you know, the flan idea . . . so . . ." I say, looking around as if I have important business here. I must be in a weakened state because of the whole Montecito fiasco. I simply don't have the energy to turn Margot down. And the horrible truth be told, I don't want to be alone right now. Despite all of my objections.

"It's perfect fall weather for once—the temperature won't

affect the pumpkins at all. So will you join us?" She asks again.
Samuel stares at me. Margot tucks her hair behind one ear, and
her sun hat lifts with the breeze.

"Sure . . . sure," I say. I hate how weak I feel. We head over
toward the pumpkin stall; I'm still attempting to make excuses.
I drop in that my stomach is a little upset this afternoon, so
best not to take on the winding hills of Silver Lake. Margot suggests I buy a steaming mug of yogi tea from a turban-wearing
gentleman under a tent that's decorated with bright orange and
pink saris. Yogi tea. Uh-huh. Hey, Margot "I have the perfect
marriage" Decoudreau, maybe it's not a glass of goddamn tea
I need. Do you think the guy with the turban might conjure a
man who could stick around for longer than a couple of days
without wanting a motherfucking medal?

We buy eight pumpkins. As Samuel and I load them into
my car, Margot wanders off and finds herself some gluten-free
bread and a pair of baby overalls made from hemp.

I follow Samuel and Margot through the winding streets of
Silver Lake. The yogi tea smells incredible, and shockingly, it
does settle my stomach a little. I think about my apartment and
briefly entertain the idea of buying a house of my own someday.
Briefly. Even without all my philosophical reasons for not wanting to buy a home, it would still be just out of reach financially.
My salary minus my monthly expenses equals a comfortable
enough living and a nice savings; I'm definitely never going to
go hungry.

The obvious addendum to this issue is my parents' standing offer to give me the money for a down payment. They
always made it very clear that Rascal and I weren't going to be
trust-fund babies. Dad had made it on his own, and we were to
follow in his footsteps and not the Foster Family Tradition of
breeding social climbers with no work ethic. Our educations

were paid for, but beyond that, we were supposed to support ourselves. However, we were each given the option of "borrowing" money for our first house. Rascal immediately took them up on that offer and bought his bungalow in Santa Monica. But I can only see bars on the windows of any house that comes from my family's money. Let's face it, I can see only bars on the windows of anything as all-consuming and permanent as owning a home.

We park. I make sure my tires are cranked the right way; the hills in Silver Lake can get pretty steep. Samuel opens Margot's door and helps her out of the passenger seat as her linen skirt flies up. He smoothes down her skirt and leans in and kisses her. They speak quietly with each other and then share that little smile. My face flushes but instead of feeling anger and frustration, I'm overtaken by a wave of sadness. The void in my life seems to open up in front of me. Would I have missed that exchange completely if not for the past couple of days? I breathe in deeply, set my jaw, and push back any sadness and regret. On with the day. Stiff upper lip. I grab my purse from the passenger seat, get out, and beep my car locked.

The house is quintessential Silver Lake—gorgeous yet ramshackle. Set on the side of a hill, the entrance is hidden by overgrown hedges. You can't tell how big the house actually is. We file past the open-house sign and creak the door open. Samuel holds the door to let Margot enter first.

"Hellooo! Welcome!" It sounds like an extra from *The Stepford Wives* is greeting us. Samuel immediately slows down, causing me to bump into him. It feels oddly childish and a little slapsticky.

"Hello, Miss—" Margot says, taking a moment to read the woman's name tag. "Hughes?"

"*Mrs.* Hughes, and you are?" The very married Mrs. Hughes extends her overly manicured hand, revealing an obvious zirconia solitaire on her finger and a Rolex knockoff on her wrist, flanked by a diamond tennis bracelet Mr. Hughes probably purchased at a mall somewhere. She catches me taking inventory. I know I'm bitchy, but I can't help myself. Jewelry 101 is a required course in the Foster Family, right up there with prudent investing.

"We're Margot and Samuel Decoudreau," Margot says. There is an awkward moment as Mrs. Hughes looks at me. How do I fit in to all of this? Is this some weird surrogate-parent thing? Is Margot carrying my baby?

"And you are?" Mrs. Hughes arranges her hands in that weird triangle pose television presenters adopt when they dish the newest celebrity gossip. She's standing with her feet in a perfect L—the pose that slims. She must have learned that in her broker seminars at the Learning Annex. That and the now overused statement "And you are?"

"Elisabeth. I'm a friend," I say. Mrs. Hughes takes my extended hand and shakes it vigorously. I politely unravel myself and begin to walk through the house, leaving Mrs. Hughes to focus on the happy couple.

I can hear loud congratulations about the upcoming baby as Mrs. Hughes goes on about the great schools in the neighborhood, saying "inclusive" and "diverse" a few too many times. After the introductions, Mrs. Hughes leaves Samuel and Margot to investigate the house on their own. The three of us meet back in the dining room. The current owner decided to paint the beautiful high ceiling brilliant blue, in contrast with that of the living room, which is painted crimson red with a bright yellow sun around the tacky apartment-style chandelier.

"You have to look past the paint, love," Margot says to Samuel.

Samuel and I are both standing, mouth open, staring at the blueberry-colored crown moldings. I decide to leave them alone again. I wander off down a claustrophobic staircase. It leads to a personal gym that looks like it was inspired by a Bret Easton Ellis novel. Mirrors everywhere.

I start to look at the real nuts and bolts of the house.

If I were thinking about renting this place, I wouldn't care about any of the things a prospective buyer would. I'd look at the location and the price. That was what I did when I rented the apartment I live in now.

Do I look at men this way, too? As rentals? "Perfect in their transitory nature." Have I been giving notice and finding something new every time a problem arises? Afraid to invest in anything permanent because it may turn out to be decaying, given closer inspection? Fearing that one day I'll come in and find my cozy home is back on assignment in Venezuela?

"Elisabeth? Where'd you go?" Margot calls, startling me out of my trance. I run my fingers along a massive crack in the wall as I pick my way carefully up the narrow, dangerous staircase to find Margot and Samuel.

Where'd I go? That's a very good question.

chapter eleven

Like all pastry chefs in top-rated restaurants, I spend my week working until the wee hours of the morning. On the nights when I don't take Julie up on her offer for an after-hours glass of wine, I stumble home, throw my chef whites into the washer, and get my running gear ready for the morning. The occasional glasses of wine with Julie are merely a political maneuver, allowing me to keep her close and on good terms. I figure this way at least I'll have some kind of psychological red flag as to when—not if—she plans on climbing over me in order to get my job. But maybe I'm being naive. If Julie's worth her salt, I won't see her coming at all.

Most nights I have to wind down before I can fall asleep. I brew a mug of chamomile and watch some Tivoed shows— guilty pleasures, mostly: teen-angst dramas, BBC America mysteries, and reality shows. I spend several minutes staring at the ceiling before I finally doze off, thinking of the hundred or so desserts that went out that night. Revisiting each one. Could I have done better? How can I strive to do better tomorrow?

I wake at eight-thirty every morning, even on my days off. I make my bed, wash any stray dishes, and/or Swiffer if need be. If Mom doesn't call, I won't speak to another soul until I reach Joan's on Third at the end of my run. After Joan's, I come home, shower, and dress for the day. I wear a variation on the same outfit: checked pants and T-shirt. If it's chilly, I'll throw on my cashmere wraparound sweater. I have two—one charcoal gray, one black, so when one's at the dry cleaner I can wear the other. I slip on my clogs, put my hair in a ponytail, and hold my freshly laundered chef's jacket over my arm. I lock up my apartment, then walk down the staircase and into the communal courtyard, past the burbling fountain, and find my car in its space. I beep it unlocked, open the back door, lay the jacket neatly along the seat, and slam the door closed.

Depending on the day, I drive to one of five farmers' markets in and around Los Angeles. Some restaurants employ a "produce wrangler" to alleviate some of the stress of the job. But if it weren't for these daily adventures, I would be without the only variable in my day: the night's feature. The restaurant always carries a fruit feature along with the dessert-menu regulars—the bread pudding, the crème brûlée, and the moelleux chocolate cakes, the desserts that sound simple but are extremely complicated and involved. I wander through the tents, daydreaming, running through the Rolodex of recipes in my head. Unhurried. Content. Breathing easily. The more complicated the taste profile of a dessert, the more I relish the gathering of the ingredients. I load my purchases into the hatch of my car on the white sheet I keep there for this very reason. I drive to work and start my routine. Over and over and over and over again.

The idea of having any kind of a social life is laughable, with this kind of schedule. I haven't stayed in touch with most of the kids I grew up with, save Will. Once I left school, I realized rather quickly how little I had in common with them. I still get e-mailed photos of new babies, receive wedding announcements in the mail, and hear about those who made partner or took over the family business in my alumni newsletters. I'll send a card, flowers, or a congratulatory e-mail depending on the situation. But that's mainly because Mom would kill me if I slipped even a bit in the etiquette department.

As I walk from my car to the restaurant this Saturday morning, I notice the neighborhood school is having a big Halloween hoedown. I'm juggling a flat of Rome Beauty apples for the baked-apple feature when I see some strange figures approaching me. A witch/mom fights with the huge black brim of her hat to keep it from flying off in the afternoon wind. Her daughter, a combination Tinker Bell/wood nymph, stomps her tiny ballet-slippered feet impatiently. She's anxious to get to the hoedown. Behind them, the father, in full cowboy garb, rounds the corner carrying a baby dressed as a red M&M and holding hands with a barely-able-to-walk Jedi knight. I love this time of year.

When I get to the restaurant, Louis, the maître d', greets me with his usual two kisses and warns that Chef Canet is already in the kitchen. Wow, twice in one month. I feel my shoulders rise in anticipation.

Working in a kitchen of this caliber is like walking a tightrope every minute of every day. On one hand, I admire the passion and enormous talent that boils up from each and every corner. But the cutthroat competition, microscopic scrutiny, and almost daily temper tantrums are beginning to take a toll on me. I know it's the price we pay for being number one in a city where big numbers, opening weekends, and being "in" are coveted far more than a James Beard Award. Chef Canet has two. People would kill to do what I do. Shit, I would have killed me back in the day. I honestly thought the eggshells would disappear after I paid my dues.

I wonder which incarnation of Chef will be here tonight. Jolly, wine-spilling *Christian,* who slaps your back and tells you he loves you—he *really* loves you. Or *Chef* Canet, who fires you because you bought Gala apples instead of Fuji. The night I got fired for choosing the wrong apples, I sat in the walk-in for fifteen minutes, waiting for him to cool off. He did. All was forgiven after I apologized profusely for my stupidity. Of course, this pales in comparison to what went on in my years as an apprentice in Lyon. And one could argue that none of these instances hold a candle to what I grew up with. Christian Canet is a rank amateur next to Dad.

The kitchen is silent except for the vigorous, almost violent sound of knives on cutting boards. Chef is already in the corner with a glass of wine, whispering to Michel, his chef de cuisine. I notice his eyes are a little more bloodshot today, the dark circles a little more defined. The wine is being poured a little earlier, and his face is looking more haggard. Neither man looks up at me as I walk to my corner of the kitchen. Samuel and Julie haven't arrived yet. I have a couple of minutes to myself. I set the apples on the counter and make a beeline for the coffee.

"Chef Page—you will do an apple tonight?" Chef Canet breaks his conspiratorial conversation with Michel. Michel, who would say yes if Christian asked whether he could shoot Michel square in the eye with a double-barreled shotgun. "Oui, Chef Canet, whatever you want, whatever I can do to further your greatness" will probably be Michel's dying words.

"A deconstructed baked apple with Tahitian vanilla bean ice cream that we'll make here. Very simple—but." I make an A-OK sign that tells him I know it'll be great.

"It *is* good. It is not . . . the pumpkin flan you make last week—that was working-class, yes? Not even French." Chef Canet searches for his words, settling on the perfect one to make me feel like shit. How masterful. I guess the mystery of which incarnation will be joining us tonight is solved.

"*Oui,* but it *was* far and away the most popular dessert that week, so . . ." I offer, my eyes fixed on the floor.

"If we served candy bars and Reddi-wip, *they* would eat it, Chef Page. Is this what you tell me—you want me to serve candy bars? Oreo cookies?" Michel stifles a laugh. There's always a collective sigh of relief when Chef Canet chooses a victim and it's not you. Tonight it's apparently my turn in the barrel. "No, Chef." I'm making imaginary patterns out of the tiles on the floor. The geometric pattern allows me to form flower after flower.

"So, don't make caramel apples out of these, yes? And make us bob for them." Chef Canet picks up his conversation with Michel. I make no effort to correct him. He has obviously mixed up two Halloween traditions. I stifle a smile as I envision the ridiculous spectacle of hot caramel and the bobbing wet heads of our upscale clientele.

"Yes, Chef," I say. He puts up his finger to let me know he's done speaking to me.

My stomach is still churning despite two more Pepto-Bismol chewables, so I bypass the espresso machine and grab an Earl Grey tea bag and pour hot water into my mug. I have yet to perfect my own recipe for yogi tea—I always seem to add too much cardamom. I'll get the recipe right if it kills me. I inhale the deep lavender aroma of the Earl Grey as I walk back to my station. I feel someone take hold of my arm. I whip around, spilling my tea a little. It's Laurent, the fish specialist.

"Can I help you?" I take my arm out of his clutches. Remnants of the working-class-flan remark are still bubbling just below the surface. I clench my jaw. I can hear my teeth grinding.

"I want you to hear from me that I . . ." Laurent shakes his head back and forth, and I get the gist immediately—or is every movement he makes sexual? He continues, "With *your* Julie." I *thought* I smelled the faintest whiff of patchouli on him.

"And?" I say.

"Just passing this along," Laurent whispers. He dramatically turns back to his fish, managing the slightest look of pride. I continue to my station, thinking that if what I have with Will can be likened to an apartment or a pied-à-terre, Julie and Laurent are like some motel that rents by the hour. I wonder if she might have the right idea.

Samuel and I have started washing and halving the apples when Julie rounds the corner. Her face is flushed. I look up. "You're late," I say.

"No, we're supposed to be early all the time. I'm actually still early, just not *as* early as everyone else." Julie twirls her long strawberry-blond hair into a ponytail and begins tying the gingham handkerchief around her head. She walks over to Laurent, and they share a creepy moment. It's fast and barely noticeable, but it's enough to make me want to take a shower. The entire kitchen slows down to take stock of the new lovers. It's not a rarity in kitchens. Schedules being what they are, it's logical to hook up with someone in the trenches with you. I've certainly had my share—Jean-Claude with the Small Turd Under His Nose, for example.

"You're just dying to know, aren't you?" Julie says, walking back over to the pastry station as she buttons her chef's coat. Samuel continues washing.

"But he *is* married," I say. To Julie, the fact that a potential conquest is married is merely an invitation—a challenge, a throwing down of the gauntlet, if you will.

"She's in France," Julie explains.

"That still counts," I say.

"Oh, it won't affect his marriage," Julie says. She's so driven to be memorable in all parts of her life—except when it comes to relationships. Takes one to know one, I suppose.

"Go get the berries out of the walk-in and start prepping them," I say, moving on.

"Yes, *Chef* Page," Julie says, dripping with sarcasm.

I sip my tea as I replay the scene with Julie. Maybe normal, loving relationships—not pleasantries—are the first victim of a streamlined kitchen. People at the top of their game trying to find someone who'll tolerate them on the outside. Tolerate them enough to put up with coming in second to the jealous mistress that is their chosen profession. Rage-filled tantrums, drunken flirtations, drives to nowhere, death-defying trips to Venezuela, and jobs that take up every iota of the soul. Is there hope for any one of us?

Then I think of Samuel and Margot. There are exceptions to every rule. I have to wonder, though, how long the two of them can last. I'm sure every marriage *starts out* looking like theirs.

chapter twelve

E lisabeth!" Mom floats across the crowded ballroom floor. She's wearing a pressed white blouse with a majestic, sweeping collar and a long black skirt. She's not wearing any jewelry this evening, and her makeup is minimal. She looks beautiful. I haven't seen her since Montecito. I lug my basket of goodies over to where she's holding court.

"Hi, Mom," I say. She kisses me on the cheek and wipes away the smudge of her lipstick, as she always does. She motions for one of her worker bees to take my basket. She tells me, "Go say hello to your father." She picks up my name tag and pins it to my dress. She straightens the tag and gives my shoulder a gentle squeeze. She is quickly distracted by a well-heeled couple who have just arrived. She waves as I scope out the room for Dad over her shoulder. It's easy. I just look for the circle of adoring twenty- to sixtysomething women and a floor littered with panties à la Tom Jones concert.

The Ritz-Carlton Huntington Hotel was built in 1907, and it's been the hub of Pasadena's social scene ever since. The ballroom we're in tonight boasts large arched ceilings, enormous chandeliers, and paneled walls, with Pasadena's elite packed in like sardines. Waiters in tuxedos move through the crammed space, offering appetizers even Chef Canet would take a second bite of.

The silent auction is set up on long oak tables at the far end of the ballroom. I can see the exotic floral arrangements from here. I thread through the crowd like a concertgoer through a mosh pit. I'm spit out by the long tables that hold the silent-auction items.

* Surfing lessons: two bidders
* Walk-on part in a future blockbuster: eight bidders
* Lakers courtside seats: five bidders
* Two VIP tickets to the Academy Awards: six bidders
* Signed first-edition Ben Page: twenty-three bidders
* Signed first-edition Rascal Page: fifteen bidders
* Basket of pastries and a computer-generated cer-
  tificate Mom must have printed out for a free series
  of private baking classes with "World-Renowned
  Pastry Chef" Elisabeth Page: two bidders. Rascal
  is the opening bid with five dollars, and Mom has
  outbid him at twenty.

Awesome.

"Can I have your attention, please?" Mom is at the microphone. The room falls silent.

"Welcome to our annual benefit for the irreplaceable Grace Center of Pasadena. The Grace Center is a safe haven for women in abusive relationships. They can get help for themselves and their children and start their lives anew." Applause swells.

"We're so thankful you've made the commitment it takes to make this program a successful one. I'd like to introduce you to a woman who will guide you through this evening's festivities, the silent auction, introducing you to the newest members of the Grace Center family, in addition to giving you as many opportunities as possible to help fund the important work the

Grace Center does. Please welcome my friend and right-hand woman, Roberta Huff." The crowd applauds politely.

While Roberta Huff is speaking, I turn around and double Mom's bid for my pastry basket and private baking series. I write down Julie's name and contact information. Then I grab another pen from my purse and, using my left hand, bid again. This one is Margot's. She must really want this amazing basket of pastries. Not only has she doubled Julie's bid, she's added a dollar out of spite. I look around the room. Roberta Huff is introducing a group of college basketball coaches who are going to start volunteering their time regularly at the Grace Center house with the kids. I take a second and marvel at how all of the men look and stand the exact same way. Mom used to sing a song to Rascal and me when we were kids as we passed houses that looked exactly like one another. She would sing from the driver's seat of that old Mercedes wagon, about the ticky-tacky houses on the hillside and how they all looked just the same. All different colors, but one indistinguishable from the next. I'm reminded of that song as I look at the men on the stage.

Losing interest in the ticky-tacky people, I grab the pen once more. It seems Julie doesn't take kindly to Margot's bid. She doubles her bid once more, plus a dollar.

The crowd erupts in applause. I am startled out of my imaginary bidding war and drop the pen. It hits the floor and rolls under the table. Great. My pen is gone. How will Margot and Julie ever increase their bids now? I quickly step over to the clipboard for Dad's book, snatch his pen, and carefully place it on my clipboard.

"I'm tired of people bidding on me anyway," Dad says as he sidles up beside me, hugging me and grabbing the pen from my clipboard.

"You're just using me as a ruse so you can nab that pen," I say, picking up the clipboard next to mine. I try to make out exactly what people are bidding on, and continue in horror, "From this clipboard for Lakers courtside seats. They're worth thousands. The lowest bid is thirty-seven dollars. And it's *Rascal.*"

"Lakers courtside seats? Are you kidding me? Hand me that, for crissakes." Dad takes the clipboard and writes down his name with a bid of $250, blowing Rascal and his bid out of the water. He hands me back the clipboard. I take a long hard look at him as he leans in front of me. Are we back to normal? He keeps the pen and puts it back on his clipboard.

"How come *you* don't have to wear a name tag?" I whine. Dad lets out a small scoffing sound and smiles at me. "You're getting more and more petulant in your old age," I say, bending down and picking up the pen that I dropped before.

"Who are you calling old?" Dad picks up my clipboard and gives it the once-over. Then he looks at me. *The* look.

"What? No one was bidding. What was I supposed to do? There's even more bids on"—pointing to the clipboard next to mine—"ringing the opening bell at the New York Stock Exchange. Jesus, my pastries are looking like a steaming bag of shit next to this stuff." Dad laughs as he studies my clipboard.

"A steaming *basket* of shit, honey," he corrects. I'm holding the Lakers clipboard as if my life depends on it. Dad writes down a bid on mine and sets the clipboard on the table. He puts his hands in his pockets and ambles slowly across the parquet ballroom floor. The crowd parts like the Red Sea.

I sneak a peek at my clipboard and see that Dad has made a bid of $250. Julie will be so upset. Her bid of $163 looks embarrassingly paltry.

"May I?"

I look up. All I see is a baby-blue-and-yellow-striped tie. A ticky-tacky person. It seems to want the clipboard I'm holding.

"*You* want a series of baking lessons?" I joke. The minute I say it, I feel like a jerk. My face flushes, and I clear my throat in an attempt to regain my composure. I stop fidgeting for a second and look up at him. His height is deceptive. He's a lot younger than I thought. His features are full and rough. Thick neck, wide chest, and a haircut only an ex-marine would sport. I imagine most women would find this man attractive—in that lumberjackian, real-men-eat-chili kind of way. Me? I seem to prefer a man whom I need a picture of to remind me what he looks like most days.

"Why wouldn't *I* want baking lessons?" he says, settling into his stance. His voice is low, and his words meld and run in to one another. He holds out his hand, and I pass him the clipboard.

"No reason," I offer. "Are you sure you're not looking for the Lakers courtside seats?" I ask as politely as I can.

He scans the other clipboards and then proceeds to fill in his name and an amount. The smallest smirk creeps across his face. "A little full of ourselves, aren't we?" he says, handing me back the clipboard.

"Why would it be full of myself to assume you didn't want baking lessons? *I* certainly don't have anything to do with it," I say, playing it cool. I scan the clipboard. "Wait, this *is* the clipboard for the Lakers tickets. Ha!" I say. It comes out a tad louder than I meant it to. Mom eyes me from the stage. I shrink down and make eye contact with the man. I continue in a bit of a whisper, "I was right. See?" I set down the Lakers clipboard and pick up my own clipboard victoriously. The man just smiles. "Why don't you prove me wrong?" I continue, flaunting my clipboard.

"About what?" he says.

"These baking lessons—why don't you bid on them? Not that I know anything about them, but they look pretty great. This *world-renowned chef* is legendary," I tease, calling his bluff while waving my clipboard around. The man deftly swipes my clipboard and fills in his name and an amount. I'm not sure why I've taunted someone that I might have to spend an entire day with. I don't know whom exactly this joke is on. I must be really desperate for bids other than those of imaginary people.

"Courageous," I say, taking it back.

He extends his hand and smiles in a down-home, genuine kind of way that politicians pay handsomely to perfect. "Well, it was nice meeting you . . ."

"Elisabeth. Elisabeth Page," I respond, knowing my mother is in the vicinity and has me in her sights.

"Yeah, I know. You're wearing a name tag," he says. I instinctively bring my hand up to the tag and then look quickly to the clipboard with my name in bold letters. And then it hits me. I've just been caught flaunting and teasing about my own legendary status as a world-renowned pastry chef. He watches my realization unfold. I say nothing.

"So I guess I'll be seeing you later, then," he says, letting go of my hand with a smile and walking away. I stand there flushed and completely humiliated at my own vanity.

I look at the clipboard.

Daniel Sullivan. $251.

chapter thirteen

E lisabeth? What names did you get?"

Margot's baby shower buzzes with conversation and laughter. We've all been trying to generate two baby names, one boy and one girl, using the two first names of the expectant parents. Since arriving at the shower, I've been introduced to the other partygoers as "Samuel's boss." I've been relegated to the outskirts of every conversation, smiling as I crane to hear the goings-on of the guests who actually know each other or, for that matter, Margot.

We just started playing this precious little name game. Before that, I spent the most painful hour sitting by myself, passing the time checking e-mails on my BlackBerry and getting half in the bag on mimosas. I don't know a soul here. Despite several attempts to break the ice, it becomes painfully obvious that no soul wants to know me.

I vowed I would limit my partygoing to the bare minimum when I was finally out on my own. And now I remember why. As children, Rascal and I were always trotted out for the benefit of Mom's many charitable and social events, not unlike the von Trapp children—minus the lederhosen and farewell songs.

Julie arrives a full hour late. I honestly didn't know one

could do that. My mother would certainly not approve. Julie quickly sits down next to me.

We mull over SAMUEL and MARGOT for a full three minutes, trying to find the most appropriate boy and girl name options for the new baby. Eva, Margot's sister, holds up an egg timer. "Get it?" she jokes, "an *egg* timer." The crowd roars with laughter as I hang my head in embarrassment for a group of women so obviously devoid of humor that a joke about the contents of a woman's ovaries is cause for hysteria. Even Margot and Eva's ancient grandmother, burdened with an oxygen tank to help her breathe, lets out a rumbly, belabored giggle. The egg timer is set for three minutes, and we're off. I come up with two names just as the countdown ends.

Since I'm seated closest to the hostess, I am chosen to go first. This could be my one chance to regain some of the credibility I lost in the first game. We were told to decorate a plain white onesie for the new arrival, so I wrote, SHOW ME YOUR TITS! Needless to say, it didn't go over well.

I clear my throat. "Lot and Stoma," I announce.

The room falls silent. Julie physically scoots her steel-mesh Bertoia chair away from me. Eva sniffs delicately and writes my two names on the big dry-erase board she has set up in the front of the room.

"It's biblical," I whisper to Julie.

"Samuel is going to have a field day with that one," Julie says, swirling her mimosa around in its flute.

I'm surrounded by a group of thirtysomething women, all of them married with children. I'm in enemy territory. Women hopped up on the idea of the upcoming fantasy baby, smelling clean and sweet, silent except for coos and giggles—no poop, no pitiful late-night crying—no reality. I can't wipe the fake plastered smile from my face.

A woman in a peasant top with no bra offers up Lara and Mort to the Baby Jumble gods. The hostess squeals with delight.

"Your safety pin is flipping in. No one can see it," Julie whispers to me as she flips my collar out and exposes the safety pin: the symbol of all that is evil in baby-shower games. When I first arrived, the hostess gave me the safety pin, advising me to wear it on my person somewhere. "It must be visible at all times," the woman warned. I listened intently. If, at any point during the baby shower, I were to cross my legs, another partygoer could swipe my safety pin, and I would be out of the game. Voted off the proverbial Safety Pin Island. The partygoer who manages to collect the most safety pins wins some completely useless gift: a scented candle or bath gel *and,* apparently, bragging rights to having her priorities completely out of order. Julie continues, "You're not trying to cheat, are you?" Another woman offers up Marla and Lars to the Baby Name Game.

"Yes, I'm cheating. That makes perfect sense," I reason.

"I'm just saying. Looks a little fishy." Julie stuffs a small piece of lemon cake in her mouth. She quickly spits it out and takes a giant swig of her mimosa to exorcise any unwelcome remnants from her too refined palate. I sneak a quick look around the room to see if anyone has noticed. Luckily, everyone was looking at the hostess as she wrote Sara and Al on the big dry-erase board.

"I'm going to cross my goddamn legs. I've been flashing that poor woman all morning," I say. "And will you stop spitting everything out? It's not like we're in some junior high school cafeteria, for the love of God." Julie is touching up her bright red lipstick. She hardly gives me a second glance. With her obvious disdain of all things domestic, Julie should stand out way more than I do.

"This cake is dry, and there's some kind of lemon zest, but it's just— Is it dried?" Julie picks through the regurgitated cake on her plate like an archaeologist chipping away at a dig in the sands of Egypt. God, are we *completely* incapable of acting normal in the real world? She continues, "It's straight out of one of those warehouse stores." She flicks at the cake with disgust. I take a quick sidelong glance at the cake—I can't believe someone would actually use dried lemon zest. Julie goes on, "And you can't cross your legs. It's against the rules. You'll lose your safety pin. You're the one who had to wear a skirt." She hesitates and then swipes a safety pin away from the hostess's ancient grandmother, who inadvertently crossed her legs as she bent down to check the gauge on her oxygen tank.

Eva moves on to Julie in the Baby Name Jumble. Julie gulps down her mimosa and sets the empty flute on the steel-and-glass minimalist table behind her.

"Greta and Saul," Julie says proudly. Once again, she is unable to come in anything but first. Even at a baby shower, her ambition is unnerving. Eva beams at her. I tear a sugar rose from a tiny petit four and pop it into my mouth. I fight the urge to spit the entire sugar glob onto the paper plate that's resting on my knees. Julie's right: warehouse store all the way.

"Well done! Well done!" Eva turns and writes *Greta and Saul* in print three times the size of my two names. I smile graciously, letting the room know I'm aware my names are "unusual" and that I'm in awe of Julie's Baby Name Jumble acumen.

In the end, Eva presents Julie with a neatly wrapped present; her names won first place. Julie bows and curtsies as she accepts the present. She takes her seat once again in the circle. The women clap politely while they search for faults in Julie. Thick ankles, maybe? Spinster in the making? Are her breasts

real? Does she have her sights on my husband? They will debate
these questions for the rest of the party.

"We're going to move out onto the deck for brunch and the
big finale: present opening! Margot?"

Margot is leaning over and offering her congratulations to
Julie. Eva glares at them. Margot quickly stands.

"Do you even know what a stoma is?" Julie steps down onto
the patio and holds the dupioni silk curtains open for me.

"Well, I can certainly use it in a sentence, if you'd like.
Stoma. If I have to hear about attachment parenting or the won-
ders of hemp anymore, I'm going to stab myself in the stoma.
Stoma," I say.

"So, how do you know Margot? Are you family?" a woman
asks me and Julie as I check out the deck's seating arrangements. She has a baby slung across her chest, and we've all been
treated to a view of her exposed breast more times than we'd
like to remember. I can't stop staring at her runaway eyebrows
and unshaved legs.

"We're friends of Samuel's," I say.

"You could be family," she says to me. "You and Margot look
like sisters. You two have the same build, and you know . . . it's
really in the eyes," she says as her baby whimpers at her chest.
She rests her hand on the baby's head, absentmindedly caress-
ing its wisps of hair. While both Margot and I both do have blue
eyes, my black hair is wavy and nothing like Margot's straight,
thick, and very blond tresses. While her skin is tanned and perfect, my own pale skin burns every time I go out in the sun. I
tuck a rogue bit of hair behind my ear.

"Oh, thank you," I answer. I notice that Julie is flagging me
down. She's secured two seats at a table on the outer fringes of
the party. The woman with the baby stares at me. I fight every
urge to find my purse, grab my tweezers and possibly a razor, and

just hold this lady down while I make her look a little less like the love child of Andy Rooney and the ever elusive Sasquatch.

"Is it . . ." I hesitate. I have never known how to ask a mother if her baby is a boy or a girl—it seems so impersonal to refer to the baby as an "it"—and I find myself at a loss again. Julie is still standing by the chairs. She is no longer flagging me down because she's anxiously scanning the deck area for another mimosa: her own personal coping mechanism for dealing with the thirtysomething marrieds.

"Bode," the woman says. That confuses me, and now I have that Creedence Clearwater Revival song "Lodi" stuck in my head. She waits for it to register. *Stuck in Lodi again.* It doesn't. She continues, "He's a boy." I should introduce her to Rascal and have him elaborate on how having a fucked-up name has worked out for him. The woman continues smiling, and I know The Question is coming.

"How do *you* know Margot?" I offer before she gets the chance. I switch into party mode: asking questions, giving an engaging smile, making the person feel like she's the center of the universe.

"I'm her doula. Joanne." We shake hands awkwardly as I introduce myself to her. She goes on, "I'll be helping Margot with her birth. And you . . . do you—"

"I don't know her that well, so I don't really think that'd be appropriate," I interrupt. Bode is officially crying. Joanne doesn't seem to notice. I wonder if midwifery or doula-ing or whatever you call it is the best calling for a woman so completely immune to crying and what it might mean. Pain, maybe?

Joanne laughs. "Children. Do you have any children?" Hey, speaking of children, *Joanne,* why don't you take a quick peekaboo at what might be causing your little one to become absolutely hysterical?

"Oh, no. Not yet." I smile shyly, trying to convey the proper level of regret. I catch a glimpse of Julie proudly hoisting two flutes of mimosa. I extricate myself from Mother Earth and quietly dismiss visions of pushing little yellow-headed kids on swings as I weave my way over to Julie.

The crisp fall air moves lazily over the canals near Eva's Venice home. This is my favorite time of year. The season is stubbornly changing. We Angelenos hold our breath for the days of summer to be officially over. We're constantly taunted with a few days here and there of beautiful autumn weather, slowly morphing into a lovely winter chill, and then it's back to the summer heat. I breathe in and hope this weather sticks around. I watch as a gaggle of geese waddles down the narrow walkways of this Boho-chic neighborhood. Multimillion-dollar houses averaging no more than a thousand square feet of living space. Eva is a set designer for some sitcom, so her home looks like a layout for one of those glossy lifestyle magazines, modern yet plush.

Margot and Samuel haven't told anyone the sex of little Lot or Stoma, so Eva has draped the five round tables with apricot and cream tablecloths. Translucent silvery runners spill effort-lessly over their sides. She's accented each table with framed pictures of anonymous yet diverse children in silver frames. Eva has obviously tried to be politically correct, seeing as how Samuel is African-American. She's desperately trying to incor-porate this wrinkle into her life and, far more urgently, into the party decor. Maybe that would explain why one Al Jarreau CD has been on repeat throughout the entire event.

My apricot-and-cream-striped plate sports tiny cakes and sweets that Julie still can't stop taking apart and tasting. Her blouse is covered with safety pins, as if she's a punk-rock kid from the 1980s.

Margot comes over and leans in conspiratorially. "How do you like the food?"

"Oh . . . ummm." Julie and I try to think of something vague yet complimentary.

"Eva hired the caterer," Margot finally whispers, and gives us a tiny wink. Julie and I both let out a relieved burst of laughter as Margot continues, "Samuel made a batch of his killer beignets. They're inside in a Tupper on the kitchen counter, under my coat. I figured only you guys would really appreciate them. And Elisabeth, there's a thermos of yogi tea in the kitchen as well. I was assuming your stomach would be a bit . . . iffy. Especially today. Samuel said you guys had a late night at the restaurant." Margot places her hand on my arm. I melt into her.

It's not lost on me or Julie that I was the only one offered yogi tea. I figure Margot is all free love and hugs for everyone until it comes to solidifying her husband's position at the restaurant.

As the autumn wind blows the scent of fireplaces across my face, something about the quiet and calm of the day makes me start to take a look at my life. I don't like what I see. The fact that Julie is the only person I can at all relate to here is more than a little alarming. Sure, I'm the most balanced person in the kitchen at Beverly. But that's like being crowned King of the Dipshits.

I refocus on Margot, who's presenting an adorable yellow chenille blankie. I ooh and ahh absently. Yes, *Julie,* I'd like another mimosa—shit, now more than ever. No wonder every single woman I know hates baby showers. It's too hard to be confronted with what you don't have.

I confronted Will about staying, and he said no. So where does that leave me? Do I go back to believing that love is a beautiful intangible comet that shoots through the night sky every seventy-five years? Or do I force myself to admit how empty and lonely those other seventy-four years, three hundred and sixty-four days, twenty-three hours, and fifty-nine minutes are without him?

I sip my mimosa as the world muffles and mutes around me. The partygoers clap, and Julie leans in to tell me something. I smile but can't make out her words. I look at Margot, holding up a little light green sweater that she then sets on her belly. The crowd coos in synchronization. I grind my teeth and set my jaw. My five-now-*eleven*-year plan is losing credibility as well as momentum. Separating and severing myself from the giants I grew up with, trying to create something of my own, is beginning to feel like a childlike attempt at rebellion, which usually manifests in some horrible body piercing or pink-tinted Mohawk. Except my act of rebellion has been my entire career— my entire *identity*. Not something you can hope grows out. I can feel something giving . . . something melting . . . something eroding . . . something bubbling up.

No.

I sit up straight and snap myself back to reality. It's this fucking baby shower. That's all it is. The fucking baby shower.

chapter fourteen

I wake up the next morning, still hungover from the mimosas, even though I stopped drinking midafternoon. (Champagne and I have never really gotten along.) I roll over in bed; the hardwood floors creak under the iron frame. Eight-twelve A.M. I pull the duvet cover up over my shoulders and try to get a bit more sleep before the alarm sounds in eighteen minutes. My brain is running through its usual lists of things to do. I can't stop sighing, can't stop rubbing my eyes and face. Trying to wipe away . . . everything. Feelings. Can you do that? Just wipe it all away? I decide to get up, despite the eighteen-minute discrepancy.

My apartment is already bright with the morning sunlight. I get dressed in my running gear and sit on the side of my bed to lace up my running shoes. The quiet of my apartment seems to encourage reflection and introspection. Best to head out, then. I breathe deeply and forge ahead. The phone rings. I push my pant leg down over my sock and head to the phone.

"Hello?"

"Sweetie, please don't scream into the phone."

"Morning, Mom," I say.

"Yes, darling—well, I was just calling to schedule your baking lesson. I'm sorry it's taken almost a month, but we've collected the money, and the bidder would like to know when he can begin to learn from the premier pastry chef of Los Angeles."

I wonder if that ticky-tacky Daniel Sullivan posted the final bid. Jesus, who am I kidding—of course he did. Except for me and my imaginary army of bidding minions, my clipboard was as unpopular as— Wow, I can't think of anything more unpopular than that clipboard. Awesome.

"Dear? Are you . . . can you concentrate for just a second? I'd like to set up this baking lesson before my lunch meeting with the Junior League," Mom presses.

"Who was the final bidder?" I ask.

"One of the gentlemen who donated his time to playing basketball with the kids. Some UCLA boy. Daniel Sullivan." That worked out well. I've painted myself into a corner where the only way to get out is give a cooking lesson to someone who plays basketball *for a living*. Maybe the next time I play a joke on someone, I should think about whom exactly the joke is on before going through with it.

"We can do it next Monday morning at the restaurant. I don't know if that's too soon, but if he can swing it, that would be ideal." I speak quickly, trying to get this over with as soon as possible.

◆

"We bought a house," Samuel says, his hands deep in the mixer. He's prepping the little chocolate cakes for tonight's service.

"I thought you were just looking?" I carefully ask.

"Oh, no. I've been saving, and with Margot's boutique doing so well . . . Our families chipped in a little, too," Samuel confesses.

"Oh," I say.

"You know, with the baby coming," Samuel adds.

"You bought the one I walked through?" I ask, trying to disguise my horror. I hope it wasn't that house we walked through. I'm not sure I know how to congratulate someone who might have purchased a money pit. Let's face it, though—I think all houses are albatrosses, so consider the source.

"That piece of shit? No way. But it *is* a bit of a fixer," Samuel says.

"Congratulations," I say.

"Yes, Chef. We're very excited," he says. I nod and get to work prepping the clafouti. It's going to be fabulous. It's a French peasant dish that I learned in Lyon. It's just upmarket pancake batter poured over warm cherries—succulent, warm, and homey, perfect for a fall night. And since the cooler weather decided to stay, I'm celebrating with a dish perfect for a crisp night by the fireside. Although it's not traditional, I'm going to do the clafouti in individual ramekins, served with cream added at the table. I figure no one in L.A. will know its real origins. And Chef Canet isn't here tonight. This is my opportunity to try it out.

Julie rounds the corner. She still has her sunglasses on. The skimpiest of Girl Scout uniforms is barely hanging on her pale, slightly doughy body. Fortunately, we have extra clothes in the back for nights that never really end. It's not that uncommon, though the Halloween costume is a twist. And three days shy of the actual holiday. It's going to be a long weekend.

I follow Julie into the back. Samuel appears out of nowhere with a cup of perfectly made espresso for her. Julie stands there swaying in her green skirt and black lacy bra, and gulps the espresso. She's mumbling something about where Chef Canet is and did he see her and how Samuel shouldn't be looking at her tits. We don't pay any attention to her. We've run this drill before. Burning the candle at both ends is the status quo for people who work in a kitchen of this caliber. The true art comes in making sure your function never dips below extraordinary. Because unlike showing up to work in a Girl Scout uniform with a vial of cocaine in your pocket and mascara running down your face, not performing up to snuff is grounds for immediate sacking.

"Is that badge for a good blow job?" I say, putting the green felt sash into her locker. The fragile paper badges are ripped and stained.

"I was a good little Girl Scout," Julie says, rolling on deodorant. I bet she earned a lot of badges last night.

I get Julie into some checked pants, an old concert T-shirt she had in her locker (I don't ask), and her chef's jacket. She's not that drunk, just really hungover and exhausted. Samuel returns with his special ginger-based hangover cure. She downs it in one gulp. Then he hands her two aspirin and a bottle of water.

I let her know that Chef Canet isn't here tonight. The look of relief that passes over her overly made-up face is wrenching. The cracks in her life are showing. Today was a little too close for comfort. If Chef Canet had been here, Julie would have been fired. For real. No amount of time in the walk-in, letting Chef Canet cool down, would have erased the infraction of being late and not prepared for the night ahead. Especially for someone as low on the totem pole as Julie. She's expendable, and she knows it.

"Monday is Halloween! Just come out—it would be so fun," Julie says to me later that night, firing up another crème brûlée and on her best behavior.

"Rascal and I like to go to the House of Pies. It's our thing. Even if that weren't happening, I'd still have to pass out candy."

After my morning run, I stopped at the grocery store and bought a bag of fun size candies as well as a miniature pumpkin. When I got home, I carved a smiling face into the pumpkin and proudly set it outside my door to show my holiday spirit and to say that I am open for the business of passing out candy.

"Your building is in such a commercial part of town. There are no kids there. Who are you going to pass candy out to, prostitutes?" This stings, but unfortunately, it's pretty accurate. I live in a corridor of the city affectionately christened "Ho Heaven" by the locals.

"Hos need candy, too." I check over the individual clafouti as they come out of the oven. I slide a few over to Samuel to get ready to go out into the restaurant.

"We're going to dinner at Lucques at eight and then to a great party up Doheny. I think you should at least come to the party." Julie is being quite civil—I appreciate the invitation without the accompanying "Woot! Woot!" and the bizarre lassoing dance moves that usually go along with it.

"I'll probably just go to dinner with Rascal, so—" I think aloud.

"He can come!" Julie nearly squeals. Obviously, things with Laurent have fizzled, as do all kitchen flings. No fuss, no muss.

"Yeah, I don't think so," I say, firing up the torch for the crème brûlée. Rascal was just named one of *People*'s fifty most beautiful people. The photograph of him was all black and white and shadowy. He was in a wrinkled oxford and worn-in jeans with his head in his hands, cigarette smoke slinking upward. Very tortured. Just the kind of man every woman in America loves: a fixer-upper. They trotted out our whole family for that article—Dad and Mom's history, the fact that I worked right here in L.A. at Beverly. It was a perfect segue into Chef Canet's picture, which, coincidentally, came next.

"Are you going to dress up? It's the least you can do," Julie says. Yes, I'm going to dress up, walk around my apartment, and greet the working girls of Los Angeles with fun-size Snickers bars.

"No. The least I could do is pass out candy from the comfort of my very own home," I say.

"Oh, for fuck's sake." Julie sounds exasperated.

"It's just a party," I rationalize.

"On Halloween," Julie says.

"Well, what are *you* going as?"

"A Girl Scout. The costume you . . . Well, I was wearing it earlier," Julie glosses over.

"That was actually rather tame for you," I say. Apparently, she's following the Halloween mantra—on Halloween everything is slutty. Last year Julie's costume was a slutty nun. I heard she used the ruler for more lascivious purposes than rapping at a young troublemaker's knuckles.

The restaurant is packed tonight. The cherry clafouti is selling like mad, and Chef Canet is officially not coming into the restaurant, as per Michel's teary-eyed announcement. He'll have to kiss his own ass tonight.

Louis, the maître d', rounds our little corner. "Chef Page! You have fans!" Louis is smiling from ear to ear. I don't have time for this.

"*Oui?*" I pick up a clafouti and present it to Samuel for a final inspection. He nods and sets it on the counter for Michel's final approval. Michel quickly summons the captain to take it out, not touching one thing on the plate. I question why he even checks them anymore.

"They wish to meet you. They have tried this dessert you make and want to give thanks," Louis says.

"No time, *mon cher*," I say quietly to Louis.

"Make time, my love," Louis replies, and turns around, holding the swinging door of the kitchen open for me. I take a deep breath.

"I've got it," Samuel says, deep into the clafouti phenomenon. Julie turns to me and gives me a big thumbs-up. She actually seems quite genuine. I wipe my chef's jacket quickly with a wet rag and straighten my hair. Julie gives me a nod of approval after picking off a few stray crumbs. Samuel doesn't look up. I follow Louis out into the dining room.

Louis leads me over to the best table in the house. There are two people sitting at the small table, nursing espressos and sharing the clafouti.

"This is Chef Page!" Louis announces, pulling out the empty chair for me to sit. I am appalled. Sit? I silently appeal to Louis to get me out of this, but he has Chef Canet's ear, and to offend Louis is to offend Chef Canet. He motions once more for me to sit. I oblige. I overhear the couple at the next table asking the captain if we are still serving the pumpkin flan. The captain says no and suggests the clafouti as an alternative. Louis walks quickly back into the kitchen to let Julie and Samuel know I'll be longer than expected. I can hear their heart rates climbing from here.

"Donna Martinez." The woman directly across from me extends her hand across the table.

"Nice to meet you. Elisabeth," I say.

"You're Ben Page's daughter, right?" The man to her left extends his hand across the table. He's much younger than I thought at first. He continues, "Paul Lingeman. Nice to meet you." He's wearing a well-tailored Italian suit jacket over a vintage T-shirt and pressed jeans.

"Yes . . . yes, I am," I stutter, caught off guard for a brief moment. I channel my mother, collect myself, and smile easily.

"A little bird told us," Donna Martinez oozes.

"Well, that and the nine-page retrospective he got in *Time* this month, marking the thirty-five-year anniversary of *The Coward*. There was also that thing on A&E—they finally did his biography—really the whole anti-war movement of the early seventies. God, they should totally release the soundtrack for that thing—Dylan, the Band, Joni Mitchell, Creedence, all of them . . ." Paul trails off. I nod and thank him. The table falls into an awkward silence. "I'm a big fan." He holds up his hands in a gesture of apology. I nod and smile.

"So, how do you like Beverly?" I ask, trying to hurry, *politely* hurry, this little lovefest along so I can get back into the kitchen.

"We love it. Christian invited us. We ran into him at a party over on the lot just last month," Donna says. The word "lot" has a completely different meaning in Los Angeles than it does anywhere else in the world. "Lot" in Los Angeles means movie-studio back lot. Well, that and a great choice for a baby name.

"I'm always happy to hear from a satisfied customer," I say. There is another awkward silence as I begin to make my getaway.

"Elisabeth, we asked Louis to bring you out here so we can officially out ourselves as stalkers," Donna says. Paul laughs a little too loud and way too long. I get ready. One of them is sure to hand me some combination of books any minute. The game now is to make a secret bet with myself as to which combination it will be. Is Paul a *Rick Danko* man, or is he going to go old school and pull out a tattered copy of *The Coward*? I'm going to go with *Jack Tinker*—one of the lesser-known works by Dad that the *really* cool guys declare his finest work.

"I can have them sign whatever you guys want. Do you have the book—*books* with you?" I ask. They both erupt in laughter. I look at them with utter confusion.

"Elisabeth, we're here to see you. To meet you," Donna says.

"Oh . . . Well, what can I help you with, then?" My voice oozes charm, and I plaster on a smile. If they're here to see me, why don't they tell me what they want so I can get back to the kitchen?

"We produce shows for the Food Network," Paul says proudly.

"Oh?" I say. Louis is seating a table of four. He slowly and elaborately pulls out a chair for each and every guest as he eavesdrops on our conversation.

"You're perfect for television," Donna announces.

"Thank you," I say, responding to a line that is so common in Los Angeles it is regarded as sort of an "aloha" or "shalom" statement: versatile as a greeting or farewell.

"We're starting to pitch some new shows to the network. We'd like to sit down with you and see if you'd be interested in hosting your own show," Donna says. Who are these people? How do they know who I am?

"I'm sorry, this is out of left field. You've got to back up a little bit for me," I say. The captain serves the couple next to me their very own individual ramekin of steaming batter, sugar, and cherries. He slices the top open, and I can smell its perfection from here. He slowly pours the cream over the top. The couple is breathless. I want to run back into the kitchen and hug Samuel until he can't stand it. Which, let's face it, would be pretty much right away.

"Right. I apologize," Paul says. He and Donna have a moment. Somewhere in that telepathic instant, the pitch is delegated to Paul. He continues, "We run a production company here in Los Angeles that has a nice deal with the Food Network. We pitch them an idea for a show, and they tell us whether or not they're interested. If they are, we'll film a pilot and take it to New York—at which time they'll get a chance to meet you and fall in love with you, as we have—and decide whether or not the show gets picked up for the season or shelved."

"We *rarely* get shelved," Donna puts in.

I don't know what to say. My first impulse is to immediately say no and excuse myself. Pages don't *do* television. Everything that comes out of Hollywood is trite and meaningless. This is below me. It's a disservice to all the years I've spent in a kitchen. But I think about where I go after the kitchen: home. Alone. The same routine for ten years. Kitchen. Home. Kitchen. Home. Sex with Will every year or so. Kitchen. Home. I decide to listen— something I wouldn't have considered doing two weeks ago.

"I'm listening," I say, peeling back the first layer.

"After we met Christian, we asked around town. We made several stealthy visits to Beverly and . . . I'm not going to lie, it obviously doesn't hurt that your family is quite well known," Donna says.

"But this is about you," Paul corrects. Uh-huh.

"Look at you. You're adorable," Donna compliments.

"You're the head pastry chef in the hippest restaurant in Los Angeles, you couldn't have a better last name, and you look like you should do commercials for Ivory soap or something. You're quite the hat trick, Elisabeth," Paul says.

"Let's just meet for lunch or a drink as soon as your schedule permits," Donna presses. Paul reaches into his coat pocket and pulls out a silver card case. He passes his card across the table. I take it.

I can't form one clear thought. I'm confused. I'm excited. I'm afraid and overwhelmed. Quite frankly, I'm still debating whether this is below me. And now I feel like an asshole for even thinking it. When I tell Dad about this opportunity, will he hang his head in shame? I know it's not anywhere on the trajectory he envisions for me. But it *is* a step—a move on the chess board. He'd have to appreciate that, at least. I'll meet Paul and Donna for a meal. There's no harm in that. Do the research and then make a decision. Dad doesn't have to know about any of this until it's something more serious. With the way Hollywood works, it'll never come to anything. Just a series of meetings that, in the end, will lead nowhere.

I cautiously jump in. "Do you know the Biltmore Hotel? Downtown?" It's a favorite haunt of mine.

"This is exactly why we love you—you are cooler than any of us," Donna says.

I'm surprised I don't get up from the table right then and there and bolt. But I say, "How's next Monday morning? They have a beautiful tea service in the morning. Why don't we meet there around nine-thirty?" We busily enter this new appointment into our various BlackBerries, Palm Pilots, and organizers. We finalize the details, and I stand and shake hands with them. I breathe in deeply and refocus. Back to the kitchen.

"What was that about?" Julie asks.

"Someone just wanted my dad to autograph a book," I say. Louis stands holding open the swinging door to the kitchen. He inclines his head slightly, looking intently at me. Is he playing Jedi mind tricks on me right now? *French* Jedi mind tricks? He lets the door swing shut as he goes back out into the dining room.

chapter fifteen

I spend that Sunday running the errands I'd usually save for Monday, due to my baking lesson with Daniel Sullivan. But this time it's as if I have ten-pound weights around my ankles. I'm becoming exhausted by the monotonous tiny loads of laundry, the Swiffer that picks up only eight to ten loose dust bunnies per week, the insignificant bags of garbage, and acting like it doesn't bother me that Will's policy is "out of sight, out of mind" but somehow, he argues, not out of love. My only excitement comes from trying the new yerba maté tea Margot suggested by way of Samuel the other night. It came with a note that she pinned to a long red scarf from her boutique. The note told me about the health benefits of not only the tea but the color red. I thanked Samuel for the beautiful gift. I wonder why Margot has taken such an active interest in my well-being. I'm positive she'll soon invite me over to read my chart and pull together a nice bag of crystals I should wear around my neck in a leather pouch to ward off evil spirits.

I sit on the couch and roll through Tivoed show after Tivoed show, stopping only to sear a beautiful sushi-grade ahi on the grill in the communal courtyard. I sauté some French green beans and shallots and serve them on the side. I pour myself a glass of Pellegrino and sit, TV tray in front of me, to watch yet another prerecorded television show.

My last thoughts before I doze off are anxious ones. I think about the day I'll have to waste trying to teach—at the very least, communicate with—Daniel Sullivan. I should read tomorrow's sports page to have some kind of conversation ready. Mom has taught me to ask questions, and when I don't have something to say, get the person talking about him- or herself. I'll pull out all of Mom's tricks tomorrow so this Daniel Sullivan and I won't fall into an awkward silence every other minute.

The next morning I drive over to the restaurant with my yerba maté in a thermos. I've done a lot of these tutorials over the years. They're offered as prizes at many of Mom's charity auctions. Ordinarily, the students are well-heeled matrons who want a backstage pass to the hottest restaurant and any juicy gossip that might slip out during a round of sifting, not men like Daniel Sullivan.

I typically open the lesson with a quick tour of the restaurant and then move into the baking portion by going over the various utensils found in a restaurant kitchen. At this point my society-matron "student" will impatiently pat me on the hand and launch into a description of the over-the-top dinner parties *she's* orchestrated. Then she'll proceed to "teach" me a thing or two. Or so I lead her to believe.

I arrive a half hour early and find parking on the street in front of the restaurant. I use my key to let myself in. I drop my purse on one of the tables, taking my BlackBerry into the kitchen in case of a blessed last-minute cancellation. As I push open the door to the kitchen, the stillness quiets me. I haven't been alone here in months. I take it in. A rare moment. I hang up my sweater in the back room, pull on my chef's jacket, and come out into the kitchen just as I hear him.

"Hello? Hello?" He's early. I quickly grab an extra apron from the linen closet.

"In here!" I tuck my hair behind my ear and wait. I've been nailed by that swinging door before. Best to have one person trying to get through it at a time. He doesn't peek around the corner. He's not hesitant. The door pushes inward boldly.

"Elisabeth Page? World-renowned pastry chef?" His short-cropped brown hair makes him look like a child colored him for a drawing in kindergarten. The purest Crayola brown—no highlights of blond, no auburn strands—completely untouched by the sunlight of Los Angeles, which seems to want all who dwell in its kingdom to be just a bit more blond.

I'm hit in that moment by the slightest of tingles. The tiniest of twinges.

"Yes, thanks for that. And you are?" Jesus, I'm channeling the Realtor from hell.

"Daniel Sullivan." He extends his hand.

"So the joke is officially on me, I suppose," I say, taking his hand and shaking it.

"You know, we don't have to do this," he offers.

"Oh . . . well . . . I'm all set up here, so you might as well stay, learn a little something," I say, passing him the apron. He smiles and puts it over his head. He reaches back and tries to tie it behind him. He's fumbling a bit.

"Here, turn around," I say. Daniel blushes slightly and slowly turns around, holding the apron strings out enough so I can take hold of them. I quickly check his left hand. No wedding ring. Now that he can't see me, I can look him up and down with impunity, doing my best to investigate the mysterious tingles.

He's not as tall as I remembered. He's wearing Levi's 501 jeans and has a worn impression in his back pocket where his wallet has gotten quite comfortable. This leads to another discovery—the boy has got a nice ass. I'm not talking just kind of cutting someone a break because he can moderately fill out a pair of pants. No. Daniel Sullivan has *back*. I wonder, maybe, if I partook of a little fling, I wouldn't miss Will so much. If I wouldn't hurt so much. I've tried these flings before, to no avail. But something in me wants to stop hurting, to stop the seemingly never-ending nights alone.

I pull the apron strings tight. As I'm threading them in and out of my fingers, I take in as much of him as I can. I notice that his gray T-shirt is just the right blend of lovingly worn and blessedly thin. Thin enough so I can make out the musculature of his back. I've never been one to use sterile medical terms in describing a person, but his back is straight out of an anatomy book. Every muscle defined. Each shoulder blade pronounced. His Crayola-brown hair cut straight along the base of his neck. I finish tying the apron and am mortified to see that I have run my hand across his shoulder. He turns his head slowly and looks down at me.

"You already have flour on you," I sputter. There is nary a speck of flour anywhere in our vicinity. Back to work. Back to work. I continue, "Okay. Let's get started. Have you been to Beverly before? Are you from around here?" I quickly button up my chef's jacket and push open the swinging door, leading the way back into the dining room.

"I just moved here over the summer. I'm originally from Lawrence, Kansas. You know, where the KU campus is. The Jayhawks?" Daniel hesitates at the entrance to the dining room. He stands right next to the swinging door as if he's waiting for me to tell him where to look.

"The heartland," I offer.

"Something like that," he says.

"Well, okay . . . this is Beverly," I say, extending my arms.

"Why the name? Is the owner's name Beverly or something?" Daniel asks.

"It's the street. We're on Beverly Boulevard," I say. Daniel's face instantly turns bright red. Did I sound like a bitch? I speak quickly. "It's the cool thing, I guess. In the beginning, Chef Canet originally didn't even want a name—just a color. The doors would be painted red, and that would be it—people would know to come here, but everyone else—the huddled masses, if you will—would be unable to find it. He was trying to be like Wolfgang Puck when he was the chef at Ma Maison, when Puck decided that the restaurant should have an unlisted number . . ." I trail off. These bits of trivia are interesting only to me. I've learned this lesson before. Several thousand conversations dwindling down to uncomfortable silences as I drone on about facts only I find remarkable.

"It's beautiful. It really is. I mean, you'd expect a place like this to be overdone, but it's just really easy . . . you know, to be here," Daniel says. He's walked over to the fireplace and is staring at the lone piece of art in the dining room. It's a simple watercolor portrait of varying autumn colors.

"Chef Canet wanted the food to be the art. So everything else takes a backseat."

"Do you have to call him Chef? Even though you're a chef, too?" Daniel asks.

"Oh, absolutely. It's a sign of respect," I say. The rules of a French kitchen are deeply entrenched in hundreds of years of tradition, second only to turning out the best and freshest food in the world.

"It makes sense. It's like people calling me Coach. I suppose they could call me Daniel or Mr. Sullivan. But you're right, it's a sign of respect," he says. Equating a coach with a chef? Are you serious? Um, honey, you're cute and all, but it's not really the same thing. Wait. Remember, Elisabeth—we're trying *not* to be a pompous asshole. Right. The silence is expanding in the space between Coach Sullivan and me. Apparently, when I'm not being a pompous asshole or a know-it-all, I have very little to say. Good to know.

"How long have you worked here?" Daniel asks, turning away from the fireplace and toward me.

"Just over three years," I answer. I realize that if I weren't here at this baking lesson, I'd be sitting at Joan's on Third right now, deep into the *L.A. Times* or attempting the *New York Times* crossword puzzle. Being here with Daniel means I can spend one less day alone, waiting for my comet to streak across the sky. Maybe my question about whether or not a fling is a good idea has been answered. Since a relationship with Will is out of the question, I have to admit to myself that this is as good as it's going to get. I won't get to have Will all the time, so I'll entertain myself until he returns.

"We should start with the lesson," I say. I swing open the door to the kitchen and lead Daniel to my station. I grab a plate of cheeses, fruit, and bread out of the walk-in for us to snack on while we work. I set it in front of him. He makes a face. Immediately. It's as if something . . . oh, *shit.*

"It's the cheese. The cheese is really pungent. I swear it's not . . . I mean, yes, it's stinky, but you just should try it—it's an aged Brescianella—it's . . . it's Italian . . ." Daniel pulls his T-shirt up over his nose and waits for me to finish blathering on about the damn cheese. I tear off a portion of the baguette and cut the cheese, utilizing every cell of restraint in my body not to look at the portion of skin that's been exposed right above his thick leather belt. I sneak a quick peek. Okay . . . wow. I *really* shouldn't have done that.

"You just cut the cheese," Daniel says through his T-shirt. I laugh. I laugh all the way from my gut. Nervous and all hopped up. I pass him the baguette and cheese. He lowers his T-shirt and makes another face. After one of those awkward, you're-the-only-one-laughing moments, I slowly stop laughing. Daniel takes the bread and cheese and puts the whole thing in his mouth. The entire piece of bread.

"So? What do you think? Not bad?" I say. Daniel is chewing and chewing and chewing. Bits of baguette shoot out of his mouth. He has a pained look on his face. It goes on far too long. He can't seem to swallow the giant piece of bread. He puts his hand on the counter and keeps chewing. It gives me a chance to take in his face. Where Will is polished and all-American, Daniel is rough and raw. He definitely has a bigger than normal nose. His skin is ruddy, with bits of stubble that refuse to cooperate with the razor. His lower lip is larger than the top. His eyes lead you to believe they should be brown, but now I can see they are the deepest of darkest blues. All of his features are so defined. There's nothing delicate about him.

He finally finishes chewing and affects a dramatic swallow. "I'm going to stick with the grapes, if that's okay," Daniel chokes out, plucking one from the bunch and popping it in his mouth. He chews and swallows. He continues, "Much easier, don't you think?"

"Do you want to get started?" I say. I love that cheese. Am I pretentious and shitty? First I say he's dead to me because he had the audacity to compare chefs and coaches, then I have a small orgasm because of an exposed bit of skin, and now I'm getting offended that he doesn't like a certain kind of cheese. I need to make up my mind about this man. Maybe if it were Velveeta, he would've liked it.

Remember—we're trying *not* to be a pompous ass. Focus.

"I've got to tell you that I haven't ever really cooked any-thing," Daniel admits.

I go to the walk-in and pull out the tarts I prepared ahead of time. I grab the container of berries and presliced apples and slam the door with my foot on the way out. Daniel waits by my station. He takes the container of berries and the cookie sheet with the individual tartlets from me and puts them on the counter.

"So is your girlfriend a good cook, then?" I rinse the ber-ries in the small sink, gently tossing them to make sure they're clean. I try to sound as offhand and asexual as possible. Off-hand and asexual like a *fox*.

Daniel's face colors. "Oh, I don't have a girlfriend."

"Oh, well . . ." What the fuck do I say next? I continue, "How do you eat if you don't know how to cook?"

"I'm great at the microwave. And you know, you . . ." Dan-iel trails off.

"I . . . What?" I question.

"At the auction, you said I wouldn't want the baking les-son. And I don't like people telling me what I want," Daniel confesses.

"So if I were a purveyor of colonoscopies, you'd . . ." I rest my hand on my hip.

"Hm . . ." Daniel smirks, letting me know he understands where I'm going with that, but he's holding his tongue. Were I to only have such willpower.

"So, apple-raspberry tartlets!" I announce.

"Yes! Apple-raspberry tartlets," Daniel repeats, flushing again.

"I thought these would be perfect for a dinner party or just to make for yourself. They'll make your house smell wonder-ful." I walk over to the oven, and Daniel follows. I say, "We're going to preheat the oven to three-seventy-five."

"Preheat?" he asks.

I stop. My hand is still resting on the oven dial. I stare up at him in disbelief. "Are you kidding?"

"What? I know what 'heat' means, but 'preheat'—what is that like? Well, heating before, right? The prefix 'pre' means 'before.' Why do you heat before?" Daniel crosses his arms over his chest and bites his lip. Either this is the most endearing exchange in the entire world, or Daniel Sullivan is an idiot. He adds, "Should I be taking notes?" Honey, there's not enough paper in the world.

"Wow, that whole 'never cooked anything' was pretty much the understatement of the century, huh? You know what . . ." I turn off the oven and walk back over to the counter. I grab the containers of fruit and the cookie sheet and put them back in the walk-in. Daniel is silently watching everything. He gets more and more fidgety as I put everything away. I grab the plate of cheese and fruit, dump it in the trash, and quickly wash the plate. I motion for Daniel to turn around, and he does. I untie his apron, take a quick look at his ass, and then pat him on the back to let him know I'm finished.

"You've given up on me?" Daniel tries to make a joke, but I can tell he's a little hurt. I retreat to the back room, grab my sweater, and fold my chef's jacket over my arm.

"No, I think we just need to back up a bit. Before we attempt to make pastry, we have to experience what extraordinary pastry tastes like. You up for a field trip? It's usually the third class in my series, but I figure we can mix it up. I do this with everyone," I say, coming out of the back room. I've never done this before. Not one time. We close up the restaurant, and I beep my car unlocked.

Daniel pauses. "Would it be okay if I drove?" He motions at his monstrosity of an SUV.

"Do we have to take out a small loan for gas?" I say.

Daniel lets out a forced, slightly sarcastic laugh. "I'm a big guy. I just don't think I'd be comfortable in your little wagon."

"It's not a fucking Radio Flyer," I blurt. I want to scoop up the F-bomb I just dropped and squish it back down, deep into my throat. I got so comfortable with him, I momentarily forgot I was still trying to impress him with my femininity. My mother's voice rattles around in my head: *Ladies don't use such colorful language.*

"No, no, you're right. It's not a Radio Flyer," Daniel says, beeping his SUV unlocked.

"Pardon my French," I almost whisper.

"You navigate," Daniel says, opening my door for me.

chapter sixteen

In the past year or so, I've felt a shift in my focus away from haute cuisine and back to my origins of relying on food to bring comfort and envelopment. Chef Canet likes to think we share the same culinary vision. But we don't anymore. He wants his creations to astound his audience with their virtuosity. And lately, he's been pulling in the reins on my desserts. I'm sure he'll hate that I served the individual cherry clafouti on Saturday night.

I used to buy in to it all. The more complicated a dessert was, the more I relished how certain people didn't—or couldn't—get it. I reasoned that only the most sophisticated of palates could handle the taste profiles I was mastering. Now I've started wondering what the rationale is for charging people twenty-five dollars for a tiny piece of olive-oil cake that seems only to impress, not nourish. I'm starting to care less and less about all the grandiose efforts and more about serving simple, beautiful food.

I figured this change in my thinking would lead to yet another variation in my five-year plan. A little cupcake place in San Francisco? A breakfast place with scones, muffins, and brioche in Malibu? Maybe a comfort-food extravaganza in Brooklyn? It was ever changing, but it was always mine. A place

I could open on my own. I imagined myself rolling out the dessert cart, offering up delectable treats to kids without even looking at their parents for an okay. Meeting with Paul and Donna to discuss a possible television show initially felt like a betrayal of my dream. But as I think about it more, the idea intrigues me. A new trajectory. One based on a foundation I laid. Or is it? Would they have even offered me the TV show had it not been for my last name? Maybe it's not such a new trajectory after all.

◆

"Just go all the way down Santa Monica Boulevard—oh wait, it's Halloween. Umm, go down to Third." The West Hollywood parade is one of the biggest Halloween celebrations in the country. Even on the morning of the parade, driving down the main route of Santa Monica Boulevard would take approximately three hours. Daniel steers the black Yukon down La Cienega and makes a left on Third.

The radio isn't on, and the silence is unnerving. I mention a couple of movies; he hasn't seen them. I mention a radio station I like; he hasn't heard of it. I fight the urge to stab myself in the thigh so we'll have something both of us can talk about.

"Are you going to tell me where we're going?" Daniel asks, rolling down his window. It's Halloween and approximately seventy-five degrees outside. I love L.A.

"Nope. How much time do you have?" I didn't ask whether Daniel had something else to do today. It's a holiday but a weekday.

"I have practice at four-thirty. I like to get there early, so I have until about two-thirty, three. Is that okay?" I'm driving down Third Street with someone who has "practice" later on this afternoon. Where everyone will call him Coach. Out of respect. Oh, how the mighty have fallen. "Pompous asshole" keeps a-knock-knock-knockin', doesn't it?

"Two-thirty-three exactly, huh?" I say, trying to lighten the mood by making the worst jokes I've ever attempted. Awesome plan.

"No, two-thirty *or* three . . . o'clock," Daniel corrects, glancing quickly over at me.

"Practice, huh? Oh, you're going to make a left on Fairfax."

"Basketball. I'm one of the assistant coaches over at UCLA," Daniel says.

"Oh, so that's why you moved out here? They recruited you?" I ask.

"I used to coach at a high school back home. I used to play, too—but that's not . . . I mean . . . Well, then I coached a couple of years at the city college and was basically waiting around to get called up to coach at KU. This call came first. I jumped at it. Not to mention the fact that a little sun seemed nice."

"Do you enjoy coaching?" My mouth is dry.

"Yeah, but ever since I started focusing on basketball, that's all anyone talks to me about."

I notice Daniel's arms are covered with blond hair, which puzzles me, because he has that Crayola-brown hair. Did he just say something? Should I be listening? "It's kind of like when you tell people you like frogs and then that's all anyone gives you. You know, Christmas, birthdays, just frogs." What. Am. I. Talking. About?

"Are you trying to tell me you like frogs?" Daniel asks.

"No, although I did go through a frog phase. Well, who didn't?" Why? Why? Why am I saying these things?

"Do I just keep going down Third?" Daniel, luckily, changes the subject.

"Yeah . . . yes, until Fairfax," I correct myself.

"Isn't there a freeway or something?" Daniel asks.

I nearly choke with laughter. "A freeway?" I continue to speak through my laughter. I am wiping away tears as Daniel stops at another light. "Just a note. In L.A. there are freeway drivers and city-street drivers. That's how we separate the men from the boys. You definitely want to be a city-street driver here. Just a little piece of advice from me to you." And yes, I was pointing when I was saying that. I pointed at myself and then, shockingly, when I said "you," yes, I pointed at Daniel. When did I turn into a gangster during Prohibition?

"Do your parents live here, too?" Daniel watches the protected left arrow run its course. One lone driver made it through. He doesn't have any idea who my parents are. Who my *parent* is, more to the point.

"My parents live in Montecito, mostly. But they have a house in Pasadena, too. You know, the Rose Parade?" Out-of-towners always know the Rose Parade. It puts Pasadena on the map.

"Sure, my mom loves the Rose Parade. They're actually coming out for the holidays, but closer to Thanksgiving. It's more of a business thing," Daniel says, kind of trailing off.

I will myself not to go into an hour-long diatribe about the Rose Parade—its origins, the best places to view the floats, and every other piece of useless trivia.

"Business thing?" I ask.

"Yeah, um, my dad is a professional Santa, and he's coming out for the Hollywood Christmas Parade. It's a pretty big deal." Daniel's jaw is tight. He glances quickly at me and then back at the road. I jump over the fact that Daniel's father is *Santa Claus* and right into the safety of trivia—why *is* the Hollywood Christmas Parade closer to Thanksgiving than Christmas? I've always wondered.

"How do you— I mean, how does *one* become a professional

Santa?" I'm oddly intrigued. But at the same time, who *is* this person? What utopian prairie did he frolic off of? Daniel finally makes the left turn. Now we're zooming up Fairfax.

"Dad sold insurance forever and retired a few years back. I'm the youngest of five kids, so my folks are a little bit older. He's been doing the whole Santa thing in my mom's classroom for years—he just *looks* like Santa, you know. Kind of a no-brainer." Daniel is using his right hand to illustrate what he's saying.

"If they come out to Pasadena, I'll have to give them the five-star tour. I can definitely hook 'em up." Hook 'em up? With who—50 Cent? I'm beginning to see the downside of hanging out only with family and people who have known me all my life. My witty banter definitely needs a tune-up. But it doesn't seem to matter. That frog bit would have brought me years of ridicule if I'd said it around my family. With Daniel, it wasn't cause for derision—it was just conversation, the beauty of a fling. With my family, there is a majestic trapeze act—flying through the air, the deftness of talent and the sheer brilliance of words. But one screwup and you plummet to the floor, busted and broken for not keeping up. Right now, right here, there is no high-flying majesty. I don't have to be anyone but myself. It's unnerving that my true self has revealed herself to be incredibly nerdy with a penchant for frogs, but beggars can't be choosers, I suppose.

"That would be great," he says.

I tell him to look out for Santa Monica Boulevard, and we finally make the turn into the parking lot. Daniel maneuvers through cell-phone-talking patrons and security guards to find a space.

"Where are we?" He absorbs the urban parking lot. The main focus of the shopping center is the Whole Foods Market.

There's also your usual manicure salon, florist, and tanning salon. But over in the corner—that's why we came here today.

"Follow me, please." I am giddy.

We walk through the parking lot past a girl dressed up as Wonder Woman—a slutty Wonder Woman, of course (though I wonder if a slutty Wonder Woman isn't redundant)—and a man dressed up as Malcolm MacDowell in *A Clockwork Orange*. Daniel looks each of them up and down and makes a face at me. I stop and look at him. He's already smiling. The wafting smells have hit us both.

"This is a whole lot better than that cheese. No offense," Daniel says as he motions for me to go in ahead of him.

The Stolichnaya Bakery is on the corner of Fairfax and Santa Monica Boulevard. It's one of the great hidden treasures of Los Angeles. Usually, I'm the youngest customer there by about fifty years. On one side of the bakery, a refrigerator of spinning perfectly frosted cakes tempts you. On the other side, rack after rack of cookies, breads, mandel breads, and other, more obscure Russian delicacies await.

"May I chelp you?" the woman behind the counter asks Daniel. She is outfitted in a hot-pink-and-black-polka-dotted apron and speaks in a thick Russian accent. Her hair is bottle-blond, and her orange lipstick is so thick you can barely see her thin lips underneath. Daniel looks at me and panics. He's overwhelmed. In a good way.

"I'd like an assortment, please," I say, stepping in front of Daniel.

The woman behind the counter is obviously disappointed.

"We sell by pound," she advises.

I look at the case. I can't decide. I quickly turn to Daniel. The woman is growing impatient. "What looks good?" I ask.

Daniel breathes a sigh of relief and laughs. "Everything. Just get one of everything." He puts his hand on the small of my back. Oh. Okay. If there were ever a moment when a decision was more solidified, it would be this one. I am definitely on the right track. I tell the woman we want one of each. Yes, the black-and-white cookie. Yes, one of every mandel bread. Yes. Yes. Yes. The woman behind the counter begins putting one of each cookie in a tiny bag and then in a much larger bag.

Daniel pays the woman and takes the bags from her. He brings the bag to his nose, takes a huge whiff, and stuffs a jam-filled cookie into his mouth.

"You've got a little something . . ." I motion all over my body, hoping he gets the hint that he's covered in cookie crumbs.

Daniel laughs and shoots cookie crumbs at me. "They're so good," he says with his mouth full, trying to wipe off the crumbs. I wipe myself off and dig in the bag for my own cookie. My mind races through many scenarios of the fling I'll have with Daniel. Only the setting varies: my apartment, the backseat of his Yukon, or even the cookie case at the Stolichnaya Bakery with the smell of cheap Russian perfume and mandel breads wafting during our torrid lovemaking. Maybe I'd be wearing a hot-pink-and-black-polka-dotted apron.

We sit in the SUV for another half hour. I've made myself completely sick from the cookies. Daniel reaches into the backseat and pulls a bottle of water from a maroon backpack. He offers it to me, and I take a long drink. Then he takes a long drink. Something about this touches me.

"What are you up to tonight, then?" Daniel buckles his seat belt and begins to pull out of the parking space. He puts his long arm around my seat as he looks back to make sure it's all clear.

"My brother might be coming into town, so I've got that," I say. Please don't ask me his name. Please don't ask me his name. I really don't want to wind through the whole Dostoyevsky/ *Crime and Punishment* reference right now.

"That sounds fun," he says. I never allow myself to get excited about seeing Rascal; he's never been that worried about such trifles as being on time and showing up for appointments. I'm still of the mind that I'll believe it when I see it. Daniel looks in the rearview mirror quickly. The sun is directly in his eyes. They're a deep buttercream-icing blue. Soft. I just want to hold his face right there. It's so fleeting, you almost have to look directly into his eyes to get the full effect of the color. There . . . stop looking around . . . just stare right into that sun for a full minute, is that so much to ask?

"What about you? What are you doing tonight?" I ask. My voice is rough and fast. My need to see the full impact of his eyes has made me act like I'm on the defensive in some paint-ball tournament—all twitchy and dodgy.

"We're having a BBQ at the head coach's house before every-one goes on to other, probably better things. Then I'll head on home and pass out candy." Daniel smiles. God, that was totally what I was going to do. You know, except for the barbecue and the whole "other people" thing.

We pull up right in front of Beverly. Daniel puts the SUV in park and turns the engine off. He keeps his seat belt buckled, although he started to reach across his chest when we pulled up. He brought his hand back quickly. I am sitting straight ahead.

"It was nice meeting you, Elisabeth. I hope I didn't make your job too hard," Daniel says.

"Oh, well, not a problem, but you *do* know that this is a series, right?" I blurt out. With all of my mental ranting on and on about flings, it all boils down to this moment: I find myself simply wanting to see him again.

"What?" Daniel unbuckles his seat belt now.

"A series. The uh . . . The first part of this lesson was the evaluation we did today. From there we decide how many classes you're entitled to. The gift certificate said 'series,' " I say, my hand on the door handle.

"A series? Oh . . ." Daniel trails off.

"I think you'd really benefit from it," I press. I try not to look at him.

"Does next Sunday work for you? I have a meeting with the other coaches that morning, but what about one?" Daniel asks. He's leaning on the emergency brake, his shoulder tilted toward me. A nice cool breeze blows through the open windows. I tuck my hair back behind my ear. Daniel's cowlicks are sprouting with abandon.

"Sunday at one." I smile, opening the door and climbing out. Daniel watches me get into my car safely and waves as I pull out from the curb. I have never honored the "series" thing. Most people want only the one class. But hopefully, he'll want more.

chapter seventeen

With a stupid grin on my face, I scroll through the e-mail messages that have come in on my BlackBerry. I'm going to see Daniel again. The e-mails break through my reverie. They represent a veritable *Who's Who* of everyone in my life. Julie. Chef Canet. George, the sommelier. Mom. Even one from Rascal. I open that one first.

> To: Elisabeth
> From: R.P.
> House of Pies. 6:00 tonight.
> See you there, Ras.

Ever since the time change, the days have been getting shorter and shorter. Dusk is about two hours away. I quickly check my watch. I have just enough time to go home and get ready before meeting Rascal.

After taking a short shower, I walk over to my closet and shift the clothes left and right, left and right. I relive the day as I dress. I find myself still thinking about Daniel. Thinking about him instead of thinking about . . . Will. Fuuuck. I curl my eyelashes. When I go in close, my face loses all of its definition. My features blur into one another, the tiniest of eyelashes garnering all of my focus.

I sweep on some blusher and think about how it was just me today. No Ben Page. No Rascal Page. No thirty-year history. No barking orders and maniacal French chefs. I was free of the baggage I usually travel with. I was naked. And he liked me. Well, I think he did. But more important, I liked myself.

◆

"You came dressed as Jack Kerouac?" I say, hugging Rascal in the foyer of the House of Pies in Silver Lake. He is wearing jeans and a white T-shirt. He's holding his black jacket in his hand. It's *almost* cold enough.

"What?" he says. His face is tanned. The beard is gone, and his hair is cut a bit shorter—the curls are still there, thankfully. Rascal really wouldn't be Rascal without that mop of curly dark hair. Obviously, the drive he spoke of was to somewhere that boasted a lot of sun—and a barber.

"Halloween? Costumes? The world just keeps turning, turning, turning?" I say, gesturing to the hostess that we'll be two tonight. She grabs two menus, and we follow her through the restaurant. A restaurant that looks exactly like you'd think a place called "House of Pies" would look. A lot of vinyl. A lot of regulars. And yes, a lot of pies.

"Fuck you," Rascal says lightly. A trio of teeny-bopper hipster girls dressed up in their best and sluttiest Halloween garb turns our way to see who's using such offensive language tonight. The ensuing double take is reminiscent of a Bugs Bunny cartoon. One of the girls notices it's *the* Rascal Page she saw in *People* while she was getting her nails done. She tugs on the shirt of another girl, commenting that Rascal looks taller in person. Like his father before him, Rascal has achieved a certain level of fame not usually reserved for writers. And the novels are only the half of it. It's the lifestyle that continues to intrigue people.

Rascal walks through the restaurant and back to the booth where the hostess has stopped. She puts our menus on the table. Our waitress approaches us with two waters, saying she'll be back to take our order. We assure her we don't need the time and quickly order our pie, forgoing dinner. We fall back into conversation—film rights, another book deal, the restaurant. The waitress returns with our pie.

"So what are you thinking about all this?" I ask, digging into my cherry pie (heated) à la mode. God, it's good. The crust is perfect—crumbly and light. Probably made with eight pounds of lard. This is what I was going for with the clafouti—the comfort of a well-made pie, no apologies.

"Of all the gin joints." The hairs bristle on the back of my neck. I can smell him. *Will*. I turn around and take a long, deep breath. He's back. His swipe of yellow hair is a bit longer, and he's trying to grow a beard, just like Rascal. I shift over in the booth. Rascal nods a hello.

"A wordsmith by trade, and that's the best you could come up with? A cheap *Casablanca* reference? What are you going to say when you leave, 'I'll be back'?" Rascal teases in his best Schwarzenegger impersonation. Will's face softens despite Rascal's mocking. The three teeny-bopper girls approach our booth and ask Rascal for an autograph.

"Happy Halloween. I missed you," Will whispers into my ear as the girls wait patiently for their autographs. A wave of anger quickly washes over me. Yeah, I missed you, too, motherfucker. Every second of every day. But that doesn't make you come back any sooner or not leave any quicker for your next assignment. What was it this time? *Vanity Fair* and Baghdad? *Esquire* and Darfur? The *Washington Post* and Afghanistan? I turn my head and feel Will put his hand on my leg under the table. His fingers brush my skin. Every brush, every movement of intimacy, breaks me—melts me—but I make sure the frost follows. Don't get used to it, I tell myself. My breathing deepens as my body reacts to Will. I make a point of looking directly into his eyes. They're that same surreally bright, almost ice blue, open to the public. I think about Daniel in that second. The darkest of blues visible only to those lucky enough to have a private invitation.

The girls ask Rascal if they can take a picture with him. He takes the napkin from his lap, places it carefully on the table, and slides out of the booth. The girls wrangle a waitress and ask if she'll take a couple of shots. All of the girls pass over their cameras and/or cell phones. They wrap their arms around him. Surrounding him. Rascal's expression is that of someone waiting in line at the DMV.

Will and I continue talking. "You're really doing the beard thing?" I say, tugging at it slightly.

"Mom's back in rehab," he announces, casually looking at Rascal and his adoring fans.

"Where?" I say, refocusing.

"In Aspen. Some kind of outpatient thing," Will says, leaning his head back a little, taking me in.

"How do you feel about that?" I ask, not knowing what else to say. For Anne Houghton, maybe the seventh time will be a charm. But for Will, every pronouncement of sobriety seems to harden him a bit more than the last.

"She wants me to be there. At the Aspen house," Will says. I wait, letting him talk. He continues, "I think . . . I think I'd rather be in Darfur." He forces a laugh, his eyes on his lap, his voice quiet.

"What are you going to do?" I ask, not wanting to tell him to go, not wanting to set him up for more heartache, but at the same time hoping that he has the capacity to be there for his mom—for *someone*. Will looks up and looks me in the eye, asking for some kind of guarantee that he won't get hurt again. That when he goes there, she'll really try this time. That they can be a normal family. That he can have his mom back. I don't know what to say. I take his face in my hands. And for those seconds, I feel the beauty of a love that has the capacity to streak through the night sky and leave people talking about it for the next seventy-four years, three hundred sixty-four days, twenty-three hours, and fifty-nine minutes.

"I'll go," he finally says, taking my hands in his.

"You guys done? Elisabeth? Jesus Christ Superstar?" Rascal says, standing over us. The girls have gone back to their booth with photographic proof that they met one of *People*'s fifty most beautiful people.

"Yeah, yeah," I say, bringing my hands back and straightening up a bit. Will picks up a menu and begins skimming the lard-filled fare.

"Because there are a whole lot of other places you guys could have chosen to have your little moment where I didn't have to be such an active audience member," Rascal says. The waitress comes over to the table, apologizes to Rascal, and hands Will a glass of water. He orders a Caesar salad and a sparkling water. Rascal asks if he'd like a penis with his order.

As the evening wears on, the warmth of Will next to me almost makes me ask if he needs me to go with him to Aspen, even if it's just for my days off. But I know he has to do this alone. His mom needs him and only him. I set my fork down. I've lost my appetite.

"You okay?" Rascal almost whispers as we make our way out of the restaurant.

"I don't know. You?" I volley the concern right back at him.

"Touché, young Page," Rascal says. Will is already standing outside, lighting up a cigarette.

"Are you in town for a while?" I cautiously ask Rascal.

"Definitely through Christmas. Why?" he answers. A nice breeze of cool fall air brushes my face. The Silver Lake traffic zooms past. The street is thick with people out for an evening of depravity made even more corrupt by the presence of a mask and costume. Will takes a long pull on his cigarette.

"Do you want to get together in the morning sometime soon? Breakfast? Coffee?" I ask.

"Why, so you and Will can cradle each other's faces while I watch *again*?" Rascal asks, taking out his pack of Pall Malls.

"I'm serious," I say.

"You have to be at work at . . ." He trails off. Will leans over and lights Rascal's cigarette.

"Eleven-thirty," I say decisively.

Rascal blows out a shaft of smoke. "How about Thursday around ten?" he asks.

"Eight," I correct.

"In the *morning*?" Rascal whines.

"Breakfast is customarily in the morning, yes," I say.

Rascal exhales. "Fine. Fine. Eight o'clock in the mother-fucking morning, you big baby."

"Doughboys?" I suggest.

"Parking is such a bitch there," Rascal complains.

"Parking's a bitch everywhere," Will says, stamping out his cigarette on the sidewalk.

"But not everywhere has giant cupcakes," I say.

"Fine. See you then," Rascal says.

"Up high," Rascal says, holding his hand high in the air for Will. He's been doing this to the poor boy for years. Will slaps the hand up high.

"Down low," Rascal challenges, positioning his hand low. Will looks at the hand he's never been able to slap fast enough. The words "too slow" always taunt him as Rascal pulls his hand away just before Will gets there. As they've gotten older, Will has tried several psychological gymnastics to try to deal with this seemingly straightforward offer. He's tried simply walking away from the "down low." He's attempted to slap the hand before Rascal can pull it away, always to no avail. And at one particularly memorable Easter brunch several years back, Will actually punched Rascal in the gut, asking whether or not he was "too slow now, motherfucker?" Rascal waits, his hand tauntingly down low.

"I'm going to get on the road," Will announces. Rascal eyes Will the way Mr. Miyagi proudly gazed upon the Karate Kid when he finally learned the true lesson of "wax on, wax off." Rascal waves goodbye, takes a long pull on his cigarette, and walks to his waiting sleek BMW, leaving Will and me alone.

"Drive safely," I say, pulling my purse tighter on my shoulder.

"I will," Will says. He leans in and kisses me gently.

"I'd ask you to come, but . . ." Will trails off. There's nothing to say. I'm running through everything I've said before. He knows it all, and I know not to jinx it. Instead, we stand there in silence.

"I'll call you when I know something," he says. He pulls his keys out of his pocket and turns to find his car in the parking lot. He beeps the car unlocked, and I see the lights of the Porsche blink in the darkness. I watch him walk away as the three teeny-boppers burst from the restaurant, loud and giddy with pictures and stories to tell their friends about meeting the dreamy Rascal Page on Halloween.

chapter eighteen

Y ou did what?"

Rascal and I are waiting to get into Doughboys. Why are there always ten thousand people here no matter what time of day it is?

"Will you let me finish my story?" My hair is still wet from my shower. After breakfast, I'll head over to the farmers' market on Little Melrose and figure out a feature for tonight.

"How do you finish a story that starts with you thinking about quitting the job you've spent your whole life trying to get?" Rascal demands. This isn't going quite as I'd planned.

"Havisham? Mrs. Havisham?" the hostess calls.

Rascal gets a giant smile on his face and stares at me expectantly. "You're going to have to refer to me as Pip all morning. You know, to keep up appearances," he whispers as I roll my eyes, raise my hand, and let the hostess know that it's *Miss* Havisham, thank you very much. We follow the hostess into the main room. She seats us just under a seven-foot-long cigar mounted on the exposed brick wall. I have nightmares that the cigar will fall on me one of these days. I cautiously slide onto the bench, taking care not to detach any wires or huge-cigar picture holders.

"I can't believe you," Rascal continues. He whips his napkin into his lap.

"I'm not going to call you Pip, for crissakes," I say.

"Not that—the job thing," Rascal says.

"Will you just get over yourself already?" I say. Our waitress approaches our table warily. Rascal and I switch on our well-bred manners and politely order our breakfasts. Well, I order breakfast. Rascal orders red velvet cake.

"It just seems like it came out of nowhere, that's all," he says, taking a sip of his water.

"I guess so, but can you let me finish?" I ask.

I've never really talked to my family about any of the negatives of the job at Beverly. It took so long to convince them that this was my passion that I didn't want to hear the chorus of "I told you sos" if anything ever went the slightest bit south.

"I'm only *thinking* of quitting. And I'm only thinking of it because I might have gotten a better job offer," I say.

"Are you going back to Lyon?" Rascal asks. The waitress brings our beverages. Rascal picks up his coffee and sips. I let my tea steep for a bit longer.

"I might be offered my own television show here in L.A.," I say. It's out there, and God, it sounds fucking lame. It's just not me. *Avery* gets offered television shows.

"What the fuck are you talking about? Television? This is so—" Rascal starts.

"Will you just—" I interrupt. Our waitress brings our orders, and we straighten up like two errant children who have been caught by their nanny.

"Will there be anything else?" the waitress asks hesitantly.

"Oh, no, thank you. This is perfect!" I pronounce.

"Delightful!" Rascal adds. The waitress backs away from us.

"This is fucking crazy. It just seems . . ." Rascal trails off, but I know what he's not saying—what he can't say.

"I know. It seems beneath me," I offer.

"Beneath *us*," Rascal adds.

I stab at my granola. "Yes, and dating Avery Lollipophead is the height of grace and refinement." I wipe the corners of my quickly tightening mouth.

"You mean *fucking* Avery Lollipophead is the height of grace and refinement," Rascal corrects.

"You're such a hypocrite," I say quietly.

"True," Rascal says, cutting into his red velvet cake.

"What?" I demand.

"You really shouldn't use *me* as a benchmark for anything except how low someone can go even with wealth, talent, and opportunity," Rascal says.

"You are not low," I say, now feeling bad.

"I allowed my name to be put on the writing credits of a movie called *Skeletons in Your Closet*." Rascal pauses and then continues with the rest of the title: "*The Secret Uprising.*" He shakes his head.

"Yeah, I remember that one," I admit.

"A high point, to be sure," he says.

"So why are you getting all fucked up about this?" I press.

"Because *you* can do better," he says.

"What if better hasn't worked for me? What if I want to try being happy?" I blurt before taking that split second to edit my cheesy outburst.

"That's patently ridiculous," he says absently, eating his cream-cheese icing.

"It's not ridiculous," I say, defeated.

"So you're saying, lamenting really, that you've been to paradise, but you've never been to me," Rascal toys—and with the lyrics to a Charlene tune, no less.

"I want to see where this goes, that's all," I say, toning down. I don't have to make any decisions. This may not even pan out. I'm going to the meeting at the Biltmore. That's it.

Rascal slowly looks up from his cake. His face is childlike in its mischievousness. "Does Will know?" he asks.

"No," I answer. The blur of my workweek has dulled the sting of not hearing from Will about how his mom is doing in rehab. To keep from thinking about it, I've been planning my second baking lesson with Daniel Sullivan with the vigilance of someone planning a small military coup.

"Are you going to tell Mom and Dad about all this?" Rascal asks. The threat of Dad doesn't have to be immediate to run a chill down my spine. It's absurd to think that a man I see so rarely has such a deep impact on my life. The mere possibility that he'd disapprove of my choices forces me to question anything and everything I do.

"Hell, no," I say. Rascal's face crinkles into a wide smile. I warn, "And neither are you." I shake my head and take a slow, deep breath. Rascal delicately sips his coffee.

chapter nineteen

I push open the door to Beverly's kitchen with the bags of groceries I picked up cutting into my fingers. I grab my chef's jacket and button it up. The kitchen instantly comes to life. I set out a whole chicken, along with a box of Bisquick. If Chef Canet saw the Bisquick, he'd fire me for real. In this kitchen, Bisquick is worse, far worse, than a gram of heroin.

I've been so caught up in preparing today's lesson that I haven't allowed tomorrow's meeting with the television people to enter my mind. I watch as the clock ticks.

"Hello? Elisabeth?"

A metal baking dish slips from my hand and falls loudly to the ground. I bend over quickly and pick up the dish. Just as I straighten, I see Daniel push the door open.

"Is everything okay?" he blurts.

"Oh, yeah, absolutely!" I say. I set the dish on the counter and just stand there. Then I walk up to Daniel and extend my hand. He takes it, and we shake hands for what feels like hours. I find myself trying to sneak glances at his eyes, as if the secret to life is imprinted there in the tiniest of writing. Back to work. Back to cooking. Back to perfectly measured doses of emotion.

"I thought we'd make a main course. So when your parents come to town, you can cook for them," I announce.

"Sounds good," Daniel says. I can't read him. I know exactly what Will is going to say before he says it. But I can't even tell if Daniel wants to be in the same room with me right now.

"Let's get you into an apron," I say, walking over to retrieve one. I hand the apron to Daniel. He puts it on over his head. I can't help but stand and watch. His hair is wet and almost black—no longer just the Crayola brown. The sprouts of hair are out of control today.

I lead Daniel around the kitchen while I teach him to boil water and debone a chicken. I tell him chicken and dumplings is perfect to serve this time of year. Some people make chicken and dumplings with only chicken breasts, I explain, though it doesn't taste the same. But if you're pressed for time or watching your calories, you can. We chop potatoes, celery, and carrots. His knife hits the cutting board hard. His chunks are giant and unwieldy. Not everyone uses vegetables, I tell him. I go into the entire history of chicken and dumplings. Its origins. The different substitutions and varieties. Without the sound of his knife in the background, it would be a symphony of way too much information about food, the history of food, and silences begging to be filled. Which I happily fill with, yes, more information about food.

"The great part of chicken and dumplings is that it's a one-pot meal," I say, flavoring the water with salt and pepper. I've been known to add garlic from time to time. I won't do that today.

"Why is it better to have a one-pot meal?" Daniel asks.

"Because, it's all in one. Easier to clean up. It's this simple meal that people think you've worked all day on. Makes the house smell incredible," I say.

"You're big into the house smelling incredible," Daniel observes.

"What?" I ask, caught off guard.

"You said the same thing about those fruit things we were supposed to do last time," he says, leaning up against the counter.

"The tartlets?" I correct.

"Sure," Daniel agrees, waiting for a reply to his first comment.

"I just like how cooking makes the house smell . . . well . . ." I'm fumbling through an explanation for something I didn't even know I thought about.

"Like home," Daniel finishes.

"Yeah, I guess it does," I agree, embarrassed by the accidental intimacy.

I help Daniel through the fun part: making the dumplings and dropping them into the boiling water with the chunks of chicken. It's his job to make sure the dumplings stay completely submerged. "Dive! Dive!" Daniel says, poking at them with a long wooden spoon.

"You don't want to poke them too hard; they might tear and get all crumbly," I say.

"Oh, sorry," Daniel says. "Dive! Dive!" he whispers.

"You can have this for dinner for about a week. I think you'll really like it," I say after the dumplings are done cooking and have cooled down a bit. I go to the storage racks and pull out a variety of take-out containers and bags. The idea of bringing Daniel comfort for up to a week excites me, though thoughts of Will tug at me. I push the thoughts away, employing Will's own philosophy of not muddying the time together with the "what if" game.

"Okay, it seems cool enough now. Let's get this packaged up for you," I say, ladling out the first of the chicken and dumplings.

"We're not going to sit down and try it first?" Daniel asks, leaning on the counter, looking gorgeous and irresistible. Don't do that. Please, have mercy on me.

"Oh, Chef is really weird about people using the restaurant. He barely lets me do these classes," I say, tightening down the top on one of the containers.

"Then when are we going to eat it?" Daniel asks.

"We?" I stop and look up.

chapter twenty

I grab a fairly clean tablecloth from the previous night that's in the hamper, waiting to be laundered. I take two plates from the shelf along with two wineglasses. I motion for Daniel to follow me outside in the now dusky night.

I flap open the tablecloth in the small grassy area between the restaurant and the office building next door. Not quite the lap of luxury. Daniel is holding the containers of chicken and dumplings stacked high in his arms. He sets them down in the center of the tablecloth as I go back in the restaurant for more supplies. I grab a bottle of wine, utensils, a corkscrew, and napkins.

"You can help with the plating," I say, kneeling down and dumping all of my ill-gotten booty on the tablecloth.

"Plating?" Daniel asks, taking the bottle opener and the wine. He eases down into a seated position. It's not the most graceful thing in the world. He looks like he's in pain. For an athlete, he moves like an old man.

"Yeah, you know, when you put stuff on a plate. Plating—I guess it's one of those words that you use all the time and think everyone knows, but it's really just you and your coworkers. I guess it's like 'basket' or 'two-pointer' or something," I say, setting out the plates, utensils, and napkins.

"I'm going to go out on a limb here and say that most people know what 'basket' means," Daniel says, pulling the cork from the bottle. He straightens his legs out in front of him.

"I think you might be right . . ." I trail off. Even though it's Sunday, people are out and about, meandering arm in arm out of other restaurants, browsing at the local newspaper stand, passing the time. I've never taken in the neighborhood like this. Daniel passes me a glass of wine.

"Now, this is way better than that stuffy restaurant," I say, sipping the wine and then trying to set it down so it doesn't spill. I open the containers of chicken and dumplings and plate up our dinner. Now I can't think "plate up" without smirking at my own insular vocabulary. Daniel pours himself a glass of wine and sets the bottle down on a patch of grass.

"I restored this old farmhouse back home, and I had to eat outside for an entire month while I figured out the whole kitchen situation. I came to prefer it." He takes a long sip.

Of course you did. Did you wear a cowboy hat and no shirt while you chopped wood and lassoed recalcitrant horses?

"And you're living where now?" I ask.

"I live in off-campus housing over by UCLA. It's really nothing but a dry-walled hotbox over on Glenrock in Westwood— along with a thousand nineteen-year-olds away from home for the first time. They must have slaughtered hogs on my carpet or something, I swear. When I tried to hang up the one poster I have, I pounded right through to the next apartment." He digs in to his dinner. He has a *poster*?

"So, your apartment is slowly killing you, then?" The first honest thing I've said all evening.

He smiles. "You could say that."

"You'll move out soon. You'll find a better place," I offer, taking my first bite. It's perfect.

"That's definitely my goal," Daniel says.

"A basket, if you will," I say, holding up my glass. Daniel smiles and raises his glass. His face folds into itself, his eyes crinkling in, the night emphasizing the shadows on the rough contours of his face. Our glasses clink together, and we drink. And make eye contact for the first time that day. I can't hide it anymore. I'm officially staring at him. Soaking in his deep blue eyes and smiling the stupid grin that first appeared last week.

Daniel hesitates for the slightest of moments. My entire body softens. I lay my hand on his leg, leaning in to him. He leans in, pausing again centimeters from my lips. I smile the most private smile. Just for him. He's so close I can feel the flutter of his eyelashes, the heat of his breath. He pulls me in to him and gently kisses me. It's so amazing, the first kiss.

We break from each other. There's no sound except the traffic whizzing past every now and again. He smiles and makes a little "hm" noise. Like he's made a decision. A quiet decision to himself. I look at him, trying to figure out what just happened. He picks up his fork. I tuck my legs underneath me tightly, holding on to my ankles, trying to stay contained. I think I've horribly misjudged this situation. A sharp stab of dread hits me. There's no room for Daniel and me to get any more serious than a textbook fling. What about my schedule? What about Will? I let out a long sigh. This textbook fling is no place for a genuinely nice guy like Daniel. What have I done?

"You know I'm never going to be able to make this again, right?" Daniel scoops up another forkful of dumplings. I let out another long sigh, taking him in. My breath quickens. I imagine myself in that instant as a person readying her home for a great storm that's bearing down any second. Running wildly through the house, slamming and locking windows, barring doors, throwing planks of wood and whatever else she can find over any possible opening, unable to keep the impending force of nature at bay.

The night wears on. We eat. We drink. We share our stories. We both try to gloss over that time-stopping kiss. When I present two left-over miniature chocolate cakes, it's well past ten P.M. We've been sitting here for hours. Our conversation has gone from what a caprese salad is to why basketball is like life, carefully tiptoeing around politics and religion. He's talked about his family back in Kansas. I've talked a bit about Rascal, finally broaching the whole name situation, dancing around the literary reference and sidestepping the obvious introduction of my father's profession. I've made a concerted effort to steer clear of the subject of my parents, or parent. I am loving this feeling of freedom. For once, I'm not known first as Ben Page's daughter, and Dad has never seemed to come up *specifically*. Meaning, Daniel has never explicitly asked me, "So, Elisabeth, is Ben Page your father, by any chance?" Go figure.

"Once you've been here a few more months, you'll really learn to love it. Have you been down by the beach yet?" I ask, piling up the empty dishes. I kneel and stand, trying to balance everything.

"I have, actually," Daniel says, gathering up his own dishes and slowly lifting himself up. His movements are labored.

"What's going on over there? Aren't you Mr. Athletic?" I say, still trying to balance all the dishes.

"I blew out my knee right after college. A career-ender, actually. So much was torn and shredded that it took me months to even be able to walk again," Daniel says, standing at last.

"Jesus," I say, feeling bad I brought it up. I don't know what to say next.

Daniel raises a single eyebrow. "Wanna see?"

"Hell, yeah, I wanna see," I say. Daniel lets out a bark of laughter and sets his dirty dishes back on the grass. He takes the cuff of his jeans and begins rolling it up, up, and up. Blond hair covers his tanned leg. I'm sorry, what exactly am I looking for here? Then I see it. An almost foot-long scar traveling vertically down his knee. Inch-wide stitches crossing it like railroad ties. It's so jagged. It hurts just to look at it.

"Fuuuuuck," I say, setting my dishes down on the grass and kneeling to get a closer look.

Daniel holds on to his rolled-up pant leg, bending over to get a better look at it himself. "It doesn't hurt that much anymore. I can run and stuff, but sitting down—like way down—well, I'm just not that graceful," Daniel says. I extend my finger, almost touching the scar. I look like E.T. *Elllliiooottttttttt.*

"Go ahead. You can kinda feel some cartilage rolling around in there," he says, taking my hand and bringing it the rest of the way to his knee. I run my finger over the wounded, raised skin. I get lost for a second. This is a real person. This isn't a dalliance or a fling or even a foil to my cometless skies. Daniel doesn't deserve this. I stand quickly, gathering my dirty dishes.

"You okay?" Daniel says, bending down to collect his pile of dishes. His pant leg is still rolled up as we walk inside the restaurant.

"Fine. It just . . . God, it just looks like it hurt. I guess I'm a little squeamish after all," I say, walking through the dining room, trying to get away from him—to save him.

"You deboned a chicken earlier and told me to rip through the muscle and pull out the joints," Daniel argues, following me into the kitchen. I look back over my shoulder and smile.

"I don't know what happened. I just . . ." I trail off, turning on the water and beginning to wash the dishes. Daniel sets his dishes in the sink alongside mine. He leans close.

"We're not done here, are we?" he says, tilting his head in.

"It's late," I say, wanting to scream, to warn him, warn him about me. Warn him that I'm not who he thinks I am. The heart he thinks might be his already belongs to someone else, even if that person isn't "good at it."

"Can I tempt you with a field trip of my own?" Daniel asks.

I finish the dishes and turn off the water. "Tempt": definitely an interesting word choice. I turn my body and lean in to the sink. We square each other off. Daniel again raises an eyebrow and cracks the tiniest of smirks. Before I can snatch the words back . . .

"You're on," I say.

chapter twenty-one

I follow Daniel on city streets (he's learning) all the way to Westwood. If it weren't for UCLA, Westwood would be nothing but a hodgepodge of overpriced chain restaurants and no parking anywhere. My mind is racing. I don't know what I want from all this. All I know is that right now I want to spend more time with Daniel. I've spent the last several years living my life in the two days I have off from the restaurant. Anything and everything that had to be done to keep my life on track, I fit in the refuge of Sunday and Monday. Dentist appointments. Trips to the DMV. Grocery shopping. My days off had also become a reminder that I had no social life to fit in at all. Maybe that made my "arrangement" with Will that much more attractive. But I can't think about this as I pull up in front of Daniel's apartment building.

He's right. It *is* sterile and beige. Still, I can't wait to see where he lives. What's on his walls? What's in his CD player? Does he have a CD player? Does he have an iPod? What do his linens look like? Does he have linens? Does he have a key bowl or somewhere he drops his mail? I wonder what his apartment smells like. Has he attempted cooking, or is he still the master of heating up various and sundry Hot Pockets?

Daniel tells me to park wherever I can, and he'll meet me at the entrance. Astonishingly, I find a space rather quickly. I check my lipstick in the rearview mirror, swipe under my eyes for any mascara remnants, and grab another bottle of white wine I've snagged from the restaurant. I beep my car locked and walk toward the entrance of Daniel's apartment building. I quiet myself and try to walk casually. Just be myself. Who that is, is really up for grabs.

Daniel walks through the glass door of the apartment building, closes the door behind me, and we walk to the elevator together.

"I've got it," he says, taking the bottle of wine as the elevator doors open up and we get on. "Now, the place is nothing nice, remember. It was the only thing I could rent on such short notice. Anyway, we're just stopping by to pick up a couple of sweatshirts and a blanket." The elevator chimes and lets us out on the third floor.

We walk down the most depressing hallway I've ever seen. Apparently, the butchering of hogs wasn't confined to Daniel's apartment. Bursts of awkward teenage squealing emanate from the closed doors that line the hall. He unlocks the door to his apartment and holds it open as I walk in.

"This is nice," I offer too quickly. It's horrible. There's no art except for one poster, advertising the UCLA basketball season, taped to the wall. Nothing else. Anywhere. Beige. Beige. And more beige. No decorative anything. Not even a key bowl. The only color comes from the giant plasma TV that's set up on the floor in the living room. It has some kind of video game box connected to it. "*That* didn't come with the place," I say, a little too forced.

Daniel sets the bottle of wine on a small table by the front door. He heads down a long hallway. I can only infer that his bedroom is down there.

"No, that's my splurge," he yells from down the hall. I take a few steps into the apartment. Binders filled with X's and O's drawn on tiny basketball courts litter the apartment, along with gym bags literally spilling over with basketballs and other equipment. I assume all this stuff goes along with the sport. Piles and piles of videotapes are stacked next to the television. Each is marked with a date, a team, or a player's name. This is definitely basketball central.

"So, what do you think? It's horrible, right?" Daniel asks, coming back down the hallway.

"You're near the school. You'll find something more . . . I mean, better . . ." I say. I think about that night at the dinner table and how my family destroyed Avery. I can't help but wonder what they would do to Daniel.

Daniel holds out a light blue sweatshirt for me. He's put on a dark blue sweater over his white T-shirt, and he's holding a red plaid blanket. "Here. It's going to get cold," he says, walking into the kitchenette and opening the refrigerator. I unfold the huge sweatshirt to reveal the UCLA Bruins logo emblazoned across the front. He continues, "Do you want to take a couple of beers or something?" He hangs on the open refrigerator door. In the span of eight seconds, I've become the kind of person who tailgates at home games.

"Oh, I brought a bottle of wine, but . . . Sure, we can do beer," I say. Daniel sets a couple of cans of Budweiser on the counter next to me.

"This is the perfect beverage choice!" I say, picking up one of the beer cans and cracking it open. Daniel leans against the faux kitchenette-counter thing and fidgets with another beer can. Goddamn. He's quite possibly the most beautiful thing I've ever seen. We stand there in awkward silence. I can't read him.

"You hate it," he says, pulling the tab off the top of his beer can.

"Hate what?" I ask, jumping at the opportunity of conversation. I'll admit to loathing anything at this point. Kittens? Fuck 'em. Puppies? Hate 'em.

"The apartment," he says.

"What? No," I force out. Who *wouldn't* hate this apartment? Why don't *you* hate this apartment? Daniel clears his throat. I try to quell the deafening voice of the pompous asshole, which is bordering on schizophrenic. Who cares what my family might say?

"You ready?" Daniel says, holding out his hand. He leaves the cans of beer on the counter. I leave the bottle of wine. We walk to the door. A thud bangs against one of his walls, followed by laughing and yelling. Daniel ignores the rugby game that seems to be going on next door and opens the door for me.

"You're not going to tell me where we're going?" I ask, slipping the sweatshirt over my head.

"Nope," he says.

◆

"I found this my first week here," Daniel says, setting the emergency brake. We've been driving for about thirty minutes toward the beach and up into the hills. It's freezing, and the Bruins sweatshirt is hardly doing its job. I hop out of the SUV and quietly close the door, noticing that it's way past midnight.

Daniel stands at the curb, waiting for me. I catch up with

him, and we walk along the residential street. I don't recognize any of this. I guess we're in Pacific Palisades, or maybe Santa Monica—I can't be sure. My entire body is shivering.

Daniel hesitates for a quick second. "Here . . . come here," he says, opening his arms to me.

I don't even think. I curl in close. "Thanks," I say, and our pace slows. I can see his breath in the night air. The moonlight is playing on the contours of his face. We walk to the end of the street and to a small fence. We squeeze through the loosely padlocked gate and come out on the other side. The trees are thick, and I still can't tell where it is that Daniel has taken me. I fold back into him as we continue walking. Daniel finally slows his pace. Now I can see what he sees. The Pacific Ocean. The full moon is hanging so low, it's like a scoop of vanilla ice cream sitting on top of a root-beer float.

"It's beautiful," I whisper.

"I think so," Daniel says, looking down. Our faces are inches apart. I want to dive in to him again. I swipe his lips with my fingers. Daniel is still. I pull him down closer and kiss him without giving a second thought to the logic, the math of schedules, or the percentages of a previously owned heart. Daniel takes the red plaid blanket from under his other arm. He begins to lay the blanket down on a clear space overlooking the entire ocean.

"No, let's . . ." I take the blanket, pull it over my shoulder, and open it out for him to join me. I'm sure I look like a mata-dor challenging a charging bull. Daniel creaks and pops into a seated position. I sit, covering both of our shoulders with the blanket. "Better?" I ask.

"Better," Daniel agrees. We position our bodies, getting comfortable. I tuck in right under his arm. He puts his right leg out straight and curls his left leg close. The moon hangs in front of us. We don't talk much. When we do, our conversation twists in and out of silence and kisses, one leading to another and then back again. As the night wears on, I nod in and out of sleeplessness. Losing the battle close to sunup, I fall fast asleep in his arms. No racing mind. No Tivo. Just him. And me. And this mountaintop.

Goddamn, he feels good.

chapter twenty-two

I can hear my BlackBerry. The alarm. The emergency backup backup alarm. My head shoots up. I try to get my bearings. Where am I? I think. Where the fuck am I?

"Is that the smoke alarm? The smoke detector?" Daniel sleepily asks through a yawn. I sit up and realize I'm sleeping on a mountaintop in a pile of dirt. I look down at Daniel and smile. His hair is everywhere, sticking up in ways I didn't think possible. Oh God, what does *my* hair look like? Did I put on mascara last night? Yes, yes, I did. Fuuuckk . . . I must look like Karen Black right about now.

"No, it's my alarm. I set it just in case," I say, wiping at my eyes, hoping to clean away some mascara.

"I'm a 'just in case'?" Ouch. Daniel opens his eyes, and the sunlight hits him right in the dark blue of his eyes. I love this. He hates it.

"Is it seven-thirty in the *morning*?" I am panicking.

Daniel slowly sits up, bits of leaves and dirt all over his sweater. "You slept all night," he says.

Oh my God . . . I haven't even thought . . . Oh, shit. The meeting. The big meeting with Paul and Donna is in two hours, and I'm on the other side of town, covered in dirt and leaves.

"I have to get going. I have this meeting this morning." I stop. He doesn't know anything about this. He's just staring at me. I don't know where to go from here. I haven't prepared; I don't have any clothes. I won't be able to take a shower. I'm on a fucking mountaintop. I'm . . . I'm . . . I'm . . . Just breathe.

"What's going on in there?" Daniel asks, putting one arm behind his head. Why is that sexy? Jesus. Focus. Focus.

"Remember how I told you I wasn't sure if I really wanted to stay at the restaurant?" I begin, settling myself cross-legged next to him. Daniel bends into a seated position and leans back on one arm. Ready to listen. Time stops.

"Excuse me?" An older couple and their dog stand over us. I'm startled out of my thought process and instinctively swipe at my mascara and try to straighten my hair. Daniel attempts to tamp down his hair.

"This is private property!" the old man admonishes.

Daniel and I stand, grabbing the blanket. "I'm sorry, sir . . . we really didn't know," Daniel says, brushing leaves and dirt from his pants. I attempt to do the same. The older couple stands in all of their early-morning glory, waiting for us to leave.

"You a Bruins fan?" the old man asks, pointing at my sweatshirt. In L.A. these could be fightin' words if we don't answer correctly. Two feuding camps as legendary as the Hatfields and the McCoys. The Giants and the Dodgers. The Red Sox and the Yankees. Republicans and Democrats. Good versus evil. The USC Trojans and the UCLA Bruins. Daniel sizes up the couple. I do the same. Wealthy neighborhood. A lot of bling. Definitely some entitlement issues. We look at each other and decide.

"No, it's laundry day," Daniel scoffs.

"Go, Trojans!" I add.

The man beams. "Going to be a great year!" He and his wife pass us as their dog sniffs and pulls them along the trail. Daniel and I make our way back down the trail, through the gate, and back into his waiting SUV. I tug my purse out of the backseat and find some face wipes I keep in there for emergencies. I pull down the visor and flip open the mirror. Horror of horrors. Daniel reaches into the backseat and retrieves a bottle of water from his backpack. He hands it to me, and I take a long drink, hoping to rinse some of the remnants of stank out of my mouth. I find a tin of mints in the bottom of my purse, quickly pop one in my mouth, and hold it open for Daniel. He takes one, then a long swig of water, and begins driving down the street back to his apartment, where my car is.

"Why didn't you tell me I looked like Emmitt Smith, the sad clown," I say, cleaning my face.

"You mean Emmett Kelly. Emmitt Smith was the running back for the Cowboys," Daniel corrects.

"Oh, right," I say. How do I know that? Television, no doubt. Television, or the osmosis of sports trivia, from being around Daniel, has made me start confusing sports legends with everything else.

"Tell me about this meeting," Daniel says as he drives quickly, knowing time is of the essence.

I continue my cleanup process as I speak. "These people came into the restaurant last week. They want to meet with me today about possibly filming a pilot for the Food Network. It's the beginning stages of maybe being able to have my own show—or something." The car jostles as I try to reapply my mascara. I'm tap-dancing around Daniel. I know that I'm in over my head emotionally. I also know that I can't think about this now. Thankfully.

"Really? That sounds great. I mean, it sounds like—and this is just from yesterday—you really are great at teaching and making sure people understand the history. You made it really interesting. I think it's great," he repeats.

I flip the mirror back up and throw my mascara in my purse. "I hate that I'm wearing the same clothes. Do I look like I slept on a mountaintop last night?" I ask, still wiping at my eyes.

"They're going to love you," Daniel says, zooming down Wilshire Boulevard. I look over at him. He gives me a quick smile and then looks back at the road. I lean back in my seat and try to calm myself down.

Daniel pulls up alongside my car. There's a parking ticket peeking out from behind the windshield wiper. Of course there is. I unbuckle my seat belt.

"What are you doing tonight?" Daniel asks, unbuckling his seat belt.

"Nothing . . ." I say, hoping that I've trailed off in just the right tone to encourage another invitation.

"Do you want to go on an official date? Dinner and a movie? It'd have to be a little late. How does eight sound?" he asks.

It's as if I'm gazing into a box of chocolates. I know if I eat one more, I'll make myself sick. But they all look so good. How can I not partake of just—one—more. "That sounds loverly," I say, tilting my head. Just looking. Taking him in. He leans over and kisses me. I move my hand from his face to his shoulder, pulling him close. I'm supposed to be thinking about being late to my meeting. One more chocolate. One more chocolate. I get lost but quickly realize that time is passing. And I'm late.

"I've gotta go," I announce finally. Daniel looks disappointed. His hand rests on my leg. "Tonight," I say, taking a crumpled envelope out of my purse and writing down my phone number and quick directions to my apartment. I lean in and give him another kiss. He's smiling. No, he's smirking.

"What?" I say, my lips touching his.

"Nothing. Nothing. Eight? Tonight?" he asks.

"Eight. Tonight," I say, moving farther and farther out of his car. Not wanting to. Wanting to stay here. Go up in that slaughterhouse of an apartment and laze the day away in his arms. I slam the car door and lean in the open window. I'm going to try to shove as many chocolates as I can in my mouth before I make myself sick. "Come here," I say, hopping up and squeezing my body through the window.

Daniel leans over. "Eight?" he says, kissing me again.

I hop back down and stand beside the SUV. "See you then," I say, pulling the ticket out from under my windshield wiper. I beep my car unlocked and climb in. Daniel idles, waiting. I turn the key and maneuver out of the tight parking space. I honk as I pull down his street.

I try to relax and take a deep breath. My stomach is quiet and calm. No Pepto-Bismol chewables. No yogi tea. No yerba maté. Just one night with Daniel. Well, if that's just . . . That's just ridiculous. It can't be that—*this* can't be. I stop at a doughnut shop to pick up a large black tea. All they have is *Lipton.* I'm wearing the same clothes from last night, no morning run, no Joan's on Third, no *L.A. Times,* and a goddamn Lipton tea. I merge onto Sunset Boulevard, sipping my tea and figuring out how I'm going to get to a meeting across town in under an hour and a half. This is L.A., after all. It's going to take a miracle. What comes next? I don't know how to do this. My schedule will overtake my life for the next five days. I don't want it to. *Do* I want it to? I don't want to hurt Daniel. Or maybe I just don't want to hurt.

chapter twenty-three

S omehow the waters part, and by the time I pull up to the valet at the Biltmore Hotel in downtown L.A., I'm early but officially hyperventilating. Los Angeles traffic hasn't helped me prepare for this meeting. I steady my breathing as I pull my purse tight on my shoulder. By the time the doorman opens the door to the grand old hotel, my head is high and my breathing is stable.

I walk through the majestic foyer, past the huge mural, and head down the regal stairs into the Rendezvous Court. A huge fountain in the center anchors this hangar of a room. Tables and chairs swirl around the fountain. The room is filled with chattering patrons, uptight businessmen with open files and cups of coffee and tourists who don't quite know what to make of all this pomp. I scan the room for the television duo.

"Elisabeth!" Donna is standing in the entryway with her sunglasses on and an Hermès handbag that looks like an overnight bag. I wave and approach her. She extends her hand, and we gush and smile through our good-mornings. I'm somewhat relieved. I was worried about the greeting: Would one hug? Double-kiss? Open-mouth kiss? I mean, how badly *do* I want this gig?

"Paul is on his way. How is everything?" Donna asks.

"Great, just great. How was your weekend?" I ask. Think Mom. Just ask questions.

"Great, how was yours?" Donna must subscribe to the same theory.

"Oh, fabulous. Did you find the hotel okay?" I volley back.

"Absolutely. My husband and I have season tickets at the new Walt Disney Concert Hall. What about you?"

We're at the net now—fast shots back and forth. I want to ask if the season tickets are great or fabulous "Well, I love it here, so . . ." I trail off.

Paul walks down the stairs and Donna motions for him to come over. We shake hands. He motions to the waiter that our party is ready to be seated. The tuxedoed waiter approaches and seats us.

Paul sits in a cushiony chair at the head of the little table. Donna and I sit on an antique couch. I still feel flushed from last night. Our waiter brings our water. I take a long drink.

Donna tells the waiter she already had a huge breakfast, so she won't be eating anything. Just coffee. Yeah, right. I know an L.A. diet when I see one.

"Why don't you order for us, Elisabeth?" Paul asks, studying me.

"Why don't we start with the Victorian tea service?" I ask, looking to Paul and Donna. They nod approvingly and motion for me to continue. "And for the tea, why don't we do the Earl Grey? This service comes with a glass of champagne." Paul and Donna nod again. The waiter smiles and leaves us.

"You're adorable," Paul exclaims. Donna is nodding, nodding, nodding. How am I supposed to trust these people? They can't drop the act for one second.

"Thank you," I say. Though I've had a lot of high-stakes interviews, I find myself becoming nervous. While I'm at the top of my game professionally, I also feel trapped in a velvet cage. Just enough money to survive comfortably, just enough freedom to create some good desserts. But there's a line; a boundary. Don't get too far afield with the desserts. This is a high-end *French* restaurant. Stay in line. Stay in line. Stay the same—cryogenically frozen—for how long?

Paul dives in with the pitch. "We want to start with a television show. You, in and around Los Angeles. It's a spin on the shows that focus on certain regions. Instead of a country, we thought it would be cute to have you move around L.A. We'd start with a field piece, and then you'd come back to your kitchen and bake off some recipes." I love that he uses the same terms I use. I'm more aware of this after last night, when my love of the phrase "plate up" was outed and mocked. The term "bake off" is far more arcane. I'm among friends. This opportunity might be the one puzzle piece I need to make the rest of my life fall into place. I need to abandon all preconceptions about what Dad would think and whether this job is on his trajectory or mine.

"You have such a way with people, and you know the city so well. We think it'd be stupid not to incorporate that in our pitch," Donna adds.

"Would you run it through all the way for me? Let's say this meeting is successful, and we decide to do business together. Where do we go from here?" I ask.

"Good question," Donna says, and immediately looks to Paul. He easily picks up the invitation.

"You say yes to us, and things will move very fast. Donna and I will meet with the executives at the Food Network and pitch them a beginning sketch of your show. If they're interested, they'll green-light a pilot, which we'll film here in L.A."

"You'll need to be thinking about possible themes for that first show," Donna says.

"Once we film the pilot, we'll all travel to New York to pitch to the network executives. That would be a four-day commitment on your part. You'd need to have approximately one hundred recipes—three to four recipes per theme—ready to go, as well as the field pieces that would correspond with them," Paul rattles off.

"That's your homework," Donna jokes. I'm going to have to find extra hours in the day. Is sleep really necessary? The waiter returns with our tea service and Donna's coffee. He tells us to make sure we allow the tea to steep for another three minutes.

"I would like to impress upon you that we've already gotten great feedback from the executives over at the network, so this is a very real scenario I've laid out for you. I want you to understand that if you say yes to us today, we will need you to be open to this schedule. I feel very confident about the pitch," Paul asserts. His body is relaxed and easy, but his tone is all business. Donna is nodding. She can't stop staring at the beautiful pastries that came with the tea service the waiter brought over. She sips her coffee.

Paul continues. "The network will provide you with a culinary team to test the recipes you provide. They have the best test kitchen in New York. But we'd like you to think about recruiting someone you feel comfortable with to assist you on-set. Someone who would work closely with our culinary producer." Paul pours himself a cup of tea. It hasn't been three minutes.

"Assist me?" I ask. The tiny bubbles are sprinting to the top of my champagne glass.

"The network provides everything behind the scenes. But we thought it might make a more attractive package if we gave you your choice of an assistant. He or she wouldn't be on camera, but we'd offer an attractive salary," Paul says. I think of Julie and Samuel. I can't see either of them jumping at this chance.

I hired them for their ambition; they'd be crazy to walk away from a job at Beverly for a chance at a less than glorious TV job. I'll throw it out there, but if neither of them bites, I'll ask the network to assign someone to me. Someone who is half as good as Julie or Samuel. I finally pour myself a cup of tea.

Paul mentions a salary for me that is staggering. We discuss time lines and filming schedules. I have a sobering thought. I'm going to have to ask Chef Canet for vacation time. Something I have *never* done. I'll lie and say it's for Rascal's book tour. Maybe he'll want to join me on this jaunt. Rascal's always up for an adventure.

There's no way I'm quitting my job yet. There are too many variables to even try to analyze the equation. I'll see how the pilot fares. If it goes well, I can make my choice then. I can't help but get a bit excited. What Paul and Donna are proposing here could transform my life. Completely. I know it seems like a small thing, but besides appearing on TV in front of millions of people, I'd probably get holidays off. I haven't had a single holiday off in all my years in a kitchen. Holidays are the busiest times of the year in a restaurant. I'd have to work only long enough to film however many episodes per year we agreed upon. I'd get a ridiculous sum of money. I'd have a life. I'd have a future. I'd be making a decision based on who I *am* rather than who I'm *not*. Still, every voice in my head is telling me this is not something I should even think about—except one. Mine.

"I'm in," I say.

◆

At eight on the dot, Daniel shows up at my apartment with a bouquet of flowers. The flowers make me blush at their promise of wholesomeness. Daniel is a man who brings flowers. Unable to help myself, I run my hand up the collar of his coat and pull him in for a kiss. Later, I give him the full tour of my apartment. "No slaughtering of hogs here," I joke. He doesn't think it's funny. I wish I could get Superman to run around the earth enough times to take me back in time so I could take it back. I cut the stems on the flowers, pull a vase out of the cabinet over the sink, and make a promise to myself that I'm going to hire an exorcist to get rid of the schizophrenic pompous voices that plague me.

Daniel and I decide on a blockbuster that's playing at the ArcLight in Hollywood. We get a container of my favorite caramel corn, two hot dogs, and a couple of sodas. In the brief minutes before the movie begins, I quickly recap my meeting with Paul and Donna. As the lights dim, Daniel talks about the auspicious beginnings of something called Hell Week over at Pauley Pavilion. Dinner and a movie, just like he promised.

When we finish "dining" midway through the movie, Daniel lifts up the armrest, and I fold in to him once again. I lose myself in the movie's flickering light. The movie is in English, but our date should have had subtitles. I've never felt something more foreign in my entire life.

chapter twenty-four

The next morning, after a chaste goodbye the night before, I find parking down the street from the restaurant and grab my purse from the passenger seat. I hear faint ringing from the depths and fish my BlackBerry out. I didn't stop at the farmers' market on the way to work; I've decided to do a chocolate pots de crème feature, with fresh raspberries that are already at the restaurant.

"Hello?" I answer, shifting and situating.

"You called?" It's Rascal.

"I have to go to New York. I don't know the dates yet, but it'll be around the holidays. Wanna go?" I ask, trying to butter him up to get his impossible approval.

"Sure, why not?"

"I'll e-mail you all the information as soon as I get it," I say, stopping at the door to the restaurant.

"I should probably let my agent know I'm coming," Rascal says.

"Where are you now?" I ask.

"Montana," Rascal answers.

"I thought you said you were sticking around here until Christmas."

"Yeah, well . . ." Rascal trails off.

"Okay, well, I'll get you those details," I say, and we sign off. Rascal didn't ask why I'm going to New York or explain his dire need to be in perpetual motion. I drop my BlackBerry back in my purse and enter the restaurant.

Louis greets me with his usual kisses on both cheeks. I push open the kitchen door, but he stops me.

"So?" He whips out a napkin and begins folding it expertly for one of the tables.

"*Oui?*" I keep my hand on the door. How much does Louis know about the "fans" he introduced me to on that fateful night?

"Did you have a good weekend?" Louis asks.

"*Oui*," I quickly say. I feel vulnerable about so many things, I can't guess which one Louis is asking about. He's never tried to keep me from getting into the kitchen and starting to work.

"The fans? You . . . Do you speak with them?" Louis flips another napkin into a folding frenzy.

"*Mais oui.* We had a meeting. It was nothing. Everyone has meetings in L.A.," I joke, pushing the kitchen door farther.

"You . . . you are not sure what to say, eh?" Louis asks.

"*Je ne comprends pas, mon cher.*" I'm getting nervous. I've never been afraid of Louis, but he's been Chef Canet's right-hand man since the beginning. Even Michel, the chef de cuisine, joined Chef after Louis.

"We are here, yes? This is *our* place," he says.

I don't know whether it's the language barrier or if he's trying to be cryptic, but this whole conversation has been more than a little annoying. "Just say what you need to say," I finally manage, dropping the attempt at bilingual pleasantries.

"The television is for you. The television is for the clafouti and the flan. You are not here anymore, yes?" My first thought is, You bet your sweet ass I'm here. If I know anything about

Hollywood types, I shouldn't quit my day job yet. I'm not having this conversation until I know for sure I have other options. A girl makes one fucking pumpkin flan, and you'd think the entire world flew right off its axis.

"I *am* here now," I say, looking Louis right in the eye. I kiss him on both cheeks and turn to the kitchen door.

I'll be damned if I'll forfeit everything I've worked for—not until I'm good and ready. I haven't worked my ass off to stand in some dining room holding my goddamn purse while a maître d' lectures me on how I should go into television because I'm not good enough for this restaurant anymore. Fuck that. I am certainly qualified. And I can redefine what is good and what customers want. I can show them it's okay to order a dessert and be presented with something sweet, gooey, and comforting, not a complicated Erector Set of arcane ingredients and mystery. It's okay to feel pleasure. It's okay to want comfort. Simple and pure are not inferior or pedestrian.

I hear a familiar woman's voice: "Chef Page?" I whip around, still fuming.

"Mademoiselle, we are closed. Please, please, you must leave," Louis says. It's Margot. A very pregnant and distraught Margot.

"Margot?" I walk over to her quickly. Her face is crumpled and flushed. Is it bad news? Oh God, please, no. No.

"This is Chef Decoudreau's wife," I explain to Louis. He looks at me as if to say, "So what? Why is she here? It's unprofessional."

"Can you find Samuel for me, please, Elisabeth?" Margot is almost in tears. Louis whips a napkin into yet another folding frenzy. Oh my God . . . is Margot . . . is she losing the baby? Why isn't she at the hospital? Where's her fucking doula now? I'm scared to death.

"Of course. Please sit down. Do you want water or something?" I ask.

"No. You're so sweet, but no, thank you." Margot lowers herself onto a chair. I burst through the kitchen door in search of Samuel. I find him coming out of the walk-in with a flat of raspberries.

"Samuel, Margot is here. She doesn't look very well," I say as quietly as I can. I take the flat of raspberries from him, and we hurry out to the front of the restaurant. I don't know why I'm following. And why am I still carrying the raspberries?

"Oberon is sick." Margot quivers as Samuel kneels before her, taking her hands in his.

"Oberon? You're naming the baby *Oberon*?" I blurt without thinking. I assumed Samuel and Margot were a little more grounded than that. I mean, I like *Midsummer Night's Dream* as much as the next guy, but please. There's a fine line, people.

"We named the *dog* Oberon, Chef Page," Samuel says over his shoulder. Oh. I knew that. Margot went on and on about Oberon at the baby shower. He's their giant Bernese mountain dog. Their first child, she likes to say.

"What's the problem?" Samuel purrs. Nothing matters. As long as Margot and the baby are okay, nothing else matters. And that the baby isn't named Oberon. That matters a little bit, too.

"He wasn't eating, and he didn't have any energy. I've got him in the car. We just got back from the vet." The picture of a very pregnant Margot loading a hundred-and-fifty-pound bear of a dog into their Toyota Prius makes me kind of love her even more in that moment. "They said he has Addison's disease," Margot whimpers.

"Addison's disease?" Samuel repeats. Margot is sobbing. Samuel puts his arm around her and rubs her back as he tries to soothe her. Louis brings Margot a glass of water. She thanks him. He gives me the international sign to move this along. I wave him off.

"Didn't John F. Kennedy have Addison's disease?" I offer. Samuel and Margot stare at me. For some bizarre reason, I continue butting into a conversation I wasn't invited to join in the first place. "See? JFK lived a very full life." There is an obvious lull in the room. "Oberon just needs to avoid motorcades, that's all," I add, attempting to lighten the mood. Margot wails shrilly. Louis looks over. Michel pokes his head out of the kitchen and yells at Samuel that his mixer is still on. Samuel sighs. His eyes are twitchy, and I can see beads of sweat moving down his tense face. Julie zooms right past me and into the kitchen. She doesn't give Margot's sobbing a second glance.

"What if our baby gets sick? I didn't even realize Oberon was hurting! What if I don't know when our baby is hurting? What if I don't know how to take care of our baby?" Margot is hysterical.

"Your mixer is on! Samuel? Samuel? The mixer is just on!" Julie bursts back into the dining room. "You've beaten the batter to shit, Samuel! We're going to have to start over, which means we're *already* in the weeds!" She quickly retreats into the kitchen. Samuel doesn't look away from Margot, but I can see his hand twisting tighter and tighter around the back of her chair.

"Chef Page, I'm going to need to take the night off," Samuel says, standing and unbuttoning his chef's jacket, not looking at me. He's focused on Margot.

She reaches up to him, grabbing his hands. "No, baby, you can't take the night off," she wails, looking at him, then me.

"If you need the night off, you should take it," I say. I don't know how I'm going to get through the night without him. My tone of voice makes this absolutely clear, and I loathe myself for it.

"I'll go over to Kerrie's. I'll take Oberon, and we'll go to Kerrie's. I shouldn't have come here. I'm so sorry, Chef Page. We'll be fine," Margot reasons, heaving herself up from the chair. Samuel steadies her, helping her up with a grace that only intimacy can establish.

"No, I should—" Samuel starts.

"We'll be fine," Margot says, her hands on her belly.

"If you need me . . ." Samuel's voice is barely a whisper. He's inches from Margot, imploring her to tell him the truth: the only thing he can't bear to hear right now.

"They need you here." Margot reaches up to Samuel and buttons up his chef's jacket. He bends in to her.

"I'm going to head on back into the kitchen," I say to no one.

"We'll know exactly how to care for our baby," I hear Samuel say to Margot as I push open the kitchen door. His voice is private and wrenching.

As the night wears on, I look over at Julie and Samuel buzzing around the kitchen. Samuel is intent yet detached. His desserts are even more immaculate, even more controlled, than usual as he attempts to contain and suppress what happened earlier. I watch him attempting to balance his messy, out-of-control love for his wife and child and this restaurant. Try balancing that with anything else. Impossible. My stomach lurches, and I think of Daniel.

"Hey, I'm going to the bathroom. Just real fast," I announce. Julie and Samuel don't look up. I walk hurriedly to the lockers, grab my BlackBerry, and walk into the bathroom, locking the door behind me. I dial Daniel—and quickly hang up. I can't. I can't. I dial Will. He knows me. The *real* me. He fits.

"Hello?" Will answers. I snap back into the moment. He sounds tired. I'm hunched over on the toilet with one finger in my ear. The noise from the kitchen distracts me.

"Hey, how's your mom?" I begin.

"She went out about a week ago, but she's been sober again for almost six days," Will informs me.

"She went out?" I ask.

"She said she was craving a White Russian. Serves me right for renting *The Big Lebowski*." Will's voice is quiet and beaten.

"How are you doing?" I'm asking a question people ask a thousand times a day. But when you actually mean it, it has a global giantness to it that still yields the tiniest of answers.

"Fine," Will answers.

Someone knocks on the bathroom door. "You done?"

"Just a second," I answer. "I had a big meeting today," I say to Will. My chest tightens.

"Oh yeah, Ras was telling me about that. Is this the *TV* thing?" Will says "TV" as if it's some kind of sexually transmitted disease.

"Yeah, the *TV* thing," I say, deflating slightly.

"We can talk more later—I've got to get back. See you soon, I promise." Will hangs up quickly. I sit there, and the room closes in around me. I stare at my BlackBerry and scroll through the list of calls. Daniel has left two messages, asking me to stop by after work; he says he doesn't care how late I am. I returned his call from this morning and told him that we'd have to wait until the weekend—too much to do in the morning. I need all the sleep I can get, as the homework Donna and Paul gave me is piling up. It all seemed so logical. Daniel understood. I flip my phone around in my hands. Around and around. He understood. I just can't . . . I mean, look at Samuel and Margot. Will has never even come into the restaurant, let alone caused a scene like Margot. It's just—it just can't work. It can't work.

"Will you come on!" the person on the other side of the door demands. The pounding startles me.

I stand, position myself in front of the sink, turn on the cold water, and splash my face. As I open the door, my BlackBerry begins to ring once more. Loudly. It has an old-fashioned brrrriiiinnnnngggggggg type of ring. The sous chef who was trying to get into the bathroom squeezes past me and shuts the door. I beep my phone on, trying to shut it up. I duck into the back room. "Hello?" I answer in a whisper, not recognizing the number.

"Elisabeth? Hi, it's Paul." His voice is smooth, even through the crackling phone.

"Hi, Paul, what's going on?" I say. What's going on? Who am I? Dwayne from *What's Happening!*?

"The executives loved the pitch. They want to see the pilot ASAP," Paul announces.

"Oh, wow—that's fabulous!" I say, slinking farther into the back room.

"I just wanted to confirm our next meeting and finalize the dates for New York," Paul rattles off. "We're meeting at Campanile this coming Tuesday, and the trip to New York is slated for the second week in December—the fourth through the eighth—I believe it's a Monday through Friday. You'll be back for Saturday night at the restaurant. I'll messenger over the details—flights, hotels, that kind of thing. We'll go over our schedules at Campanile so we can set up some dates to shoot the pilot. Got it?"

My mind is racing. "I'd like to have my brother travel with me," I ask, trying to keep up.

"That's fine. We usually plan for spouses, but we can make arrangements for him. Rascal, right?" Paul asks.

"Right," I say.

"That's not his *real* name, is it?"

"No, his real name is actually worse," I say.

"What shall I put on the ticket?" Paul presses.

"Raskolnikov. His full name is Raskolnikov Page," I say, and spell it out.

"You're right, it *is* worse. Okay, I think we're done here. I'll see you at Campanile with all of your homework. Congratulations, Elisabeth. This is going to be a very exciting time for you."

"Thank you, Paul. See you then," I say. I think about Samuel and his "excitement" of the night. I wonder, if I call Paul back, could he maybe bring my old life to the meeting at Campanile.

Could he do that for me?

chapter twenty-five

The days pass, and I fall into a rhythm with Daniel. We catch up about our days during midmorning phone calls as I drive from my apartment to the farmers' market. We've obsessively planned our next outing, and every time we say goodbye, Daniel makes sure to say he's looking forward to seeing me again. We're mere miles from each other, but Daniel might as well be back in Kansas. Maybe it would be better if he were.

I open the restaurant with my key and walk in through the empty, darkened dining room. I rushed all morning and arrived super-early for work. I pop two Pepto-Bismol chewables and pull my purse strap tighter on my shoulder, shuffling a bit with the baskets of fresh raspberries as I push open the kitchen door. Julie turns around; she's steaming some milk for her latte.

"Hey, you're early," I say, walking into the back room. This is the perfect opportunity to approach her about the possibility of working on the TV show.

"Yeah, I thought I'd . . . Well, I could use a few brownie points. What's up?" Julie takes three shots of espresso and dumps them into her cup.

I set the raspberries down at our station. "I have a proposition," I begin, walking back over to her.

"Spill it, Chef," she says.

"I got an offer to do a pilot for my own television show," I say, my voice calm. Julie crosses her arms over her ample chest. I continue, "It's not final; there are a few meetings still, details to hammer out. And I'm not even sure I really want it." Maybe it would have been good to know how *I* felt about this proposition before I said anything.

"Wait . . . what?" Julie is broadsided.

"Some people came into the restaurant, and one thing led to another, and they offered me a television show on the Food Network," I say.

"You'll still call, right? When you're a big star?" Julie asks, eyeing the kitchen like a fox in the henhouse.

"I want you to come with me," I say.

"Come with you?" Julie asks, focusing back on me.

"I get to bring an assistant. You'd be behind the scenes, but it's essentially what you're doing now, only for TV," I say. We're silent. Is she looking around the kitchen knowing she can hate it now, too? Visions of wide-open poppy fields. A social life. A get-out-of-jail-free card. Or is she seeing that famous shot in the Tour de France when the lead bicycle blows a tire, falls, and causes a huge pileup, but the camera catches a blur as a single cyclist zooms past the carnage, unscathed, to the finish line?

"Your *assistant*?" Julie says pointedly.

"Holidays off. Summers off. And the money is great— double what you're getting now," I explain. Shit, it sounds great even to me. Then again, I've been where Julie has wanted to be for three years now.

Julie is smiling. She begins to laugh. I laugh, too. I don't quite know what we're laughing at, but I don't want to ruin the moment. Maybe she's thinking about it. Right then the door to the kitchen swings open, and Samuel walks in.

"Hey, Samuel." I wave. Julie is still chuckling. More and more people will be arriving soon. She's going to have to hurry this along. Turn me down or laugh maniacally. Can't do both. Samuel nods a quick hello and walks back to his station.

"I'm going to stay," Julie says. She's stopped laughing.

"Yeah, I kinda thought so," I manage, allowing the laugh to crumble into my throat.

"It's just that with you gone, Chef Canet will definitely make *me* head pastry chef," she says, walking into the back room.

I follow. "I haven't quit yet. The pilot might not track well," I say. But there's blood in the water. I'm on my way out. All she has to do is circle long enough, then go in for the kill.

"I could really make a name for myself here," Julie says.

"I thought I'd give it a shot. With the hours being better, the money being so good, I just thought—" I continue.

"I'll do it," Samuel says from behind me. His voice is low.

I spin around. "Do what?"

"Yes!" Julie pumps her arm back à la Kirk Gibson circa the 1988 World Series. Samuel was the slight hitch in her plan to take over the world. The finish line is hers to burst through.

"Julie just said no to a job you offered her, right? Fewer hours . . . more money . . ." Samuel says, leaning against the doorjamb.

"Yeah, she . . ." I begin. Samuel has been working toward the goal of head pastry chef since he was eleven years old. Sneaking into kitchens as a kid, apprenticing as a teenager, and finishing first in his class at the Culinary Institute. He's pursued this dream even longer than I have.

"I'm worried I'm not going to know my own kid, Chef," Samuel says. His voice is quiet.

"Do you even care what the job is?" I ask.

"I trust you, Chef Page. I'd be honored to go anywhere with you. If you'll have me," Samuel adds.

"I'm . . . I'm flattered, Chef Decoudreau," I say, pinching my eyes shut, trying to block any emotion. Julie looks away. Samuel calmly pulls a handkerchief from his checked pants and hands it to me. "You have handkerchiefs? Who has handkerchiefs?" I ask, dabbing at my runny nose.

"What *are* we talking about?" Samuel asks, motioning for me to keep the snotty handkerchief. Julie grabs her chef's jacket out of her locker and slams the door shut.

"TV. One of those cooking shows for the Food Network. A whole L.A. thing. Local food and places of interest," I say, still sniffling. Samuel's whole face contorts into that wide, beautiful smile I saw at the Silver Lake farmers' market long ago. I can't help but smile myself.

"That's definitely—I wasn't expecting that," Samuel confesses.

"We'll film a pilot, and then I'll go to New York the second week of December to meet the executives and pitch the show. I'll know then if we get picked up. So it can be business as usual until then. Julie? Business as usual until then? Julie?" I prompt.

"Yes, I got it. Business as usual. You're not going to be here for a full week, huh?" Julie taunts, trying to change the subject.

"Just that Tuesday through Friday, as far as the restaurant is concerned. Four days. Not a full week. December fourth through eighth," I clarify.

"What's this, Elisabeth?" Chef Canet comes around the corner. Samuel and Julie quickly walk out of the back room and into the kitchen.

"Rascal has a book signing in New York, and I'd like to go, Chef," I lie.

"You're saying words that I do not understand. Rascal? Is this a person?" Chef Canet sits on the long bench in the back room.

"Rascal is my brother," I say. Goddamn my dad. He's the gift that keeps on giving.

Chef Canet laughs. "That's ridiculous."

"I didn't name him, Chef," I explain.

"So this Rascal—he's doing what in New York?"

"He wrote a book, and he's doing a signing in New York," I say. Why lie at all?

"Where?"

Oh, shit. That's right. Maybe I shouldn't make up a lie about a book signing to someone who just got back from his own book tour. "Columbia. He's speaking at Columbia." I offer.

"Hm."

Great. Now Chef Canet is going to call his publisher and ask why he doesn't get asked to speak at Columbia.

"It's for their English department. Young Lions—it's connected to the public library there," I say. I'm throwing out anything literary I ever remember Dad talking about.

Chef Canet stands. "How long will you be gone?"

"Just four days—the fourth through the eighth of December. I'll be back that Saturday," I say.

"Feh," Chef Canet huffs as he walks out of the back room. Not a nod of agreement. Not a middle finger and a big "fuck you." Not a shave and a haircut, two bits. Nothing. I stand there next to my open locker. What the hell happened? I think I just got my first bit of vacation time. I grab my chef's jacket and shut my locker.

Samuel turns the corner of the back room. He quickly looks over his shoulder, making sure Chef Canet is out of earshot. I slip on my chef's jacket and button it up.

"So the hours are good?" he asks, speaking on behalf of his wife, his unborn child, and their newly acquired home in the hills of Silver Lake. It got a whole lot more serious in here all of a sudden.

"If the show gets picked up, we'll have to film enough episodes for each season—about twenty-six episodes altogether. We'll also get substantial signing bonuses, a salary that makes this look like welfare, and . . . and it's like the great glass elevator, you know?"

"Up and out," Samuel says.

"Exactly," I say. We stand there for a couple of seconds in silence.

"We're having a little boy," Samuel says, smiling.

"Really? That's . . . Congratulations," I say, smiling back.

"Thank you," Samuel says. He and I shake hands. He takes my hand in both of his. His hands are as rough and cut up as mine.

chapter twenty-six

I 've spent all week with every cookbook I own, every slip of paper, every secret envelope with recipes written in chicken scratch, strewn out over my entire apartment. I've come up with enough recipes and field-piece ideas for my meeting with Paul and Donna this morning. I've decided to start out with a boxed lunch as an homage to my own culinary origins.

As I drive over to Campanile on La Brea for the morning meeting, I return Mom's phone call from the night before.

"Hi, Mom," I say, making my way down Third Street.

"Sweetheart, don't scream into the phone. Did you get my message about planning Thanksgiving?" Mom asks.

"We can meet this Saturday morning before work, if you're willing to come out here," I say.

"Absolutely. I can visit Roberta in the Palisades for lunch. So we'll meet at your apartment? How's eight?"

"Why don't we meet at Toast—it's right there on Third. You know, Rascal took you there the last time he came out?" I say.

"Yes, that'll do. I'll meet you at Toast at eight, then."

"See you then," I sign off. I pull into the parking lot at Campanile and stop the car in front of the valet's booth. I grab my purse and the binders filled with my "homework" and hand my keys to the valet. When I go in, I see Paul and Donna sitting in the bar area to the left of the entrance. I smile at the hostess and approach. "Good morning," I announce, checking my watch. Right on time.

"Elisabeth! Good morning!" Donna kisses me on both cheeks.

Paul places his hand casually on my shoulder. "Shall we?" He hops down off the bar stool and gestures to the hostess that we're ready. She leads us through the restaurant, to a table in the corner of the back room. I usually like to sit in the front part of the restaurant, with the beautiful fountain and natural light, but I understand the need for quiet and privacy. Our waitress introduces herself and asks for our drink order.

"Just tea, thank you. Earl Grey, if you have it," I say to the waitress, knowing that they probably don't have yogi tea, and forget about the comfort of Daniel Sullivan, to quiet my stomach.

"Oh, just the coffee. I already ate," Donna says, giving the waitress back the menu.

"Double shot of espresso, please—and keep them coming," Paul orders.

"I've pulled together all the information you asked for," I say, presenting each of them with a binder. The binders contain the hundred recipes I've collected, along with the field pieces they should be paired with. They're all color-coded, with illustrations and organized to perfection. The waitress comes back over and sets down my pot of steaming tea, Paul's espresso, and Donna's cup of coffee.

"Excuse me, I just want to wash my hands before I dive in." Paul sets his napkin on the table and walks toward the bathroom.

"This is great work. We're quite relieved," Donna confesses.

"Oh? Why?" I ask.

"Paul wouldn't want me to say anything, but we already had another pilot ready to go for the executives at the network. Edited. Filmed. Everything. We had to shelve it." Donna's eyes are wide. Her entire demeanor is that of an adolescent girl gossiping at a school cafeteria table.

"Can that happen? I mean, aren't there contracts . . ." I trail off. No wonder this is happening so fast. It all makes sense.

"The other pilot didn't track. Really bad numbers. We had to start from scratch—no pun intended!" Donna jokes. I feel sick to my stomach.

"I'm back," Paul announces, pulling out his chair. Donna slides her binder over and flips it open to the first page. The idea of shelving my show permeates my thoughts.

"So you're thinking of starting out with a Hollywood Bowl box lunch?" Donna blurts.

"Yes. I think it exemplifies what we're going for. The L.A. scene and the food that blends with it. It'll be a great jumping-off point," I say.

"By the way, the marketing people have thrown out a few ideas for the name of the show," Paul begins carefully.

"Oh?" I ask.

"We thought *Page by Page: A Singleton's Life in L.A.* was cute," Donna says, tittering. Thoughts of the velvet-blazered guy at Rascal's book signing spring to mind. That's quite possibly the worst name I've ever heard.

"Wow, that is a *great* . . . Wow . . ." I trail off. The waitress approaches our table. Trying to steady my breathing, I order oatmeal and fresh fruit. I try to figure out how being single isn't such a bankable asset anymore. Paul orders eggs Benedict. You know, *Paul,* in my profession, being single is a necessary prerequisite to being taken seriously. Donna reiterates that she's already had a "huge breakfast." My eyes dart around the restaurant.

"Did you have another way you'd like to go with this?" Paul fishes.

"Something about pastry. That's where my background is, at least professionally. It's not what the show is about, but if you do a biographical overview of me, it's going to be heavy in the dessert portion. So I thought *Life Is Sweet*," I say. Paul and Donna look at each other. We fall into an awkward silence. I know exactly what they're going to say. I break in before they can. "What about *Life Is Sweet with Elisabeth Page*?" I'm trying to find some kind of middle ground. Paul smiles widely and nods in agreement.

"That's adorable!" Donna says.

◆

I'm nearly bursting out of my skin as I park the car and walk to the restaurant. *Page by Page: A Singleton's Life in L.A.* Oh my God. Why don't you just call the show *Ben Page's Loner Kid Cooks*? I'm glad I didn't pitch that one; they might have taken me up on it. The meeting was troubling. It felt like a circus sideshow. What other things are they going to trot out? What other ideas from the "marketing department" should I brace myself for? What am I getting myself into?

I hate finding street parking when I get to work every day. I hate not having a parking spot. Once you've made a decision to move on, everything about the place you're leaving just bugs the shit out of you. I stand outside the restaurant and look up at its tasteful, nondescript visage. I make a promise to myself as the traffic zooms past and the clock ticks on—I may not know what comes next, but I can't go on living like this. Cross my heart.

"Elisabeth! You're late!" Chef Canet is leaning against the pastry corner, glass of wine in hand. Julie and Samuel are frantic behind him.

"Yes, Chef," I say, walking past him and into the back room.

He follows me. "I heard you had visitors the other day," he says as I slide on my chef's jacket. I freeze.

"Yes, Chef," I say, turning to face him.

"The trip to New York? You're constantly late. This is all because you are going onto the television!" he pronounces. I've never been late. I'm not even late right now; I'm just not as early as usual.

"No, Chef," I say, hating myself. Chef zeroes in. I take a long, deep breath.

"You were what . . . how you say . . . a stray when I found you, yes?" he starts.

"Yes, Chef," I say.

"And now you . . . you use my restaurant as . . . ummm . . . something to make you better?" Chef is struggling for words.

"No, Chef."

"Yes, Elisabeth . . . you use Beverly to trap another job." Chef's voice rises.

"No, Chef." My voice is quiet. My brain is in familiar territory.

"Beg me. Beg me to stay," Chef says, his glass of wine spilling slightly.

"I want to stay, Chef," I say, my voice calm and strong.

"Beg, *petite chienne*," Chef says, hitting the G with disdain.

"Please," I say, looking him in the eye, despite his calling me a "little dog."

"Please what?" he says, one inch from my face. I can smell the wine on his breath.

"Please, Chef," I answer, my emotional shutdown complete.

"Remember who found you, little stray," Chef says, pulling away from me and slithering out of the room. I breathe in deeply. Again. My body heaves in pain—the wails caught in my throat—silently screaming. Julie and Samuel come into the back room. I straighten my body and swallow down any outward signs of emotion.

"Sweetie . . . sweetie . . ." Julie soothes, sweeping me into her arms. Samuel holds a cup of tea in front of him. I breathe deeply, trying to get control.

"Everything's fine . . . the usual," I say, pulling away from Julie. I smile at Samuel as I take the mug of tea.

"Should I not have told him about the meeting?" Julie asks, straightening her gingham handkerchief.

I zero in on her. "No, not at all. Thank you for being so thoughtful," I say, not letting her have one iota of pleasure in my evisceration. Julie presses out a tight smile and retreats into the kitchen. Fucking bitch. Samuel watches her leave and focuses back on me.

"You all right?" he asks.

"I'm fine," I say quickly.

"I'm going to head on back," Samuel says.

"Okay, I'll be right there," I say.

Samuel walks over to me. "Don't let them win," he says. His intensity is unnerving. He waits. "You ready?"

I breathe in through my nose, closing my eyes and trying to quiet the demons. "Ready," I say.

Samuel nods. "Okay, then," he says almost to himself.

"I'm right behind you," I say, slowly buttoning up my chef's jacket. I allow myself to think about a life without tantrums in those brief moments. I used to live in an apartment that had a refrigerator that constantly ran, day and night. When I moved into the apartment I have now, I had to buy a new refrigerator. It was so quiet I couldn't fall sleep without the constant drone. Will I be able to stand the silence of a life without tantrums?

Luckily, the night blurs by. I feel like the walking dead. I can't touch any emotion. Chef Canet never says another word to me all night. Julie is on her best behavior. Samuel keeps to himself and turns out one work of art after another; as usual, his need to control something comes out in each dessert. A man after my own heart.

I climb into my car. The quiet surrounds me. My throat is burning. I try to control it. I look at the clock—two A.M. I take out my BlackBerry and hold it tightly. I dial Daniel's number, hoping he'll pick up.

He answers on the fourth ring. "Hello?" He sounds sleepy.

"Were you sleeping?" I ask, my voice cracking.

"Are you okay?" he asks, ignoring my question.

"I had a rough night," I admit.

"I'll be right there. Are you home?" Daniel speaks quickly.

"No, I'm driving home from work," I answer, leaving out the fact that I'm driving toward his apartment.

"Come over," he says.

"I'd like that," I say, making my way into Westwood. My breathing steadies. My stomach quiets, despite visions of Samuel at the restaurant trying to handle a distraught Margot, unable to be in two places at once.

I find parking and call up to Daniel. He says he'll be down to let me in. I can see my breath in the cold air. I hear the zooming of traffic in the distance.

I look in through the large glass double doors. The elevator door opens, and Daniel walks out. He has his comforter draped over his shoulders and is wearing an undershirt and boxers. His Frankenstein scar cuts a wide swath down his right leg. His Crayola-brown hair is everywhere, and he's rubbing his eyes as he approaches the door. God, I miss him. Daniel flips open the lock on the door and holds it open as I walk into the warm lobby.

"I'm glad you called," he says, tugging the comforter around his shoulders.

"I hope you don't mind—it was just a rough night," I say. My scary monotone is back. I feel awkward.

"Hm," Daniel says, pushing the button to the elevator. It dings right away, of course. What sane person would be using it at this time of night? He waits for me to walk in first. He pushes the button for the third floor, and the doors close. The fluorescent lighting is stark and unflattering. The elevator moans and slowly ascends.

I have to be at the farmers' market bright and early tomorrow morning, and there's no way I can be late. Not Chef Canet's newly crowned little bitch. It was a mistake to come here. I should have gone home.

"Come here," Daniel says, opening his arms wide to envelop me in the warmth of the comforter, my head on his chest. The tears start rolling down my face. He closes his arms tightly around me. His breathing is slow and steady as he rubs my back.

Maybe I did go home after all.

chapter twenty-seven

I can hear the alarm on my BlackBerry sounding from the pocket of my checked pants, which are lying somewhere in Daniel's bedroom. Seven-thirty A.M. Daniel slept on the couch, after making sure I was settled. I gather my clothes and walk out into the living room.

"Is that thing going to go off every morning?" Daniel says, stirring, the comforter twisting around his body. His shirt is off. I've never really seen him this . . . well, this naked. We fooled around a little after our dinner-and-a-movie date. But that was pretty tame and definitely not as well lit as I would have liked.

"Yep. I have to. The farmers' market beckons," I say, sitting on the edge of the couch next to him.

Daniel turns over. "You don't have to be at work until eleven-thirty, right?"

"Yeah, I know. But I go on a morning run and then do a breakfast thing before the market." I kiss him gently. "Thank you for letting me stay here," I say close to his face.

"Let me get ready, and I'll go with you. A run would do me some good," he says, untwisting himself from the comforter. With me? On *my* morning run? Daniel walks down the hallway into his bedroom, stretching his body, working his neck out— all of the basic exercises you would do if you were a former basketball player with a blown-out knee who had to sleep on a couch the night before.

I sit on the couch and wait. The minutes tick by. I can't be late. I can't be late. I check my watch again. What's taking him so long?

"Let's hit the road, Jack." Daniel walks down the hallway in sweats and a KU T-shirt. I stand quickly. He continues speaking as he gets to the door. "I'll take my car—that way you can go right to work." He has a look on his face. Or maybe there is no look. Maybe I'm searching for a look, a confirmation that the other shoe is about to drop.

"It's not always going to be like this," I say, looking up at him.

"Okay," Daniel says.

"I don't like it any more than you do," I say, wedging my body between him and the door. Old habits.

"Are we talking about your job or the fact that I slept on the couch last night?" Daniel asks. He raises a single eyebrow. My face must read pure surprise—I don't know why. I thought someone this stable wouldn't have the same passion or spontaneity that someone like Will has. I'd decided I'd have to give up my kitchen-floor rendezvous and settle for a weekly missionary-position kind of life with Daniel. Like there had to be something *wrong* with him—a downside—a reason to choose Will. Daniel and I are frozen in this high-stakes game of chicken.

Daniel leans in and gives me a kiss. The sweetest little toothpaste kiss. I feel his stubble on my face. I realize this kiss is morphing into something completely different. The thoughts run rampant in my mind. My schedule . . . my BlackBerry alarm . . . my morning run . . . all fly out the window.

We stumble over and stand next to the beige burlap sack of a couch. I think quickly about my undergarments. I have on a nice bra. The panties. Oh, God. Am I wearing my Superman panties? Why am I thinking about this, for chrissakes? I lift his shirt from the very bottom all the way up over his head and throw it on the ground at his feet. I slip his sweats down, exposing his boxers and that scar: the scar that stopped me in my tracks that first night. He steps out of his sweats and closer to me, his chest pressing against me. I stop. Daniel is still, his breath fast. I look up at him, the darkest of blue eyes waiting and patient. Yes. Yes to Daniel. Yes to the scar. I run my hand down the front of him. Daniel closes his eyes, clearly experiencing all of it. Trusting me. I grab hold of the bottom of my own T-shirt and bring it up over my head, whipping it onto the couch. I take his face in my hands and dive in to him again.

I had always tried hard to reserve and isolate certain parts of my personality, out of some blind sense of protection of self. Don't get too attached to people, because you'll just have to go without them. I had to stay in control. I had to know what's coming next. If I know it's going to be nothing—*probably* going to be nothing—then I'm not crushed. I couldn't be a victim of the roller coaster if I didn't get on in the first place. That's why I made a career out of baking—it's an exact science of measurements and timing. But then I turned my career into my whole life. I thought being with Will was hard. But this? *This* is terrifying. More terrifying than anything I've felt with Will.

As we lie on the floor later that morning, I prop myself up on one elbow, grab the sheet off the couch, and wrap it around me. The chill is sneaking in through the paper-thin walls. I seize the moment to take in every inch of him.

Daniel yawns and turns over. "You're looking at me like a piece of chicken you just deboned," he says. He is completely naked. No sheet. No clothes. Just sunlight and everything God gave him.

I blush. "You caught me."

Daniel reaches up and pulls me in to him. "Come here," he says. He sounds more relaxed than earlier. He's got a youthful drawl now. I adjust the sheet and look down at him. Isn't he supposed to get up and tell me he's leaving for Venezuela? I feel strange. I'm sitting here looking like a cross between the Schmoo and Buddha, and this beautiful man wants me to "come here." I shift the sheet and put my head on Daniel's chest. He strokes my hair. I can hear his stomach gurgling.

"Go ahead and check the time," Daniel taunts sleepily, his voice deep in his chest. I hop up, leaving the sheet behind, and find my BlackBerry. Nine-thirty A.M. I quickly do the math. If I stop at Whole Foods on the way to work, that'll take about an hour off my morning routine. I don't need a run now; my mind is clear, and my workout is taken care of, thank you, Daniel. I tap the buttons on my BlackBerry, resetting the alarm for ten-thirty, which allows me enough time to get ready, stop at the store, and make it to work on time. Daniel creaks his way into a standing position. I finish programming the alarm just as Daniel takes my hand and leads me back to his bedroom. He falls into bed, pulling the covers open for me. I crawl in and curl up next to him. My stomach at rest. My mind calm. I close my eyes and go back to sleep. Just like that. I haven't slept this hard, this peacefully, in I can't remember how long.

chapter twenty-eight

I drive from Westwood that Saturday morning to meet Mom at Toast, one of several breakfast places along Third Street, to go over the Thanksgiving dinner menu. I've been staying at Daniel's apartment every night since that first time. I bought a quart of Greek yogurt at Trader Joe's, some fresh fruit from the farmers' market, and made a batch of yogi tea to keep at Daniel's. If I had to choose between our apartments, mine would be more attractive—I don't have Hell Week or hog butchering happening right outside my door. But since I'm always the one arriving last, it makes sense for Daniel to stay at his apartment instead of waiting by himself at mine. Plus, I don't have a PlayStation.

I left Daniel lying in bed, half naked and with several invitations to stay. It took everything I had to go. He's leaving later this afternoon for the Maui Invitational, a weeklong tournament. Paul and Donna have set up the big pilot shoot for this weekend—perfect timing. I'm supposed to show up at the first location shoot tomorrow morning at six A.M. Apparently, sleeping in isn't an option just yet.

I valet the car and walk to the hostess stand outside of Toast. "I'm meeting someone," I say, motioning that I don't need to be seated. The hostess/actress/model acts like I've insulted her in some way: She apparently wanted to reject me before I rejected her. I weave in between wooden tables, through couples who are both on cell phones, celebrities meeting and "eating," your basic morning rituals. I stop.

Mom. Rascal. Will.

All sitting around a table. One chair vacant. Mine. It's odd, seeing Will now. I can feel my heart contract a little. Mom stands and kisses me on the cheek, wiping off the lipstick. Rascal leans back in his chair, holding out his already empty coffee mug as he tries to get the waitress's attention. He nods a distracted hello. Back from Montana, I suppose. Will. I can't even look at him. He'll know. I don't know what it is he'll know. I'm not sure what *I* know right now. I sit down next to Will. That smell. It's him. It's *him*. He wraps his arm around the back of my chair. I turn my head as the waitress comes over with a pot of coffee for Rascal. I sneak a quick glance at Will. He turns and makes a face, letting me know that I'm wearing the most bizarre expression. Like I've quantum-leaped into this body and I'm acquainting myself with these new surroundings for the first time. It's actually not that far off. His eyes crinkle up, and he smiles, whispering that he missed me. I feel like I've betrayed Will in some way. Not because I'm sleeping with Daniel, I suddenly realize, but because I'm starting to fall in love with Daniel.

"What are we having?" I ask. The waitress looks directly at me. I'm the only one who hasn't ordered. I quickly order a bowl of yogurt and granola and a big side of fruit. And an Earl Grey tea. I just keep adding things. Mom is horrified at my lack of decorum.

"Darling, we're going to have Thanksgiving at the Montecito house this year. Your father is already there. We'll arrive on Wednesday—have just a small gathering on Thursday—and then you can join us on Sunday morning. We'll have

Thanksgiving dinner at four that afternoon," Mom says, cracking open her organizer.

"Sounds good," I say, my head spinning. I'm kind of glad that I have to get to work. I wouldn't be able to . . . I just . . . it's easy to think I've changed when there's no opportunity for relapse. My feelings for Will are stowed away in places I have yet to uncover.

"My mom's out of—" Will quickly stops himself and gauges the table. We all know. Even Mom. He continues, "She made it through the outpatient program. Clean and sober since the White Russian incident. She says she's going to roast a turkey."

"You won't be joining us this year?" Mom asks.

"No. What are you guys going to do without me?" Will jokes. I laugh too loudly. I know he's afraid to feel even the teensiest light of hope about his mom.

"You're leaving?" I ask.

"Well, yeah. To go meet Mom back in Aspen. I'm here for a couple of days on a gig for *Rolling Stone*. I turned down a great story for *Time* that would have taken me to Nepal for at least two or three months. Nope. It looks like it's home for the holidays," he says with a hint of sarcasm. He stares at me a little too long. Turning down assignments? It's what I've always wanted. His mom is clean and sober. Why am I not excited for him? God, I hope he doesn't get that I think it's all too good to be true. I don't believe things until I see them. He used to be like that, too. It was like piña coladas or getting caught in the rain—we never trusted that people would actually do what they said they'd do.

I quickly turn away. "That sounds perfect. It . . ." I trail off and take Will's hand. Then I make eye contact with him for the first time this morning. I squeeze his hand tight. Will softens and puts his other hand over mine. His iridescent blue eyes blaze for a second in fear. Even I'm afraid to get my hopes up about Anne Houghton and her promised Norman Rockwell Thanksgiving.

"So they've already hired someone to adapt the book for film," Rascal blurts. He's not a blurter. All of us take note.

"Oh?" Mom asks. Rascal had to have a special intervention with Mom and Dad about the impending movie version of *The Ballad of Rick Danko*. It was like a weekend retreat, complete with trust walks, couples massages, and role-playing games. In the end, Dad told Rascal he was fucking crazy, and Mom took him aside and told him everyone was proud of him, "everyone" once again being code for "Dad." This could explain the trek to Montana.

"Some girl. Met her the other day. Calls herself Dinah," Rascal announces.

"Like 'someone's in the kitchen with—'" Will starts.

"Exactly! Fucked up, isn't it? You literally can't get it out of your head when you're with her." Rascal sips his coffee. Mom flips through her organizer, penciling in, erasing, penciling in.

"Is she doing a good job?" I ask. The waitress brings me my tea.

"I don't even know what . . ." Rascal is sputtering. Suddenly, he looks over my head at something.

I hear a voice behind me. "Elisabeth?"

I look over my shoulder. Daniel. In all of his morning glory. Wet Crayola-brown hair. A Kansas T-shirt. Wait—what? What is he doing here? I stand quickly, and my chair tips over and hits Daniel. He catches it and sets it back in place. The family has gone into a complete catatonic state. A quick slide show of Averyesque evisceration flashes in my mind. Mom slowly closes her organizer. Will repositions his arm around the back of my now-empty chair.

"You left your BlackBerry in my car. It's been going off nonstop." Daniel's voice is low, and he's leaned in to give us privacy.

I sway and giggle, trying to act as indifferent as possible. Daniel takes in the people at the table. He straightens his T-shirt, obviously cursing the casual outfit he's chosen. He attempts to tamp down his wet hair, to no avail.

"Oh, God, I'm sorry. Daniel Sullivan, this is . . ." I start, trying to stop his downward spiral. Mom's eyes bore into me.

Rascal stands, extending his hand across the table.

"Rascal Page. I'm Elisabeth's brother . . . *older* brother," he interrupts. His napkin is tucked into his belt. Mom sighs and pulls it free, folds it, and places it at the side of his plate. "Have you heard about me, or are you as in the dark as I am?" Rascal asks. Will is watching this interaction with a heat that burns the side of my face.

"I saw a picture of you on her kitchen counter," Daniel offers.

"I'm three in that picture," Rascal says, staring at me.

"You've really grown up," Daniel says. Rascal laughs as he sits back down.

"This is my mom, Ballard Foster. Mom, this is Daniel Sullivan." My voice changes into a softer, more proper tone. Daniel moves behind the table. Mom stays seated as Daniel shakes her hand. She tilts her head coyly as he tells her it's a pleasure to meet her. I must have done something right in a past life not to have Dad sitting at this table this fine morning. My farce can continue for just a bit longer. Oh, wait . . .

"Will Houghton, this is Daniel Sullivan." Hello, yes— Daniel, meet Can of Worms. Can of Worms, meet Daniel.

Daniel turns, and they just know. The realization sweeps across both of their faces. Will is steadfast, his gaze fixed. For the briefest of seconds, I see confusion and apprehension flash across Daniel's face. He extends his hand. I can see him tensing his jaw, unsure of the backstory. What haven't I told him about this Will Houghton? Will stands. He's the only one at the table who's not dwarfed by Daniel. He takes Daniel's hand, and their handshake is tense yet cordial. I'll say this: They both have impeccable manners.

"Can you join us?" Will asks. His voice borders on the patronizing.

"Oh, no. No, thank you. I have a plane to catch," Daniel says. Will eases back into his chair. I didn't want him to find out this way. Maybe I didn't want him to find out at all.

"You travel?" Will asks, looking directly at me.

"Just for the week," Daniel says. His smile is tight.

"I'll walk you out," I say to Daniel. He looks shell-shocked.

"It was nice meeting all of you," Daniel says. I've gotten so used to him, his body, but right now, in this situation, I don't know how to be with him. How to touch him. We have to walk out of this restaurant together, and I can't figure out how to do that without holding his hand. I don't know if I can do it in front of Will. I run through scenario after scenario. Sensing my apprehension, Daniel turns and begins to walk out of the restaurant. I catch up to him. I take his arm to slow him down, and slide my hand all the way until it meets his. He clasps my hand tightly and sighs.

"I'm so sorry . . . I'm so sorry," I say once we're outside.

"Tell me about him," Daniel says, his dark blue eyes squinting in the sunlight.

"He's a friend, a family friend since birth. We have a *history*," I say.

"I'm not sure he thinks it's in the past," Daniel says, his voice low and calm.

"I can't help how he feels," I say, taking both his hands in mine.

"Yes, but you can certainly clarify how *you* feel," Daniel says, looking down at our clasped hands. We look ridiculous. Both of us let go. I kiss him.

"Be good," I say, close to his face, brushing his lips with mine and actively dodging the whole "clarifying" comment.

Daniel hesitates. "My parents are coming out after Thanksgiving, you know, for the Hollywood Christmas parade. I thought you might be able to come to one of my games, meet them, and all of us could have dinner together or something? On your night off, of course."

"I'd love to," I say.

"Great," he says. His jaw is tense.

"What are their names?" I ask.

"Why?" he asks, smiling.

"I just have a thing. I like to know names," I say.

Daniel's body relaxes a bit. "Nick and Marilyn."

"Your father is a professional Santa . . ." I trail off.

"Yeah," Daniel agrees.

"And his name is Nick?"

"Kind of funny, huh?" Daniel says.

My chest tightens. "You'll call when you land?" I ask, already missing him.

"Absolutely," Daniel says, his eyes still unsure. He leans in and kisses me once more. A long sigh and a flood of unsaid words pass between us in those moments. He smiles and turns to leave. I watch him go. He waves when he gets to his car, and then it disappears down the street. The sounds from the restaurant seem to come back up. I walk back in. Dreading what is waiting for me once I sit back down.

"What was that thing on his shirt?" Will asks as I smooth my napkin over my lap.

"It was a Jayhawk," I say.

"I like him," Rascal announces, digging into his bacon and eggs.

"What?" Will is flabbergasted.

"He seems like a nice young man. Real salt of the earth," Mom says, giving me the tiniest of smiles.

"'Salt of the earth' is a nice way of saying 'white trash,'" Will insists.

"Fuck you," I say. The cracks in the foundation are showing.

"Elisabeth. Language," Mom scolds. I deflate into my chair.

"He's very . . . what's that catalog . . . the one that's all . . ." Rascal is posing as if he's throwing a football.

"Abercrombie and Fitch," I offer dejectedly.

"Yes, exactly! That's it! Abercrombie and Fitch. He's *very* Abercrombie and Fitch." Rascal takes another giant bite of eggs.

Will looks over. I can feel him trying to get a read on me. He bends over the table a couple of inches, trying to make eye contact. I can't. He'll know. He'll *know.* No one has ever come between us. The waitress reaches over my shoulder, placing my breakfast in front of me. I thank her. I pick up my fork and take a bite, forcing the food down my closing throat. My chest is tight and pained. Is it wrong to want to erase Will? Scoop out the parts of my heart that still love him, worry about him and want him to be happy?

After we eat, we finalize the Thanksgiving plans, and now we're all standing in front of the restaurant waiting for our cars. Mom's arrives first. She tips the valet; he opens her door as she waves goodbye. He closes the door behind her. Immediately, we all relax our posture. Rascal and Will reach for their cigarettes. Rascal hands the valet our tickets as Will's Porsche rounds the corner. Hearing the rev of the engine, Will turns his head.

"You're welcome to come to Aspen. It'd be nice to hang out with someone other than my mom for a couple of days," Will says to me. Rascal stands by the valet station, sensing that Will and I may need a moment.

"Oh . . . I have work. And you know, Mom has plans . . . lots of plans," I joke, not wanting to hurt him.

"Is this about that guy?" Will says, motioning to the valet to hold on a second. He zeroes in on me. Rascal walks over to us.

"No . . . no . . . I just have to get into work," I say. Will's face contorts in a mix of confusion and worry. I am still. My breathing quickens. I hold eye contact.

"Up high," Rascal blurts, raising his hand high in the air. Will slaps his hand automatically.

"Down low," Rascal taunts.

"Fuck you," Will says.

"Well, now, that doesn't even remotely rhyme with 'down low,'" Rascal says, pulling his hand back.

"I'll call when I get to Aspen. Wish me luck," Will says, handing the valet a tip and hopping into his car. The valet shuts the door behind him, and Will speeds off.

Rascal turns to me. "So, was it about that guy?" he repeats.

"Yeah, totally," I say, putting on my sunglasses.

"Thought so," Rascal says almost under his breath.

"Yeah," I say, my mind elsewhere.

Rascal takes a long look at me, sizing me up. "So, I was watching this high-speed car chase the other day," he begins. "And they're chasing this guy on a motorcycle—which, as you know, switches shit up—you can't do a spike strip, you can't pull a pit maneuver. I mean, hell, you can barely track the guy, the way he's snaking through traffic." Rascal pauses, casually taking a drag on his cigarette.

"Wow, are you really telling me a story about a high-speed chase?" I ask. In Los Angeles, televised high-speed chases are a cultural phenomenon. The art of watching and studying them has become as popular as handicapping the Kentucky Derby.

"If you could maybe be quiet for half a second—" Rascal pauses for effect. I zip my mouth shut. He continues, "So, this guy is zooming in and out of traffic, and the only thing we know is that a police helicopter is overhead—no cop car could keep up with this guy. It's five o'clock on a weeknight, and traffic is getting pretty heavy, and all of a sudden, the news copter's camera pans back, and there's this one lone LAPD car right on the guy's tail. *No one* saw this coming. Now, right as this is happening, a civilian hears the lone cop's sirens and starts to pull over to the side of the road and, in so doing, wedges the guy on the motorcycle in—trapping him. The LAPD car pulls right up, the cop in the passenger seat hops out, and he takes the guy down. Perfect."

"That's a beautiful story," I say as Rascal's BMW rounds the corner.

"You're not alone in this, Bink," Rascal says, stamping his cigarette out on the sidewalk and kicking it in the gutter.

"What?" I say, caught completely off guard.

Rascal pulls out his wallet and starts for his car. "If you want to take Will down, you don't have to do it alone. Some civilian could come up and inadvertently wedge him out. As long as you trust someone to have your back and pull up alongside, all you gotta do is hop out of the car." Rascal puts his sunglasses on. "See you next Sunday. I'm bringing blankets infested with smallpox instead of mashed potatoes. You?" He smiles widely, handing the valet a tip and bending into his car.

"Apple pie," I answer.

He pulls out onto Third Street without looking back.

My little wagon rounds the corner. I take out my wallet and hand the valet a tip as he opens the door for me. I sit down, and the door slams behind me. I set my purse on the passenger seat and then just sit there. Silence.

I don't know how to juggle this new life. First it was the one flaming torch: Balance the job. That was it. Keep that torch in the air. And every once in a while someone would throw another torch in. Balance the family. Then they'd take the torch, and it would be back to the one. Keeping it in the air. And then maybe someone would come along and throw two torches at me. My family and Will. And it would get a bit more difficult. Juggling the three torches. Keeping them all in the air. Balancing each one's time in the top position. Then two torches would be taken away. But then there was a new torch. The TV show. So I was juggling two torches. Then I met Daniel. Three torches. And now I get the other two torches back. Family and Will. I'm juggling five torches all at once. I'm barely catching that one, and this one almost dropped. And that one called me a little dog, and that one has the deepest blue eyes, and this one has impossibly high standards, and that one is the only love I've ever known. And that one—that one offers me a way out. Keep 'em high. Balance it all.

My arms are tired.

Someone honks behind me. I'm jolted out of my thoughts. I put the car in drive and pull out onto Third Street. All five torches are high in the air.

◆

At the end of my shift that night, I check my phone. There's a message waiting. I dial my voice mail and wait as I walk through the restaurant and out into the crisp fall air. The blur of the kitchen has given me exactly what I wanted tonight—oblivion.

And now, as I wait for this voice mail, my chest tightens again—not knowing. Which one is it? The call log says the call came from an unknown number. It could be Daniel calling from the hotel in Maui, or Will calling from his mom's house in Aspen. I push the buttons that walk me through a voice-mail center. It's apparently designed for people with the IQ of a woman Rascal would date. I beep my car unlocked. I have one new message, the phone tells me for the eighth time. I slam the door behind me, and the silence of my car surrounds me again. I wait.

"Hey, it's me. I just wanted to let you know I landed and I'm all settled in at the hotel. I've never been to Hawaii before, you know. This . . ." I can hear Daniel move around and then the distinct sound of the opening of hotel curtains. He continues, "It's beautiful here. Just incredible. We definitely have to come back. Okay . . . Well, sleep tight. Talk to you soon." Daniel pauses, and I hear him fumble a bit with the phone as he hangs up. The voice-mail lady asks me if I'd like to delete the message, press seven, or save it, press nine.

I press nine.

chapter twenty-nine

W e're going to do a shot of you driving up to the parking
lot. You're going to stop the car right where that tape is,
stick your head out the window like we went over, and say the
line that's written on the card. From there we'll go into your
show opener." It's eight on Sunday morning. I'm about to shoot
my first shot for the pilot of my very own television show.

I'm being talked at by Hunter, my director. He looks like
he's fifteen. Paul is standing behind him, on the cell phone.
We're filming the field piece right outside of the CheeseStore
in Silver Lake. This will correspond with my overall theme of
building a box lunch to take to a performance at the Hollywood
Bowl.

"Got it," I say.

I have on more makeup than three women put together.
My hair, which took hours, is in a beautiful 1930s-style wave.
A wardrobe girl put together a flirty little skirt, a pink tank top,
and a vintage-y cardigan for me to wear.

We're starting by filming the field pieces. Each episode will
have one destination that opens up the show; this is threaded
through the rest of the episode and coordinated with what we
decide to cook. Then we'll go into the kitchen and film three

recipes that relate to the theme. For the field pieces, we work with two cameramen. Each camera has two guys whose whole job is to wrangle all the cords. A smallish woman keeps checking sound; the boom mike hangs over my every word. The amount of people it takes to film anything always astounds me. I put my Audi in reverse and pull up the street to where a production assistant (to whom I will have to learn to refer coolly to as a P.A.) stands with a walkie-talkie. My car idles as the P.A. and I wait for our cue. He holds on to that walkie-talkie as if it's—

"Go! Go!" the P.A. screams. My car lurches forward.

"Cut! Cut!" the P.A. yells. Jesus H. Christ. The P.A. listens to the walkie-talkie and walks over to my car.

"Hunter says that you have to drive *smoothly.* Can you *do* that?" Mr. P.A. has quite the attitude for someone sporting cargo shorts and a Grateful Dead tattoo on his ankle.

"Yeah, uh-huh, but if you can stop screaming in my ear, that'd be great." I put my car in park and wait for Jerry Garcia to give me the go-ahead again. He listens to the walkie-talkie. Then he points at me. I see Jerry Garcia dabbles in the passive-aggressive. I put the car in drive and glide smoothly into the parking lot. Stop at the tape. Stick my head out the window.

"When you come to Los Angeles, a night at the Hollywood Bowl is a must. Today we're going to put together a meal of some of the best local offerings that'll fit nicely into a box lunch. Just like when we were kids, only better. My first stop is always right here—the CheeseStore in Silver Lake." I'm supposed to pull away and park in the specified parking space. I do. I hear Hunter yell cut. I do this same thing ten more times.

After we get past the first shot, Paul pulls me aside while Hunter sets up our first shot inside the CheeseStore.

"Our kitchen fell through. A water main burst or something. Anyway, I think we're going to have to rely on this field piece . . ." Paul trails off dejectedly.

Even I know that's not a good idea. "What kind of kitchen are we talking about?" I ask.

"It would have to be double the size of a normal kitchen. That's why this—or that's why the kitchen we lined up was so perfect. It was in the middle of a renovation, so we could pull the cameras back as far away as we needed to. Ummm, just let me . . ." Paul begins dialing.

I break in. "I know someone who has a kitchen that big." Paul passes me his phone.

She picks up on the first ring. "Hello?"

"Mom?" Paul's cell phone is sticking to the five layers of foundation on my face.

"Good morning, darling! You're up early," Mom says.

"Hi, Mom. I . . . I need a favor," I say.

"Of course. Wait, are you okay?" It's not hard to see where my whole "come down to the station to identify the body" thing came from.

"Oh, I'm fine, Mom. Everything's fine . . ." I trail off. How do I begin?

"Five minutes!" Jerry Garcia yells, coming around the corner of the building. Okay, quickly. I'll begin quickly.

I put my hand over the receiver. "When are we going to need this kitchen, Paul?" I whisper.

"Tomorrow morning. Six A.M. We need enough time to shoot the entire pilot episode. All three recipes."

"Mom? Okay, umm—I have a really great opportunity and . . ." I can't get this out.

"Darling?" Mom prods.

"It's still pretty tentative, but I was offered my own television show. You know, like on the Food Network?" I say.

"That's fabulous!" Mom sounds excited. I don't know what I thought she'd sound like, but . . .

"We have to shoot the pilot episode so when we go to New York, we have something to show the network—like me in action kind of thing. If they like it, we get picked up for the whole season," I explain.

"Two minutes!" Jerry is staring right at me. Paul shushes him.

I continue, "We had arranged for another kitchen to film the whole cooking part of the show, but a water main broke, and now we're kind of stuck. And I was wondering . . ." I look at Paul.

"Absolutely! Oh, I'm so proud of you, Elisabeth. This is so exciting! Iris! Iris!" Mom is calling to Iris with her hand over the receiver.

"It's just for the pilot, so it would only be this once," I say.

"Darling, it would be such fun. When do you need it?"

"Tomorrow morning at six A.M. And we're talking around twenty people with a lot of equipment."

"Darling, I know. We had that horrible man from *60 Minutes* here that one weekend. You'd have thought Ben was being interviewed by the pope himself." I remember that weekend. She's right.

"Speaking of Dad," I say.

"He's in Montecito this weekend, working on the novel. It'll be just you and me, darling," Mom assures me.

"This might turn into nothing, so I'd rather he not hear about it quite yet," I say tentatively.

"It's nothing to be ashamed of," Mom says.

"I know . . . I just . . . It's the Hollywood thing. The pilot may not get picked up. It's . . ." I trail off.

"Well, I think you should be the one to tell him, so I'll respect your wishes," Mom allows.

"Thank you," I say. Mom and I sign off. Paul breathes easy.

"Ms. Page? Ms. Page? Hunter really needs you now!" Jerry Garcia is beside himself. I finish getting brushed and sponged by the makeup girl and walk into the CheeseStore behind another P.A. and stand right on the taped X, just like Hunter and I went over.

The day flies by in a haze of taped X's and cue cards filled with information. I stop using the cue cards about halfway through. All the information is in my head already, and reading from the cards is throwing me off. Hunter doesn't trust me at first, but after I ask for one take where I'm off the cue card, he allows me to go free for the rest of the shoot. I do a short interview with the sommelier about the different types of wine you'd bring to a party, versus wines you'd take to an outing at the Hollywood Bowl. We choose a goat cheese called Midnight Moon and pair it with a baguette. I go over all the cheese options: goat, sheep, cow, and blue. I talk a little bit about how I adore blue, but emphasize that it's definitely a choice—a strong choice and maybe not the best one for an outing with friends whose tastes you're not sure of. We touch on the cupcakes the CheeseStore has on display. I introduce the red velvet cupcake specifically. This will be the lead-in for the beginning of the cooking portion of the show.

"Cut!" Hunter says from behind a screen where he can see what the show will look like. I freeze on my taped X.

"That was great. Just great. We'll resume tomorrow at . . ." Hunter looks to Paul.

"We'll be in Pasadena, filming in Ballard Foster's kitchen," Paul says.

"Tomorrow, everyone. I'll e-mail directions. Call time is six A.M.," Hunter announces. The crew begins to break down the equipment. They vacate the CheeseStore in under five minutes. It's as if we were never here.

chapter thirty

"D arling!" Mom greets me at the front door with a kiss on my cheek. She swipes off her lipstick just as the makeup girl dives in for any opportunity to put more foundation on my face. I hug Mom tightly and walk in. The rest of the crew is pulling up and readying for another day of shooting.

Mom and Dad's house is south of Caltech and the Huntington Library in a pocket of Pasadena that melts right into San Marino. The houses are beautiful and massive. Unlike in Montecito, they're visible from the street and pruned to perfection, waiting to be ogled by all who drive by.

This house has been in the Foster family forever. When we were growing up, there were whole wings of this house off limits to Rascal and me. Actually, to anyone except patrons and foundation chairs. The paintings and tapestries on the walls would be at home in any museum. The traditional furniture was designed to be adored from afar, not used. The Montecito house is more of a testament to Mom's real style, which explains the ever evolving nature. It's as if she has never felt comfortable putting her stamp on this house because it belonged to the Foster family, not just to her. Mom's search for her own personal style has been a lifelong battle. But, it's not as if she doesn't try. A team of designers would attest to her vigilance.

"Thank you so much for doing this, Mom. It was really a lifesaver," I say, noticing that Mom has set out coffee, tea, and pastries for the crew. I look at her, and my whole body puffs up. I don't think I've given enough credence to the characteristics I've inherited from Mom; she's always overshadowed by Dad's influences. But over the last couple of days, I've thought about how remarkable it is that I'm so easy and confident in front of the camera. I have to believe that this poise is something I picked up from Mom.

"Oh, it's my pleasure. I also wanted to mention what a delight it was to meet that young man at breakfast on Saturday," Mom fishes.

"Yes, Daniel," I answer as briefly as possible.

"Daniel. He certainly was well mannered," Mom fishes again.

"Yes, he's very well mannered," I agree.

Mom settles into her stance as people stream into the house. She is unmoving. "Elisabeth?" she presses. "Is it serious, darling?" I've never had to define something like this for Mom. I'm honestly not sure how she's going to react. I don't know if she's loyal to Will or if Daniel's less-than-noble bloodline will bother her.

"He's . . . he's lovely, Mom, and yes, it's serious," I offer, not really knowing what "serious" is. Mom tilts her head slightly and lets the smallest of smiles break across her face. I take this as an unspoken declaration that I may continue to see Daniel. I breathe a sigh of relief as Mom quickly changes course to more pressing matters.

"Now, while I have you here, I know you're feeling like you don't want to stay in the Crow's Nest anymore, so I've set you up in one of the guest rooms. Thought you might want to try that."

"Mom, Rascal and I have to fly to New York for . . . Well, I have to go for the show, and Rascal has to meet with his agent and his editor," I say.

"Sounds wonderful, darling," Mom says absently.

"We can't stay the night on Sunday. I'll just drive up for the day. We have to be back at Rascal's by six o'clock the next morning to leave for the airport," I say.

"What?" Mom's eyes lock on mine.

"Mrs. Page?" Paul walks through the large wooden door.

Mom glares at me and turns to greet her guests. "Ballard Foster," she corrects, extending her hand to him. They shake hands as Paul looks around the house. I worry for a second that Paul is going to kiss her hand.

"It is *such* a pleasure. Your home is breathtaking, Mrs. Foster," Paul says.

"You can call me Ballard," she clarifies.

"Ballard, then. May we?" Paul points to the rest of the crew, waiting outside. They're ready to come in and officially take over. Mom nods delicately. Paul beams and waves the crew in. Just then Samuel and Margot pull up in their Prius. Margot walks over as Samuel opens the hatch of the car.

"I'm just dropping him off. Don't worry," Margot says, leaning in to me for a big side hug. She must be due any day now. She passes me a thermos filled with yogi tea. "For your first day."

"Oh, thanks. But I'm not Samuel's boss anymore, so . . ." I say awkwardly.

"What?" Margot brushes an eyelash from my face.

"You don't have to do this anymore. I'm not his boss here," I say.

"I don't do this because you're his boss," Margot says.

"Then why do you do stuff for me and not for Julie?" I ask.

"Because she's a bitch," Margot says, not missing a beat. Oh. Samuel comes up behind her with his knife set and gives me a quick wave. It's the cutest little excited, first-day-of-school kind of wave. I hold my thermos of yogi tea that my *friend* gave me because I am apparently *not* a bitch, and we all walk inside the house. They don't quite know what to do with it.

"You grew up here . . ." Samuel trails off. They take it all in.

"How is *everything*?" I ask Samuel. "Everything" meaning the impending baby. Samuel and Margot have purchased a birthing pool and installed it in their new Silver Lake house. In a matter of weeks, Margot will climb into the pool and give birth to their first child with Joanne, her doula, proud mother of Bode, the whimpering, perpetually breast-fed baby from the shower.

"*Everything* is taking his sweet little time," Margot says, putting a hand on her belly. Samuel could not be smiling more.

"Mom? I'd like you to meet someone." I pull Samuel and Margot over to where Mom is overseeing the lighting and camera placement for the day's activities.

Mom turns effortlessly. "Yes, darling?"

"This is Samuel and Margot Decoudreau. He—"

Mom breaks in. "Of course, of course! Samuel, Elisabeth has done nothing but sing your praises. And Margot, it's a pleasure. I have to guess—are you a little over eight months?"

"Yes, almost exactly," Margot says, extending her hand to Mom. Someone calls Mom from the kitchen, and she politely excuses herself. Paul walks over and looks from Samuel and Margot to me and back to Samuel and Margot.

"Paul Lingeman, this is Samuel Decoudreau from Beverly. He'll be my culinary assistant." The men shake hands. I continue, "And this is his wife, Margot, and . . . Well, we have yet to meet the new arrival." Paul and Margot shake hands.

Margot laughs. "Soon. Very soon." "I'd better get to the boutique. Good luck." She gives Samuel a peck on the cheek and slowly waddles out of the foyer.

"Samuel, I'd like you to meet our culinary producer. You'll be working closely with her. Bring your knives and come with me." Paul leads Samuel back into the kitchen. They are deep in conversation as they walk.

We blow through the day, cooking the three recipes I pitched to Paul and Donna at Campanile. I start with the red velvet cupcakes from the CheeseStore in Silver Lake, letting those bake off while I prepare a decadent Monte Cristo sandwich. It's a recipe I "borrowed" from the CrepeVine restaurant in Pasadena. I pair that with a salad of field greens, heirloom tomatoes, and light crumbles of the Midnight Moon goat cheese for contrast. I frost and package the cupcakes and put everything together in a picnic basket Mom whisked out of her entertaining closet. I add a six-pack of Stella Artois: an homage to Daniel. We make time for the three commercial breaks, and at a little past four in the afternoon, our pilot episode is ahead of schedule and officially "in the can," i.e., finished.

"I want to thank Ballard for welcoming all of us into her home. Wish us well on our upcoming pitch. Cheers!" Paul holds his glass of champagne high. It seems this is the crew who'll work on the show—if it gets picked up. I look around at all the faces and breathe deeply. We've done all we can, and I feel confident. I feel good. I lock eyes with Samuel. He's never looked more at ease. Mom has her champagne glass held high, and she's beaming right at me. I smile back and get lost in the perfection of the moment.

chapter thirty-one

We're doing a Gâteau Saint Honoré tonight," I announce as Julie and Samuel walk over to me. I'm already knee-deep in tonight's feature.

"That's a little ambitious," Julie says.

"The patron saint of bakers," Samuel says.

"The what?" Julie asks.

"Saint Honoré is the patron saint of bakers and confectioners," Samuel explains.

"We're going to do a lighter, more deconstructed take on it. I have one here for you to take a look at. You can see we'll still do the basic look, with the layers of puff pastry and the choux cream on top, then surround it with the cream puffs. But I want it to be smaller and not as heavy. So take a look at that, and we'll get started," I say, then jump into an in-depth conversation with Samuel about the mechanics of what I want for tonight. And what I want is to knock one out of the park.

Ever since my run-in with Chef Canet, I've made it a point to feature some of the most decadent desserts I've ever attempted. I won't be put through that again. It helps that Daniel is out of town, leaving me to my own devices and the routine that got me to this level in the first place. One less torch.

"I thought we might be able to do another batch of that belle-hélène with the leftover pears. We could add some kind of ice cream to it. I mean . . . because I would want to expand on your idea a little bit—maybe a caramel something?" Julie says.

"Great suggestion, but we're going with this," I say, and fall back into my conversation with Samuel.

"But the gâteau doesn't even have a fruit component to it," Julie says, still not doing what I asked her to do.

"Once again, great suggestion, but we're going with this," I say. This time Samuel and I don't fall back into conversation.

"I think we should go with my idea," Julie says.

"How far are we taking this?" I ask, stepping forward.

"I just think that if you and Samuel are on your way out, you should allow me to assert my creative vision," Julie explains.

"I understand that you're anxious to 'assert your creative vision,'" I say. "But right now you're just being disrespectful." Samuel excuses himself to gather the ingredients for the other menu standbys.

"I think *you're* being disrespectful by not allowing the new guard to express herself," Julie says, taking a step back. I take another step forward. Our faces are inches apart.

"I am *still* your boss, and if you refuse to follow my orders, I will take it as a sign that you no longer want to work here. Are we clear?" I say, unblinking. Julie thought she'd circled long enough. The fact that her first charge at the castle was on the back of a dessert I already created is a bad sign. If she wants this head pastry job, she'll have to come up with her own ideas. She obviously thought tonight was the perfect time for the kill. She miscalculated. I refuse to go out until I see fit. I will not leave a job I earned through toiling in the trenches for ten years. So help me God, I'll leave when I say.

"Yes, Chef," Julie spits out. Samuel rounds the corner with an armful of ingredients.

"Now go throw those leftover pears away," I say.

◆

I drive home that night after stopping at the twenty-four-hour grocery store for the supplies I'll need for the desserts I'm bringing to Thanksgiving. I'm doing the usual apple and pumpkin pies. I'll also bring a bread pudding from the restaurant: Dad's favorite. I drop my keys in the designated bowl and head into the kitchen, overloaded with grocery bags. My apartment stayed clean while I was at Daniel's. I'm actually happy to be home for a while. I got a parking ticket every night I spent at his place, and I'm pretty sure I have some horrible creepy-crawly fungus from his slaughterhouse hallway. But I also sleep on the left side of the bed and wear his Kansas T-shirt as pajamas. It's so easy to get used to someone. Dangerous, I suppose. I pick up the mail that's strewn on the floor, where it's been pushed through the mail slot.

I'm dead tired. Daniel has been gone for a full week at the Maui Invitational. Somehow his trip to a basketball tournament in Maui doesn't quite pack the same punch as Will's dodging bullets in Iraq and/or Lebanon. He's due back late tomorrow night. He says he'll come over to my apartment after he gets settled. I'll leave the key under the mat. He'll be waiting for me. I'll get to come home to someone tomorrow night. We'll have a few hours together before I drive up to Montecito. Then I'm off to New York, and he'll fly to Oakland for another exhibition tournament.

My BlackBerry rings from the key bowl. Apparently the key bowl is multitasking. I walk over to the phone. A late-night phone call: now one of three people.

"Hello?" I head back into the kitchen.

"I Googled Daniel Sullivan," Rascal announces.

I tuck the phone into the crook of my neck. "And what, the entire country of Ireland came up?" I say. I find the large envelope that was messengered over by Paul, containing all the travel documents for New York. Now that we're into the production phase of the show, I am dealing with Paul only. Donna's expertise is development.

"Yeah, just about," Rascal says.

"It's two o'clock in the morning," I say.

"I'm hiding in the guest cottage. When are you getting here?" he asks.

"Sunday morning. Early. I got the tickets for the New York trip. Paul hired a car to pick us up at six in the morning," I say.

"So you'll just spend the night at my place?" Rascal asks.

"It's going to be a hassle, but it should work. What did you find on Daniel?" I ask.

"Well, he coaches for UCLA, right?"

"Wow, you remembered," I say.

"I *am* a writer. I get paid to remember things," he says, dripping with sarcasm.

"I thought you got paid for being a Page," I taunt.

"Ba-dum-bum," Rascal parries.

I laugh. "I had to."

"Your little Daniel blew out his knee right after he was recruited by the Chicago Bulls from the Jayhawks. He started coaching about two years later at some Podunk high school in Kansas and then on to the city college," Rascal says. I knew about the knee injury, but not what it cost him. He did say it was a career ender—I just figured it was his college career, not his *professional* basketball career. I'm not the only one with secrets.

"Ummm, I've gotta go," Rascal says quickly.

"Oh, okay," I say.

"Dinah's on the other line. We're working on the adaptation," Rascal says.

"Is *someone* in the kitchen with Dinah?" I tease.

"Stop. That fucking song haunts me. I'll see you Sunday when you get here," Rascal says, quickly signing off. I beep the BlackBerry off and ready the house for tomorrow night, when Daniel gets back from Hawaii. I can't wait to see him. I also can't, or won't, deal with how much I've missed him. My chest tightens as I search my brain for something else to think about. Something less terrifying. My mind drifts to Rascal. I wonder why he's working on his adaptation at two o'clock in the morning. A little late for anyone to be in the kitchen with Dinah, if you ask me.

chapter thirty-two

Will called for you," Daniel says as soon as I walk in the door of my apartment. I'm holding a bottle of wine and leftovers from the restaurant. I haven't seen Daniel in over a week, and these are the first words out of his mouth? There's a definite edge to his voice. My entire body deflates.

I'm not ready for this conversation. I know where my heart is. It's with Daniel. I also know that I can't completely erase Will from my life. He's gone from all the important parts of my heart, but those faded images replaying in the pantheon still haunt me. He's like the *Where's Waldo?* of my life—he's in every picture, you just have to look for him. Being with Will defined my whole life, and that's not— Wait, that's it.

"He got to me, you know. He spelled his name for me, real slow. Like I wouldn't know how to spell 'Will.' I'm not stupid. And this . . . I'm sick of not knowing shit about you."

I think that's the first time I've heard Daniel cuss. Am I a bad influence? But then I think about the Chicago Bulls and those two years. I look up. I can't lie anymore. Omission *is* lying. "He was my . . . my everything. *Was*," I whisper. Honesty. Trust. New frontiers. Cliffs. Plummeting. Forgetting. Leaving. Grab the words, stuff them back in. Grab 'em before they get to

Daniel. My arms are at my sides; I'm still holding the wine and leftovers. Did I think they could stop the chickens from coming home to roost? How clueless and oblivious *am* I?

"Oh?" Daniel asks, walking over to me, pushing the front door closed. He stands over me—so big. Most of the time I forget how big he is.

"I don't want to sound— *I* feel stupid," I say.

"Why?" Daniel says, taking the wine and leftovers and setting them on the floor next to the couch.

"I think I didn't know how fucked up it was with Will until I met you," I say, rubbing my face.

"Really?" Daniel's voice is lighter.

"I had gotten so used to it—I didn't even see it. Will would travel for months and years at a time following these stories. At first I thought it must be hard for him to leave me, because it hurts not to be around the ones you love. Then a couple months ago, I realized he didn't love me at all. Not the . . . not *this* kind of . . ." I'm unable to finish the sentence. I dodge the left-out word and continue, "I do care for Will. I want him to be happy. But I realize now that you alter your life to be around the person you really . . ." I trail off once again, still unable to say the word. I think for a moment. How deeply do I want to get into this? Fuck. It.

"Elisabeth?" Daniel asks.

"It's not just Will," I say.

Daniel looks like he's afraid I'm about to recite a laundry list of lovers he can look forward to meeting at breakfast cafés all across the L.A. basin. "It's not?" His voice wavers.

"Will was just copying my brother, who was copying my dad. I pretty much thought that's what love looked like: Don't get too attached. Be indifferent. And be ready for them to leave if something more compelling comes up," I say, tears burning my throat.

"Your dad?" Daniel asks.

"Yeah." Daniel is quiet. I continue, "Ben Page is my dad." I've been dancing around this information for over two months.

"I know who your dad is," Daniel says quietly.

"You do?" I ask, honestly caught off guard.

"My dad has every one of his books. He was in Vietnam, too—said your dad really nailed it," Daniel offers.

"Why didn't you say something?" I ask.

"Because it didn't matter. It *doesn't* matter," he says without missing a beat.

"Right, right," I say, letting out the first sneaking tears.

"I understand. I really do. I thought the same . . . I thought I knew what was important." Daniel stops. Our words are coming fast. Obviously, both of us are anxious to let our cats out of the bag.

"And?" I ask.

"Ever since I could walk, I had a basketball in my hand. There was a basketball in every picture of me. All-state. Scholarships. I got drafted to the Chicago Bulls right out of college—I never told you that. Thirty-ninth-round draft pick. That's pretty good, by the way," Daniel adds with the trace of a smile. I step closer to him. He rubs his jaw and looks off in the distance. I want to reach out to him, but I don't want to pressure him or make him uncomfortable. I keep my hands at my sides. "I was going up for this rebound. Stupid, really. It was a scrimmage, not even a game, and it was the weirdest feeling. It was more of a sound—just this pop. It didn't even hurt right away, and nothing in the rebound made me think it was as bad as it was. I mean, I'd landed on much worse." Daniel runs his hands through his hair and sits on the couch.

I sit next to him and put my hand on his leg. "You don't have to," I offer.

"No, it's good. I sat on the bench for the rest of the season in my suit and tie. In the beginning, the rest of the team tolerated me—kept me in the loop. I mean, I thought these guys were my family. It was everything I'd ever wanted. When the news came down that the injury was a career-ender . . ." Daniel pauses and lets out a small laugh. "They didn't want to have anything to do with me."

"I'm so sorry," I say, bending toward him to make eye contact. I need him to look at me. Daniel takes my hand, squeezes it tight, and swipes at his eyes. He takes in a deep breath, collecting himself.

"I went home, and my parents—I'd kind of left them behind while I was in Chicago—well, they . . . My mom drove me to every physical therapy session. Dad installed all these ramps all over the house." Daniel laughs, sniffling a bit. He wipes at his eyes again, taking an even deeper breath; it's obviously getting harder and harder for him to collect himself. The tears are clogging in my own throat. Daniel looks directly at me, his eyes moist. "I found out the hard way what was important—what *is* important."

I'm silent. My whole body is leaning in to him. I've never said "I love you" to anyone outside of my family; and we usually say it with a smirk or an eye roll. "So banal," we quip. I don't think I know what love is. Not in that Foreigner, huge-eighties-hair-band kind of way. I mean the amazing scope of it. How one word can define everything from the absolute love I have for Mom and the caramel/molasses look she gives Rascal and me, threading through my soldier-like loyalty to my brother and on to the more complicated love I have for Dad, all the way to this. Where I am right now.

"I love you." I barely whisper it. Daniel looks at me. He's wearing that smirk. Is this funny? Is it cheesy and all after-school-special-like? *A Lesson in Love for Sally Anne,* probably starring some now-aging *Beverly Hills 90210* alum. Oh, shit. Well, goddamn. How are you supposed to tell someone that and really mean it without sounding absolutely ridiculous? I feel like I want to ooze away in this self-made puddle of cheese.

"I love you," Daniel says. I like how he doesn't say "too." His smile is broadening, and a giggle is erupting just under the surface.

"What?" I ask.

"I know how much you hated to say that. And not because you didn't mean it or anything. I know you mean it." Daniel gently kisses me. "But the pained look you had on your face was priceless." He almost can't contain himself.

"Well, I try," I say, breathing easier.

"Yes, you do," he concedes.

"Thanks for telling me that stuff," I say, looking directly at him.

"Thanks for letting me," he says.

◆

I wake up the next morning bright and early. Daniel is on his side of the bed, fast asleep. It's nearly impossible to get up. I should be able to be in Montecito by ten and then drive right back tonight with Rascal. I'll spend the night at his place so we can meet the car that'll take us to the airport in the morning. Daniel's hair is sticking up everywhere, and the blankets are around his ass. I've got quite the good view from where I'm standing. I lean over and give him a gentle kiss on the forehead. He smiles and sinks back into the bed.

"Happy belated Thanksgiving," I whisper.

"Drive safe, fly safe, and call me when you get there," Daniel says, his mouth full of pillow.

"I will. Have fun in Oakland," I say.

"I will. And why don't you take a picture, it lasts longer," he says, pulling the blankets tight over his shoulders.

chapter thirty-three

"C an you pass the rolls?" I ask Rascal. The table is smaller than it's ever been. No added leaves to accommodate the many guests we usually entertain. Just the four of us. Iris and Robert took the week off. The Pages. Giving thanks.

"They're one inch from your hand," he answers.

"It's impolite to reach," Mom corrects.

"See? It's impolite to reach," I chide.

"Jesus H. Christ, will someone just pass the girl the goddamn rolls?" Dad asks. Rascal pushes the basket of rolls over to me with great effort.

"Why, thank you, sir," I say, placing the tongs back in the basket after serving myself.

We've been eating Thanksgiving dinner for over an hour now. Rascal and I spent most of the afternoon in the guest cottage, just staying out of the way, passing the time as we usually do: arguing, laughing, playing Scrabble, and drinking good wine. I made a point of telling Rascal that being in the kitchen with Dinah at two o'clock in the morning brought a far more lascivious angle to the song. He assured me it was just business. I asked how large her lollipop head was. He revealed that she was not the proud owner of the requisite lollipop head. I nearly fainted.

I have to admit that being here without Will feels a bit unsafe. He has always been my sanctuary during these tense family gatherings. Someone to look to when it all seemed insurmountably crazy. I've found myself relying more and more on Rascal this Thanksgiving. I'm sure he's already annoyed by the role.

"Are we all on board for the Children of the Homeless fundraiser in December at the Mayers'?" Mom announces. We all drone that we are, as usual, on board for yet another charity event.

"I'll e-mail you the details," Mom says. This means she would like us to e-mail back what it is we're donating. "So, when do you two leave for New York?"

"Tomorrow," I announce.

"What's in New York?" Dad asks.

"Empire State Building," Rascal answers.

"Carnegie Hall," I add, digging into the mashed potatoes. Dad lets out a long sigh. So, who's going first? I ask myself. Rascal and the adaptation that's going far better than we ever thought possible, or the fact that I'm not just going Hollywood. I'm doing *television*.

"More wine?" Mom asks Dad. Nice dodge, Ballard. Nice.

"Sure, sweetie. Thanks," Dad answers. "So, what's in New York?" he asks again. Why don't we just offer him some Ambien? Maybe a crack over the head that'll render him not only unconscious but with a touch of amnesia. Rascal is quiet. No Will to look to. Mom has done what she could for us.

It's all me.

"I got an offer to do a pilot for my own television show, Dad. I'm going to New York to meet with the executives." I choke out the words that are undoubtedly going to be my last.

"You're doing *television*?" Dad echoes, shaking his head slightly.

"Yes," I answer.

"What *kind* of television show?" Dad asks. No question is just a question with Dad. Every conversation is a chess game, and he's always ten moves ahead.

"It'd be on the Food Network. Me in and around L.A.," I recite. Rascal sips his wine. Mom watches Dad. It's not computing. It's more horrible than he ever could have imagined.

"You're leaving the restaurant, then, I assume," Dad clarifies.

"If the meetings in New York work out, yes," I answer, feeling like I'm on the stand defending my life.

"So, no James Beard Award," Dad points out.

"They have a cookbook category, so there's still hope," I answer.

"Five-year plan?" Dad asks.

"Was actually the eleven-year plan and was in need of an overhaul," I answer.

"*Television,*" Dad ruminates.

"Yep," I answer.

"What the fuck happened?" His voice is quiet.

"These people came into the restaurant—" I begin.

Dad cuts me off. "No, I mean what the *fuck* happened? How did this happen?" he asks no one in particular. The entire table is quiet. "Answer me, Elisabeth." Dad's eyes bore into me.

"What do you want me to say, Pop? Anything I say at this point will just piss you off more," I say, finding words I didn't know still lived in my throat.

"You're right about that," Dad says, slamming his fork down.

"I've made my decision," I say, the words barely crawling out of my mouth.

"What? To be a fucking sellout?" Dad says, flashing that smile.

"Yes, Dad, to be a fucking sellout."

"Don't be a smart-ass," Dad warns.

"Okay, I'll be a dumb-ass," I respond. Dad bends forward over his plate. I sit still.

"Ben, I think it's a great opportunity," Mom offers.

He turns to her, and it clearly takes everything he has to eke out a smile for her. He's *never* yelled at Mom. "Sweetie, please don't. Our kids . . . what the fuck happened to our kids?" Dad says to her.

"I think they turned out rather great," Mom says, giving me and Rascal that caramel look of hers. Unconditional. Rascal and I shrink down in our chairs.

"For what it's worth, I think it's a good decision, too," Rascal adds.

Dad zeroes in on him. "Of course *you* would," he says, sarcasm dripping.

"Okaaaay," Rascal says, drawing the word out.

"I'm not going to apologize. I know it's the right way to go," I finally say.

"Unbelievable," Dad says, almost to himself.

"I'm happy," I say.

"I guess that's what worries me," Dad says.

I pick up my wineglass and take a long sip. We're pretty much done here, I'm thinking.

"I don't think it's such a bad thing," Rascal starts in again. I turn to him, my eyes pleading with him to leave it. He shakes me off, homing in on Dad.

"Rascal, stay out of this," Dad says, honestly meaning it.

Rascal shifts in his chair, straightening slightly. "No. This adaptation thing . . . it's awesome, Pop. I mean, this girl . . . she gets me. She gets the book—and I . . . I really think this movie is going to be pretty great," Rascal says.

"Once again, *you* would say that," Dad says, sloughing Rascal off.

"Pop, I'm serious. You know the part in my book—" Rascal begins.

"I didn't fucking read it," Dad growls.

Rascal recoils slightly. Takes a second, then leans in to the table. Leans in to Dad. The equivalent of full steam ahead. "What?" Rascal's voice cuts.

"I knew Rick Danko. I don't have to read your book about him," Dad says.

"The book isn't actually about Rick Danko, Dad. There's a funny little thing we in the writing biz call 'metaphor.'" Rascal uses air quotes with "metaphor." He's bending now, contorting his body over the table.

"Yeah, well, when you actually live life, you don't have to use bullshit smoke and mirrors like metaphor. You just write from the gut," Dad says, his voice easy and taunting.

"Now, had you actually read the book, you would see that this is exactly what I was talking about. You guys, you were going to change the world. And instead, you all drank yourselves to death. You don't . . ." Rascal trails off.

"Don't what?" Dad says, his voice rising just that much.

"Do you honestly think . . . Do you honestly even . . ." Rascal's face is bright red.

"Think what? What? Without fucking metaphor, you can't even form one goddamn real thought?" Dad's voice is getting louder and louder.

Rascal breathes deeply and situates himself. "Do you think people go see the Rolling Stones to hear 'Love Is Strong' or a nice cut off of *Steel Wheels*? No. They want to hear 'Sympathy for the Devil,' 'Paint It Black,' or even 'Brown Sugar,'" Rascal says.

"Get to the point, son," Dad says, his voice calm again.

"It's the Robbie Robertson factor," Rascal says.

"A point, son. I need you to make your point and stop throwing out random names of people I knew and you didn't."

"My point—the point of my novel—is that part of greatness is knowing when to move on. When to evolve and, most importantly, *how* to evolve," Rascal finally gets out.

"Evolve into what?" Dad asks.

"Into something other than a relic of a time long past," Rascal spits out.

"A relic?" Dad says, his voice beginning to climb again.

"Yeah," Rascal says, nearly bending out of his chair.

"What do you know about relics?" Dad asks.

"How often do people ask you to autograph your last book, Dad? Or are they just constantly quoting *The Coward,* maybe *Jack Tinker*—and without the movie adaptation of *The Plantation Band,* that book would hardly get the attention it does," Rascal says, taking his deepest breath after the last words.

"These are pretty weighty theories you're bandying about," Dad says, his voice the low growl his prey would hear for only a brief second before the lights went out.

"The legacy you've left is in some time capsule that plays on A&E every other week. Do you realize what a huge impact your voice would have on the antiwar movement going on right now? But, no—all you do is insist on being a part of the retrospective cheese-fests that just want to jack you off. I mean, where's your relevance today? Who are you now?" Rascal says.

"Relevance. That's what all this is about? Hm. What does that make you? I mean, what kind of creature latches on to a remora?" Dad sets his wineglass down on the table. His voice is eerily calm.

"You tell me. My book went where yours couldn't. *I* went where you couldn't. *That's* why you didn't read it," Rascal says.

"I didn't read your book, Rascal, because I can't seem to justify how I was saddled with a kid like you. *That,* son, is why I didn't read your book," Dad says, breaking out that patented smile.

"That's enough, Pop," I snap.

"Elisabeth, be quiet." Dad doesn't look away from Rascal.

Rascal takes his napkin from his lap and stands. "Dad, this may come as a shock to you, but you not being able to justify being saddled with a kid like me . . . Well, I take that as a compliment," Rascal says, beginning to walk out of the room.

Dad quickly gets up, standing over him. "Don't you get up from this table," he says.

"We're done here, Dad," Rascal says, his voice fixed in a monotone.

"Sit your ass back down," Dad says, moving closer to Rascal.

"No," Rascal says, his body tight and unmoving. Dad's entire body is shaking. Rascal powers past Dad. Dad swings and connects directly with the corner of Rascal's left eye. Rascal whips to the side, his wiry body hitting the wall of the dining room. I recoil into my chair. Mom immediately stands.

"Ben, that's enough," Mom cuts in, going over and seeing to Rascal. Dad looks horrified.

"How long have you wanted to do that?" Rascal says, his hand over his already swelling eye.

"Rascal, I didn't . . . you—" Dad's voice is still a low growl.

"Probably about as long as I've wanted to tell you to fuck off," Rascal says, low and controlled. Dad is taken slightly aback.

"I said that's enough," Mom says again, a little louder, but not at a yell. She looks at Rascal, taking in his reddening face. Not one tear. His eyes are clear and defiant.

"This is Thanksgiving dinner, and we are all going to sit down like a family and finish this goddamn meal," Dad announces.

Mom comes over to the table. "Kids, I want you to go back to the guest cottage. Your father and I need to talk."

"Yes, Mom," Rascal and I say together.

"Ballard?" Dad says as Rascal squeezes past him. I stand and set my napkin on the table.

"Ben, I need you to be quiet until the children leave," Mom says. She says to Rascal and me, "I'll come out to the cottage when I'm done. Please give us some privacy until then."

chapter thirty-four

H oly shit . . . holy shit . . . holy shit . . ." I say, opening the
door to the cottage and going directly into the kitchen for
some ice. Rascal follows, his hand over his eye. He looks completely dazed. I crack the ice from the trays, bundle it in a dish
towel, and hand it to Rascal. He puts the bundle on his eye and
collapses onto one of the bar stools in the kitchenette.

"I totally thought you were going to bring up Avery," I say,
breaking the odd silence.

"No, no, Mom doesn't need to know about that," Rascal says
absently.

"You okay?" I ask.

"I'm fine. I'm fine," Rascal says mechanically, his face reddening more.

I drag the other bar stool over and sit next to him. "You
stood up to him. You held it together. That was fucking incredible," I say, taking the bundle of ice and holding it on his eye
myself.

"He fucking hit me, Bink. Dad fucking hit me." Rascal's
good eye is glassy.

"I know. I know. I can't explain . . ." I can feel my throat
closing and burning with tears.

"I'm moving to Montana. I bought that cabin—the one I wrote the novel in. I can't . . . I've worked too hard to try and stop this. I can't keep running."

"So you're leaving?" I ask, sniffling up the welling tears.

"I think I have to," he says. I shift the melting ice. He cringes at the pain this action brings.

"I can't believe this." Anger bubbles over, spilling out onto the counter.

Rascal looks shocked. "What?"

"If you ever want to pinpoint the moment, you know, run it back in your head—the exact moment your little sister figured out you were full of shit—yeah, it's this moment. Right here," I say.

"What the fuck are you talking about? This is the least amount of shit I've been filled with in my entire life." Rascal's voice is soft.

"You finally stand up to Dad, say you don't want to run anymore, and then you announce you're moving to Montana? I thought you liked being in the kitchen with Dinah. I thought there was something . . . You don't see the irony in all this? I'll wait for the light to go on." I stare right at him.

"Don't be a smart-ass. My eye hurts too much for you to be a smart-ass." Rascal pleads.

"One step forward, two steps back," I say, taking the dish towel and dumping some of the melted ice in the sink.

"Oh, stop it. Calm down. Sit. Just . . . Will you sit down?" Rascal stands and takes my hand.

"What?" I say, bringing the ice back over and resting it once again on Rascal's eye. I sit.

"It's not like that. At least it didn't sound like that when I worked all this out earlier." Rascal runs his hand through his unruly curls. I bite the side of my cheek and wait. He sits back down and scoots his stool in.

"I just can't be around him anymore. I have to find my own place. I have to put down roots and try, at least try, to see this thing through," he says, his voice cracking.

"Why does it have to be in Montana?" The tears let loose down my cheeks.

"I'm so sick and fucking tired of it. The heir apparent. The scion of this, and the prodigal son, and fuuuck! I don't want it. I don't want to *be* him. I don't want to be like him. But I can see I'm turning into him. Sometimes, at night, I'd just sit there and . . . there'd be nothing keeping me here, you know? Nothing worth sticking around for." Rascal turns his face away and wipes at his good eye.

I lean in. "What are we talking about here?"

"I had these fantasies where I'd take his Colt .45 right out of that Shrine to Manhood. Maybe even let my blood splatter on the pages of his next masterpiece. Poetic, right? My book would sell millions. Posthumous shit always sells tons." Rascal's jaw is tight and cruel. He scoffs out a small laugh and turns away.

"What? You're joking? You're making jokes about . . ." I can't even say it.

"It's not as if it's something that I'm *still* thinking about." Rascal breathes deeply and tries to compose himself.

"I'm so sorry . . . I'm so sorry . . ." I get out.

"No, it's . . . Jesus, you're the only thing that kept me around sometimes," he says, reaching across the counter. I lean over the counter in tears. The bundle of ice falls to the ground. Rascal scoots his stool around and puts his arm around me, holding my head tightly to his chest. I look up, my eyes wet, and try to smile. Rascal kisses my forehead. Always the big brother.

"Montana, huh?" I say.

"Yeah, I don't know what's worse. Death or Montana," Rascal jokes.

"Not funny," I say, looking up at him.

"I know," Rascal says, wiping away one of my tears.

"Are you still coming to New York with me?" I ask, sniffling and heaving, trying to regain a modicum of composure.

"My kind of town," he says, letting my head fall back on his chest. We hear the door to the cottage open and close. Rascal wipes his face, and I hop down to pick up the fallen ice. Mom walks calmly through the swinging door into the kitchenette.

"Your father needs some time by himself. I've asked him to spend some time at the studio in Laurel Canyon," she says.

"Mom, I'm so sorry," Rascal says, standing.

"Oh . . ." Mom bites her lip. Her eyes well up. She continues, "You're sorry? *You're* sorry? Oh, my sweet, sweet boy . . ." She pulls Rascal to her. Only then does he crumble into tears. I hold on to the bundle of ice and feel tear after tear roll down my face.

"Come here, sweetheart," Mom says, holding out her arm to me. I dump the ice and quickly fall in to Mom's embrace. She holds us tight. Tighter than she ever has. "I'm so sorry. Please . . . please . . . you must forgive me," she says, her voice breaking with each word. Rascal and I pull back from her, taking her in.

"Mom, you didn't do anything," I say.

"Exactly. I didn't *do* anything. I was so horrible to Anne. I was so judgmental about how she treated William all these years. How she'd neglected him for whatever it was that caught her fancy. I thought I was so much better. My perfect little family. And here I was, so blind. I need you . . ." Mom's eyes are on fire, boring into us. "I need you to know that I will never allow something like this to happen ever again."

"Okay, Mom," Rascal and I say in unison. He leans on the counter, picking up the bundle of ice and resting it once more on his swelling eye.

"I just didn't see it . . . see how bad it had gotten. And now I can't look at myself in the mirror. I made a vow to myself—God, I must have been sixteen—it was right after Daddy died, and I was spending yet another Christmas at boarding school. Such a . . . It was lovely. They really tried to make us feel at home. But I swore that when I had a family, I would keep it together no matter what. I just never . . ." Mom trails off.

"How could you know?" I ask.

Mom looks at me, right at me. "You know. They don't change, darling."

"But—" I begin.

"They *don't,* darling," Mom says. It's clear to me that she's also talking about Will. I now understand why Mom was so alarmingly keen on Daniel. Had she been secretly hoping I'd find someone . . . anyone?

"Okay, okay," I say, nodding and not knowing where to look—where to focus my eyes. I can't look at Mom. I can't look at Rascal. This whole time they've known. They've known. Everyone's known. Will is never going to be the man I need him to be. Ever. He'll never change.

"You're feeling pretty good about that high-speed-chase story right about now, huh?" I say to Rascal.

A smile breaks across his face. "Yes, I'm truly a prophet," he says. He wipes snot off my face.

"So where do we go from here?" I ask.

"You and I go to New York," Rascal says.

"No, I know that. I just . . ." Rascal and I look to Mom.

"Your brother's right. You go to New York," Mom says.

"But—" I start.

"This is something your father has to make right. We didn't do anything wrong. *You* didn't do anything wrong," Mom says.

"But—" Rascal tries.

Mom cuts in, her voice final. "You didn't do anything wrong, sweetheart. This is *his* mess to clean up." Rascal softens.

"What about you?" I ask.

"I've decided to take Anne Houghton up on her offer to join her in Aspen. I got a flight for first thing in the morning," Mom announces.

"Holy shit, Mom," Rascal yelps.

"Language, dear," Mom corrects, giving him the smallest of winks.

chapter thirty-five

Rascal and I are packed up and riding in the back of a Town Car on our way to LAX. It's just after six in the morning. We've already made a Starbucks pit stop in search of tea, coffee, and a nice caffeine buzz. I eagerly await my tea to cool from temperatures like those found near the center of the Earth. Last night is still thick in our throats. Dad left within minutes. He had scribbled a long manifesto to Rascal, apologizing for his behavior, and left it on the kitchen counter. By the time he was entering the 101 in his Corvette, Dad had already left three messages on Rascal's cell phone, apologizing and pleading with him to call. Rascal couldn't bring himself to listen to the messages but saved them anyway. The limousine service to LAX picked Mom up first thing in the morning. The house was near empty within hours of the punch heard around the world. How am I going to explain last night to Daniel? Oh yeah, my family got together for Thanksgiving—it was great, we had turkey, mashed potatoes, and a fistfight.

Rascal's cell phone rings from his jacket pocket. He takes it out, checks the number, and beeps the phone on. "Hello?" He's quiet, listening. Who's calling him at six o'clock in the morning? Dad?

"Who is it?" I mouth.

He waves me off. "Oh, good. Tell her we're thinking of her."

"Who is it?" I ask again.

Rascal mouths, "Will." He says into the phone, "Yeah, she's here." He listens and then answers, "Oh, thanks, man, but we can't. We're flying to New York for a business thing."

"What? What is he saying?" I whisper.

Rascal whispers back, "Shut the fuck up," and turns his body away from me so he's looking out the window. I notice the morphing of the pumpkin patches is finally complete; Christmas-tree lots have sprouted on random corners throughout the streets of Los Angeles. The odd mixture of holiday cheer and melancholy is thick in the morning air. I don't know what it is about this time of year that makes me feel so dreamy and elsewhere. Maybe it's the twinkle lights that make every house look that much more fairy tale–ish.

"Okay, well, give our regrets to your mom," Rascal says, signing off. I wait. He says, "Mom called Anne from LAX. Her plane is on schedule."

I look out the window.

"It's weird that he called, right? That's weird." I say.

Rascal puts on his sunglasses over what is now officially a black eye. "Things aren't important if people aren't important," he muses. One high-speed chase story and the guy thinks he's Aesop.

"Oh, okay, Yoda," I say, digging my own sunglasses out of my purse. It's not even gray dawn yet.

"Copycat," Rascal says.

I put on my sunglasses, sigh as loudly and dramatically as I can, sip my tea, and promptly burn my tongue.

◆

Rascal and I walk through the revolving door and into the large lobby of the W Hotel in Times Square. The weather is crisp and beautiful. Not snowing yet but definitely thinking about it. Rascal wears his sunglasses inside. We head toward the registration desk.

"Welcome to the W Hotel. What can I help you with?" asks the impeccably attired woman behind the counter.

Paul and Donna have each left a message on my BlackBerry, telling me a car will pick me up at the hotel tomorrow at eight A.M. for our pitch meeting at nine. Donna's message is very specific about what to wear (something wholesome yet current) and how I should do my hair (down but out of my face). Paul tells me to relax, that the pilot looks fabulous and everything is looking really good for us.

"We have a reservation. Elisabeth Page and Rascal Page," I say. Rascal holds his messenger bag across his chest and yawns.

"Oh, yes. Here you are. You're on the same floor but separate rooms? I'm so sorry, Mr. and Mrs. Page, I'll remedy this oversight right away."

"We're brother and sister, ma'am," Rascal corrects.

"Oh, pardon me." The woman fusses with her collar and then taps incessantly on the computer's keyboard.

"Thank you," I say, taking the key card she hands me.

Rascal takes his and looks at the room number. "Do we have any messages?" he asks. The woman taps a few more keys on her computer and tells me I have four messages. She'll print them out for me. She has two for Rascal.

"Thank you," I say, taking the paper. The bellman whisks our luggage away, and Rascal and I walk to the elevators.

"Mom's already called," Rascal says, reading his messages.

"Yeah, she called me, too," I say.

"And Dad," Rascal adds.

"Yeah, me, too," I answer.

One of my messages is from Paul Lingeman. He must have left messages both at the hotel and on my BlackBerry. A tad much, I think. The final message is from Daniel. I already left a message for him when I landed. I smile. After last night and Mom's words of warning, every last shred of love—*that* kind of love—I had for Will feels as if it's been exorcised. My chest tightens nonetheless. I try to blame it on the peculiar holiday air. But it dawns on me that this feeling isn't about the melancholia of the holidays, or even Daniel, for that matter. It's about Will. Or rather—the absence of Will.

"Dinner tonight?" Rascal says, pressing the button for the elevator. It comes immediately.

"Sounds good," I say, stepping into the elevator.

"Meet you out front at eight. Where do you want to go?" Rascal says as we climb to our floor.

"I've already called in a favor. Just meet me downstairs at eight," I say. The elevator doors open at our floor, and we walk to our separate rooms in silence, both of us lost in thought. Uncharted territories of thought.

Rascal and I eat at wd-50 on the Lower East Side. Our last-minute reservation is thanks to a few well-placed phone calls to old friends. We are joined by Rascal's literary team: agents, editors, and their adoring assistants, who no doubt pulled strings to be invited to dinner with Rascal. He's been vague all night about how he got that black eye, alluding to barroom brawls, foiling a bank robbery, and being caught in flagrante delicto by a jealous boyfriend. He's trying to make light of it, but he hasn't quite been able to spin one of his famous yarns.

After dinner, Rascal retreats to his hotel room minus the buxom assistant who's been throwing herself at him. It's more than a little unnerving: Rascal climbing into bed alone? I stop off at the hotel gift shop for a magazine, and while I'm waiting in line, I decide to call Daniel. Once I'm done paying, I move into the lobby and dial.

"Hello?" he answers. The time change means he's just getting home from practice.

"Hey," I say, melting.

"Hey yourself." Daniel's voice softens.

"I just got in from dinner with Rascal." I haven't told Daniel about the fistfight. I don't know how a conversation like that even starts.

"Elisabeth?"

I spin around. It's Will, and he's standing a mere five feet in front of me. His leather overnight bag is slung over one shoulder; you can see the brush of yellow hair and the icy blue eyes from a mile away. He's still carrying a coffee from the airport terminal.

"You have all your big meetings tomorrow?" Daniel asks me.

I'm staring at Will. He stands there. Listening. "First one is at nine sharp," I answer.

"I'll cross my fingers at six," Daniel says.

"Okay, well, I'll let you get some sleep," I say distractedly.

"It's eight o'clock here, Elisabeth," Daniel says.

"Oh, right. Right. Then I guess I'd better get to sleep," I say. Will takes a sip of his coffee. I focus on Daniel.

"Okay. Sleep tight and good luck tomorrow," Daniel says.

"You, too." We're both quiet. I breathe deeply. "I love you," I say, looking away from Will.

"I love you," Daniel says back. We sign off as Will fidgets with his messenger bag.

"What are you doing here? I thought you were in Aspen." I don't want to cause a scene in the lobby, so I walk out onto the sidewalk. Times Square is lit up around me, a landscape of flickering advertisements. Tiny flakes of snow have started falling.

"I had to come," Will says.

"I don't even know what to do with that," I say. I can see my breath.

"Yeah, well, if you don't know what to do with that, this is going to be even worse." Will digs through his messenger bag and pulls out two plane tickets.

"What . . . what are those?" I ask, feeling the chill on my face.

"Two tickets to Vegas. You, me, and the Little White Wedding Chapel. I had it all planned—" He sees that the expression on my face isn't one of happiness. After dreaming of this moment for as long as I can remember, now all I can think is that I wish it were Daniel asking me those words, not Will. I don't want a life with Will. I've already lived that life, being afraid of Dad. I don't need to repeat it. "But . . ." Will trails off. The tickets ruffle in the wind.

"What?" I ask.

"I'm never going to remember that you have some meeting at nine sharp."

"I know," I say. Will and I stand there, silent, our bodies squared off. He watches me, almost studying my face. I take him in, too.

"I'm never going to tell you I love you without . . . well, without some excuse about why I never seem to act like it."

"I know," I say.

Will breathes in deeply. "I'm going to go back to Aspen. Maybe stay with Mom for a while." His hand is tight around the tickets, crumpling them.

"That sounds good," I say. I can't stop this wave of sadness. Loss.

"I do love you," Will says at last.

"I know. I love you, too," I say, meaning it.

Will hooks his hand on his messenger bag, letting out a little "hm" noise as he begins to turn. "He's a good guy?" he asks, almost as an afterthought.

I smile. "Yeah."

"Okay," he almost whispers. I watch him walk away alone in the falling snow. It's over. Or it's just begun. Sometimes it's hard to tell.

chapter thirty-six

The meeting at the Food Network passes in a fog of shaking hands, rushing through long corridors, watching the pilot, and listening as Paul and Donna pitch the show. My show. The executives seem receptive; as far as I can see, the meeting is going well. My fingers and toes are numb again. One of the execs asks me the inevitable Dad question. I joke that he and Rascal have promised to give me the official Page varsity jacket and teach me the secret handshake when I publish my first cookbook. I don't tell them that the varsity jacket comes with its very own black eye. Everyone laughs heartily. Paul and Donna breathe a sigh of relief.

The three of us wait in the greenroom for the execs to come out. Apparently, we have to meet with another set of executives. This is a good sign. We made it past the first gatekeepers. I sit and watch *The View*, thankful that the sound is turned down. Paul and Donna speak in hushed tones in the corner. I sip my bottle of water and check my e-mail. I got the confirmation that the Christmas present I ordered online for Daniel has been sent out: a poster from the 1952 Summer Olympics in Helsinki, Finland. The Olympics where the American basketball team was led to victory by the beloved University of Kansas Jayhawk Forrest "Phog" Allen. Finding the poster was a huge coup.

◆

The next morning I'm in Rascal's suite, waiting for him to get ready, when my BlackBerry rings from on top of the small desk. My heart races. I'm waiting on the call from Paul. *The call.* This little ringing BlackBerry holds the answer to my future.

Rascal comes out of the bathroom in his towel. "Are you going to fucking get that, you drama queen?"

"Hello?" I say breathlessly, getting to the phone just in time.

"We've been picked up!" Paul announces. I give Rascal the thumbs-up with a giant smile. Rascal looks genuinely thrilled. He digs through his suitcase and finds a pair of boxers and the same jeans he's been wearing for three days.

"What? That's incredible!" I squeal. Rascal's cell phone rings from his jeans pocket. He looks at it, mouths that it's Dad *again,* and sends it to voice mail. He tosses the cell phone on the bed and walks back into the bathroom.

"The executives went nuts over the pilot. They said that with a little work in post, they're going to air it and get a feel for the numbers and demographic. I'm sure Donna told you that we were behind the eight ball on this one. That pilot being as good as it was really saves our asses. Great news, Elisabeth. Congratulations!"

I can't stop smiling. I can't stop smiling. "What happens now?" I ask.

"Depending on how well the pilot does, we'll film anywhere from thirteen to twenty-six episodes. The network is pushing for a set here in New York for the cooking pieces. We'll probably have to shoot all of the field pieces back in L.A. during one week. It would mean spending a lot of time in New York, but we've gotta do what we've gotta do. This is the opportunity of a lifetime for you." Paul is speaking quickly. My mind is swimming. I remember Daniel talking about how he finally figured out what was important. Telling him I'm going to have to start dividing my time between New York and Los Angeles would be like a sucker punch to the life I was just starting to get excited about. Have I gone from the frying pan into the fire? I can't let this happen. I *won't* let this happen. I am more than comfortable pointing the finger of blame at Will's obsessive travel as the proof of love, or lack thereof. What I need to come clean with is that I was in no hurry to stop my own compulsive climb up the ladder of success.

"What's the hang-up on the kitchen?" I ask.

"It's just too hard to find a house we can use long-term. It's easier to build a set." Paul is talking distractedly. What's important? Rascal's moving to Montana. Mom and Dad are staying more and more in Montecito—that is, if they stay together at all. If I stay in Los Angeles, it means investing in a life with Daniel. It means putting something besides my career first. It means I'm willing to alter my life and change the very DNA of my future.

It means I get to love and be loved in return.

"What if we—or rather, I—*bought* a set . . . I mean, a piece of property that we could make into a permanent set. Ina Garten—I mean, the Barefoot Contessa—does that, right? Paula Deen does, too?" I babble. I can't even *say* the word "house." Rascal rounds the corner into the suite. He walks over to his suitcase and pulls on a white T-shirt.

"What exactly do you mean, Elisabeth?" Paul asks.

"I mean, I put a down payment on a house with whatever advance money you can wrangle, and we build a permanent set for the show in it," I say. Rascal stops dead in his tracks.

"That might work." Paul allows.

I breathe deeply. "Okay, so, tell that to the network people.

When do I need to have this set ready?" I ask, getting a sheet of paper from the desk. Rascal throws me a pen.

"Shooting starts the last week in December," Paul says. That's under three weeks. I almost throw up.

"Okay, then. Get me all of the specs for what I'm going to need for this kitchen, as far as all the technical stuff goes, and I'll go ahead and . . . find a set . . . I mean . . . I'll find a house." I sign off with Paul, sink onto the bed, and hold my BlackBerry loosely in my hands. I wonder if Samuel and Margot still have that Realtor's phone number. I wonder if I can speak to her without hyperventilating and excusing myself so I can breathe into a paper sack for five minutes. What the fuck have I just done?

"What the hell was that about?" Rascal asks.

"I don't know," I say, wishing I had a paper sack right now.

"What did you just do?" Rascal presses.

"I think I just . . . I've got to stay in L.A. He was saying that I would have to spend half my time in New York, and I just can't. I took this job so I could slow down. That kind of setup— I might as well stay at Beverly," I say.

Rascal is toweling his hair dry. He stops and slowly pulls the towel off his head. He looks at me and raises a single eyebrow. His hair is out of control. "Why don't I just transfer my house in Santa Monica over to you? You can take over the mortgage. We can work out the rest of the details later. I mean, even if I come back from Montana, I'm going to want something different, so . . ." Rascal runs his hands through his hair. This is his definition of "brushing it."

"No, I—" I stand, pacing, still unable to abide the handout from Mom and Dad, even secondhand.

"It's got that great ocean view. The kitchen isn't big, but you could bust out a couple of walls. No big deal. All of my furniture is already out of there. I'm sleeping on an air mattress until the house in Montana is ready. Mom has every designer in the Los Angeles basin in her Rolodex. You give me the specs, I'll call her, and she'll get someone on it." Rascal is calm.

"I don't know—I just . . ."

"Look, you're picking up the mortgage—it's not like the Foster Foundation is handing you a house along with the silver spoon in your mouth," Rascal reasons.

"It is kind of . . . I mean, it's . . ." I stutter.

"It's going to keep you in L.A.," Rascal says.

"Yeah, but at what cost?" I bite back.

"Look, you can make this about that if you want, but the way I see it, you're simply investing in your future, both professionally and personally."

"Personally, huh?" I question.

"I don't think Columbia or NYU has quite the basketball program that UCLA does, but what do I know?"

"What about you?" I ask.

"I'm moving to Montana, Bink. I'm getting out." Rascal pauses just long enough for me to notice the black eye once more. He continues, "I was just going to put it up for sale; we might as well keep it in the family." We stare at each other. What's important? It is that simple, isn't it? Love is altering your life to be around that person. It doesn't really make a lot of concessions for ego and fear of permanent residences.

I nod before I even know I'm doing it. "Yes, let's do it," I say, picking up my phone and redialing Paul to tell him the news.

chapter thirty-seven

I pull in to the UCLA campus, skipping a song on my iPod so I can avoid thinking about any of the things that are distracting me right now. As Rascal and I sat in the airport, waiting on our delayed flight, I hired movers, canceled my phone service, called all my credit cards with the address change, and made several lists of all that this move would entail. I'm not sure you can check some box next to "overcome fear of buying a home due to the lack of consistency in one's love life," but I'll give it a shot nonetheless. On top of everything, I've decided I'm going to walk into Beverly tomorrow and quit.

I know this is all exciting. I know it's as if I've been presented with the keys to a brand-new mansion and told that it was mine to keep. But it seems like I'm standing in the oversize foyer, not knowing where anything is, not knowing where the light switches are, and not knowing the sounds of the house settling. The velvet cage I was so used to—however claustrophobic it was—I knew every nook and cranny of that life. In all of its fucked-up glory, it was mine. This—I don't know who I am in this new place. Maybe all of those outside definitions of me—Ben Page's kid, Rascal Page's sister, Five-Star Pastry Chef, Will Houghton's childhood sweetheart—maybe I defined myself with them as well.

I park my car, get out, and pull my purse up on my shoulder. I proceed through the UCLA campus toward Pauley Pavilion. I just want to see Daniel. I want to tell him everything, but I'm petrified of telling him anything. I feel raw and exposed. I can't get the weight of that house off my shoulders. I feel bound to its permanence already. I get to the front of the will-call line and am handed an envelope with *Daniel Sullivan +1* written in Sharpie pen on the front. I pull my purse strap tight around my shoulder and walk my little +1 self right through those giant stadium doors.

The stadium is bustling and alive. A ten-piece band of kids on the far wall plays what seems like one long song with pauses and drum solos. I dig in my purse and find two Excedrin. I pop them into my mouth and swallow them dry. The game is already in full swing, and the players rush up and down the court. They look more like boys than young men. I walk up into the stands and find my seat number on one of the long benches. Because this is an exhibition game, the stands aren't filled to capacity, so I set my purse down beside me. I'm behind a group of women talking to the referees. They seem to know someone who plays for the team.

I look down the sidelines for Daniel. He's sitting three seats away from the head coach, who's pacing up and down the sidelines in shirtsleeves and a tie. The coach's coat hangs on the back of his chair. Daniel holds a dry-erase board and is focused on the game. He's wearing his suit and a baby-blue-and-yellow tie tied tight. I allow myself to envision, for the quickest of moments, Daniel putting up a basketball hoop in the driveway of the new house. Maybe we could set up a barbecue in the backyard. I have a backyard, for the love of God. We could even invite people over for a barbecue—pipe in one of those mix CDs with a martini glass on the cover.

"Oh, come on now! Show him now, come on! Show him!" the woman in front of me yells at the court. Apparently, this isn't the place for deep introspection. I focus on the game. Wasn't I supposed to be sitting next to Daniel's parents? Since I've never been to a basketball game, I don't know if there's some kind of VIP seating. If that's the case, why aren't I there? I look around at the crowd some more. On the other side of the bleachers, I see a group of kids wearing the same shirts and cheering. I focus in. UCLA. Hm. I look at the people around me—a lot of orange paws painted on faces. So, that means I'm sitting on the—

"Go, Bearkats! Go, Bearkats!" the girl to the left of me screams. Shit. I'm surrounded by Sam Houston Bearkats, not UCLA Bruins. I didn't even think about it. Who doesn't know that the coaching staff would be set up in front of their own crowd, behind their own players? I just wanted to get a good view of Daniel and not have to walk behind the court. I scan the crowd on the opposite side of the auditorium. It doesn't take long. Marilyn and Nick. Front-row center. The man *is* a dead ringer for Santa Claus. He's wearing a Tommy Bahama shirt under a light jacket and jeans. Daniel's mom looks like Mrs. Butterworth, all soft and cushiony. This is ridiculous. I clap as the Bearkats make a three-pointer. The girl next to me smiles. I notice Daniel looking over at his parents during a time-out. They make some sort of motion, like they don't know where his flake of a girlfriend is.

The clock ticks down, and it's finally halftime. The crowd disperses, and I make my move over to the other side, then grab my purse and walk down to the court. My mouth goes dry as I approach Daniel's parents.

"Mr. and Mrs. Sullivan?" My voice cracks. Dammit. I subtly wipe my hand on my skirt and extend it to them. They look up and take me in.

"Elisabeth?" Daniel's dad says.

"Oh my goodness, we thought something must have happened to you, sweetheart," Daniel's mom says as she stands and takes my hand.

"I sat on the wrong side," I explain, taking Mr. Sullivan's hand.

"Oh, well, that's worse than we could have imagined," Mr. Sullivan jokes. His belly—it is like a bowlful of jelly.

"Oh, now, Nick, let the poor girl sit down." Daniel's mom scooches over and pats the bleacher. I already feel calmer.

A group of cheerleaders hop and bounce out on the court. There are lots of "Okays!" and "Let's gos!" yelled at the crowd. The band plays some unrecognizable song as the cheerleaders dance and form pyramids—you know, rocket science. Nick and Marilyn clap. They each have a little Bruin pillow under them, along with a foam finger resting up against the bleacher. There is a travel-size cooler between them. How much time have these two spent watching basketball? They are professional parents, right down to the accessories. I again remember what Daniel said about figuring out what was important. They built ramps around the house. Adorable.

"So, tell us, Elisabeth—Daniel says you're a great cook," Nick says, leaning over to me as the cheerleaders whoop and holler themselves back to the sidelines.

I blush. "I can hold my own, Mr. Sullivan,"

"Oh, please call me Nick, little one," he says. Oh. My. God.

"You know, we always wanted Daniel to settle down with a nice girl. He just works so darn hard, we thought we'd never see the day," Marilyn confesses.

"Oh, now, don't embarrass the poor girl, Marilyn," Nick prods. My eyes fall to Marilyn's hand, and as usual, my Jewelry 101 training overtakes my better judgment. She's wearing a tiny solitaire diamond engagement ring along with a simple gold band.

Marilyn sees me looking. "Oh, this." She covers her hand. "Nicky and I got married real young. He had this beautiful car . . . What was that car, hon?" She tugs at Nick.

"It wasn't a car, Marilyn, it was a GTO," Nick corrects.

"Well, he sold the GTO to buy a ring—*this* ring. We never had the heart to upgrade." Marilyn pats my hand. My entire body melts. The pompous-asshole voice in my head is officially shamed into submission.

Nick offers me a "pop" from the cooler. I take it and crack it open. Halftime ends, and the UCLA team runs back out onto the court to the roar of the crowd. Daniel trots behind the team. I see him look toward us, and it's beautiful. Our presence registers. His face completely folds into itself as he smiles. He quickly focuses back on the team, clapping and huddling up with the boys.

"Watch the fouls, ref!" Nick calls out. Marilyn looks to see what the infraction was. I look at these two and can't help but soften.

"Danny needs a new suit, don't you think?" Marilyn whispers to Nick during a time-out.

Nick looks at Daniel. "Oh, don't embarrass the poor boy in front of his girlfriend, hon. He's fine." I guess adults *do* still use the word "girlfriend." Nick pats her leg and makes a face at me. I just want to go sit on his lap. Hop on up there and ask for the world. I want a home with a fireplace in it, Santa. And can you put happiness and love in my stocking? How about adorable little buttercream-icing-eyed babies under the tree this year, Santa? I've been good, I promise. Well, I'm trying . . . I'm doing my best.

For the first time, I feel like the light at the end of the tunnel is actually within reach. I mean, this person who sits here today has a shot. I allow my brain to float up into the clouds a bit. There I am: sitting on the deck, reading a good book, a cup of tea steeping on the teak table. I look up in time to see Daniel glide down the driveway, gracefully flipping the ball in the basket for another two points. I look away from the game and get lost in thought.

"Oh, come on! Traveling! He might as well as have a passport for that trip!" Nick stands, yelling with his fist pumping. Daniel glances back at his dad and then finds me again.

Flash.

That's the image I want to remember forever.

◆

"I'll have the . . . uh . . . Northshore?" I hand the menu back to the waiter at Islands, a Hawaiian-themed chain restaurant located on nearly every beachy corner in Los Angeles. The waiter won't take it from me; he points to the place on the side of the table where the menus are supposed to stay. Daniel takes my menu, smirking as he slips it into the designated spot. How convenient, I think. Why don't we set up a trough and we can all eat from that? God, I sound like Chef Canet. Enough—no more pompous ass. It was shamed into submission, remember? Marilyn orders a salad that has "Wiqui Waqui" in the name, while Nick and Daniel order burgers.

"Anything to drink?" the waiter asks. He's wearing a loud Hawaiian shirt with shorts. It's so cold outside you can see your breath, and this poor kid has to wear a short-sleeved shirt and shorts.

"Diet Coke, please," Marilyn orders.

"Can I get a hot tea?" I ask.

"What do you have on draft?" Daniel asks.

"Bud, Coors, and Heineken," the kid says. Please choose Heineken. Please choose Heineken. At least it's imported.

"I'll have the Heineken," Daniel says. *Pompous ass. Pompous ass.* But I breathe deeply.

"I'll have the Bud," Nick says. The waiter writes down our order and walks away.

Daniel straightens his tie. "What did you guys think of the game?"

"The reffing was pretty nonexistent," Nick says. Kids have continually slowed down as they pass our booth. They can't help themselves. One little boy is staring at Nick from across the restaurant. But Nick seems used to it. Hey, it's not so different from going out with my family.

"Well, the better team won. That's all that matters," I say. Daniel looks over and smiles. My arm is situated underneath his so my body melds under him, protected by him. I lean in to him, and he pats my leg under the table. Nick and Marilyn are talking about the hotel, and I take my opportunity.

"You were great out there," I whisper.

"How can you tell?" Daniel presses.

"You looked happy. In the zone," I say, trying to use a sports reference to help my street cred.

"In the zone, huh?" Daniel smirks, squeezing my hand under the table.

"Tell us about this television show," Marilyn says to me.

"We got picked up for the entire year, so we'll shoot twenty-six episodes. And it's definitely a lot calmer than working at the restaurant," I say.

"Where will they do the filming?" Nick says.

"I just love the Food Network. I love that Paula Deen," Marilyn exclaims. Daniel keeps his hand on my knee under the table.

"The first bit of the show is going to be like a field trip around L.A. Then the rest will be filmed in a kitchen," I say.

"I always wondered if those were real kitchens or not," Marilyn says, sipping her Diet Coke.

"Most of the shows are filmed in New York on a set at the Food Network. Rachael Ray. Emeril. But because my show is all about L.A., we had to find a kitchen that was out here. Stuff kind of fell through, but luckily, my brother is moving to Montana, so we . . . I . . . we transferred his house into my name yesterday. And now we're doing some renovating . . ." I trail off and sip my tea.

Daniel whips his head around and looks at me. "You bought Rascal's house?" His voice is low and calm. Marilyn and Nick are quiet.

"Oh, that's adorable. Your brother's name is Rascal?" Marilyn gushes.

"I can't believe you're buying Rascal's house. How long was I in Oakland?" Daniel asks. His ears are turning red.

"Now, now, son, it sounds like it was just for work," Nick says. Right. Right. Like you, sir, investing in a nice red suit and maybe eight flying reindeer.

"They were saying I'd have to move to New York and film on a set they'd built there. I didn't want to leave L.A., so I thought of this," I say, looking up at Daniel. He's not looking at me. My visions of barbecues, graceful two-pointers, and steeping tea are starting to fade.

"Oh, well, isn't that sweet. See, now, honey, she didn't want to leave L.A.," Marilyn says to Daniel. Daniel nods to his mom, clearly as gently as he can manage.

"Can you . . ." A tiny girl approaches the table and presents Nick with a place mat with a big Santa colored on it—this one dressed in a Hawaiian shirt, like the one Nick is wearing. She has tried to write what she'd like for Christmas around the picture of Santa. But since she's only five or so, the writing looks more like circles and lines completely unconnected. The little girl's mom stands behind her, nervous and hoping the gamble will pay off.

"Oh! Ho! Ho! Ho!" Nick says, twisting around in the booth and swooping the little girl up on his lap. She wriggles with delight. The entire restaurant lets out an audible "awwwww." I watch the little girl and then turn to Daniel. His head is down, and he's staring into his beer. I put my hand on his leg under the table. He looks at me.

"I'm sorry. I should have told you earlier," I whisper as the little girl asks for an American Girl doll and an invisible-ink pen that writes and then disappears—so her little brother can't read it, she explains.

"Are you going to live there?" he whispers back.

"That's the plan. They wanted me to move to New York, and I . . . just . . . I guess— Well, I realized what was important," I say, trying to recall our conversation.

"Finding out what's important doesn't usually involve buying property," Daniel says.

"It does when it means staying. Altering your life," I say, once again using catch phrases to try and trigger something in him that would make him see that I did this for us.

"Altering your life. Altering *our* life is more like it," Daniel says. My stomach has that hollowed-out feeling. I was right. I was completely right. The cost of this house will be too high. Wait. Have I horribly miscalculated what Daniel and I have? Was he some kind of philosophical stepping-stone of a relationship so I'd stop pining for Will? No. No. What am I missing here?

"It's a beautiful house. It wouldn't be the worst house to move into, and if I'm paying the mortgage there, I might as well live there." I move my head so he has to look at me, make eye contact with me. "I didn't want to leave you."

"This is about the whole slaughterhouse thing, isn't it? God, you joked about it before, I just never thought . . . We should have talked about all of this. I should have been in on this."

The little girl gives Nick a quick peck on the cheek and hops down. Nick waves at the mom, and she thanks him. The little girl waves and waves and waves as she walks out of the restaurant.

"Everything okay?" Marilyn asks Daniel and me.

"Yeah, yeah—let's talk about Dad's big day, huh?" Daniel announces.

Nick lights up, but Marilyn looks over at me, concerned. I didn't even think about telling Daniel before I decided about that house. It never entered my mind. Two steps forward, one step back. Sounds a bit too familiar. And it didn't sound all that bad when I was working it out in my head. I make a decision that relies simply on what's important, and I get bitch-slapped for it? This isn't going quite the way I planned. All I knew in that moment was I didn't want to divide my time between New York and Los Angeles; it's not that I wanted Daniel to move in with me or anything. Well, I kind of did, but not officially. I just thought he'd fall in love with the place and decide to stay, night after night. I guess this is an example of the conversation I should have had with him rather than rattling it around in my own head. I'm slowly realizing what a *Lord of the Flies* kind of life I've been leading—looking out for myself, killing my own pigs, and never showing weakness.

Daniel and I are quiet as we walk down that slaughterhouse of a hallway. It seems all the more ridiculous. For the first time, we don't make love, even after the long week apart. Lying in bed later that night, I can't sleep. The chill between us is haunting, and I can't shake that I've maybe made not so much the wrong decision but the far riskier one. Though I don't see how making a decision that will keep us in the same city could be an infraction I should be ashamed of.

"You up?" I ask.

"Yeah," Daniel answers.

"I'm sorry I didn't tell you about the house," I say again.

"I know," Daniel says, turning over to look at me.

"Are we done then? Over?" I quietly ask, assuming he wants nothing further to do with me.

"What are you talking about?" Daniel asks.

"Well, I—" I start.

"Elisabeth, I just want to be in the loop. It's nothing to break up over." Daniel almost laughs.

"Oh. I just . . ." I trail off.

"You didn't buy any other houses while I was gone, did you?" Daniel jokes, trying to lighten the mood. Something about this hits me right in the gut. I close my eyes and try not to see it: Rascal's black eye. Try not to hear it: the constant ringing cell phone of a father attempting to apologize for what he did. Try not to feel it: this pain. The pain I've been running from my whole life.

"No, no more houses," I whisper.

"It was a joke, I'm sorry. I didn't mean to," Daniel says, propping himself up on one arm.

"I didn't . . . I don't have any houses to tell you about, but I . . . think I might have some other stuff," I say, crumpling over. The burning in my throat, the desperate attempt to swallow it—breathe through it.

"What happened?" Daniel asks. I look into his eyes in that second, my eyes used to the darkness of his bedroom. The bluish shadows that fall across his arms and body, the black shadows dipping in the space between us.

I try to force a smile. "I don't know whether to start or end with Dad giving Rascal a black eye," I say.

"You might want to start with it," Daniel says.

chapter thirty-eight

I walk into Beverly bright and early the next morning. I can't help but feel this bizarre civil war of weightless and unburdened, versus vulnerable and exposed. Something about sitting in Daniel's bed and telling him everything has made me uneasy and off balance. I no longer wear my usual suit of armor. There's nothing that Daniel doesn't know. There's no question that I need him. There's no question that I love him. He knows it undeniably. I'm officially in uncharted territory.

I have a busy day—nothing to do with the restaurant. I confirmed that Chef Canet will be in today. Samuel and I agreed to meet here, quit together, and then go over and see the progress that's been made on the house. Mom told me she hired the perfect designer for the kitchen and can't wait to introduce us.

I walk through the dining room. The beautiful dining room. It really is stunning. Louis gives me a small wave. I make it a point to flash a giant smile and an even more gigantic wave. I'm not carrying a flat of anything. No baskets. I push open the door to the kitchen.

"Elisabeth!" Chef Canet stands in the corner with Michel. They're going over the specials for the evening.

"Yes, Chef," I say, walking up to him in my street clothes.

"What's this?" he asks, flipping the lacy collar of my sweater.

"May I speak with you privately, Christian?" I ask. Michel looks absolutely stunned that I would deign to use Chef's first name. Christian, however, immediately senses what's coming and motions for me to step into the back room.

"What is it, Elisabeth?" he asks. His voice is low. I've lucked out. I've somehow managed to get the happy, backslapping Christian on the day I planned to quit. Samuel turns the corner, his eyes scanning the room for us.

"Chef Decoudreau, we are speaking privately. Can you excuse us?" Chef asks.

"This concerns me as well," Samuel says.

Now Chef looks downright scared. "Both of you, eh?" he asks.

"Yes, Chef," I say.

"To the television?" he asks.

"Yes, Chef," I say.

"Today?" he asks, looking at Samuel.

"Yes, Chef," Samuel answers.

"I'm opening a little patisserie at the Grove next year. I thought you two might run it," Christian throws out. Fucking perfect. I can't look at Samuel. I don't know if he's thinking about it. Shit, I don't know if I'm thinking about it.

"No, thank you, Chef," I force out, turning down the job that could have been next up on my five/eleven-year plan.

"No, thank you, Chef," Samuel adds. My face breaks in half with the widest of smiles. I want to take Samuel's hand and skip right out of here, out into the swaying poppy fields that should be right outside the restaurant door. Movie-magic fantasies in a movie-magic town.

"Well, then . . ." Chef says, his hand on his hip, looking dejectedly out into his kitchen.

"Thank you, Chef, for this opportunity," I say.

"Thank you, Chef," Samuel says.

"You leave me with—what—this Julie tonight?" Chef asks.

"She has talent," I say.

Chef smiles. "But it is not in the kitchen, yes?" Samuel and I don't answer. I won't go out talking shit, no matter how much Julie has pissed me off. "Do you know the girl at Bastide?" Chef asks.

"The head pastry chef?" I correct.

"*Oui.* She is talented, no?" Christian asks.

"She's incredible. She's revolutionary," I respond.

"Do you have her number?" Christian asks. Samuel looks to me. Unbelievable.

"Yes, Chef," I answer.

"Get this to me before you go," Chef says, waving his hand in dismissal. Samuel and I thank him again and walk into the kitchen.

"I'll be right out," I say to Samuel. I walk over to the pastry corner and lean on the counter next to Julie, my purse still hanging on my shoulder.

"I'm totally in the weeds now, you know," Julie huffs, bustling around the pastry station. Christian sends over two sous chefs to the pastry corner. They await Julie's command.

"I just wanted to . . ." I dig in my purse, pulling out a recipe box that I've filled with blank index cards, setting it on the counter right next to Julie. I continue, "If you're going to make it in this business, you're going to have to charge the castle on your own horse." I stand tall, pushing myself away from the counter. Julie picks up my gift and sets it beneath the counter. She doesn't make eye contact with me as she begins my recipe for the almond cake with mission figs.

I catch up with Samuel outside the restaurant. No poppy field, but the sweetest chill air wafts past the both of us. Freedom.

"You ready to see the set?" I say, beeping my car unlocked.

"Hells yeah," he says, smiling wide.

I pull up in front of Rascal's—my—Santa Monica house. All the crew trucks are here already. I creak open the front door, and my heart soars. The house is empty, save the ebony hardwood floors. The high ceilings. The huge windows. The arched doorways. It's gorgeous. I walk quickly through the rest of the house. The front bedroom is adorable, perfect for an office or a guest room. Rascal's air mattress rests in the corner with his overnight bag of clothes spilling out across the floor. I walk into the master suite. The rounded Spanish architecture allows the room to feel soft and warm. The hardwoods are flawless. They anchor the room and give it such depth. It's breathtaking. I walk over to the window and get my first look at the incredible ocean view.

"You coming?" Samuel yells. I turn away from the window and take a last look around the master bedroom. Once Daniel sees this house, he'll certainly want to spend more time here. A sleepover—that's all I ask.

I walk through the rest of the house, finding the kitchen. I am stunned. It's beautiful. I'm excited to meet the designer Mom hired, and on such short notice. What she's done is truly a miracle.

The entire room is painted a pale robin's-egg blue. The exposed beams are a deep chocolate brown. The crown molding and trim are a creamy white. The camera setup occupies half of the room, cords and cameras and a bank of computers. I look up and see about twenty lighting rigs hanging over the room. I can feel the heat on my face. There is a lovely island made from that same deep chocolate butcher block in the middle of the room, with a stovetop on one side and a sink on the other. Samuel and the culinary producer are going over the ingredients for the hot-cocoa recipe we're going to do in the next show. Samuel's whole body looks loose and easy, his shoulders relaxed, his smile constant. The culinary producer is wearing the headset and carrying a clipboard she's never without. Paul and Hunter are sitting behind the bank of computers, and I can hear them running the show opener over and over again. There's more counter space on the wall behind me, along with a pair of convection ovens. All along the top of the wall are old black-and-white photographs.

I look closely. They're of us. My family. The classics. Rascal and me—me trapped in that godforsaken ice cream bucket, Rascal giggling wildly. Dad in his official navy portrait. Mom posing on a jetty looking like a pinup girl. There are a few new ones I've never seen. Mom and Dad when they were probably younger than I am now. Rascal's little curly mop of a head behind a sea of wheat. All four of us together in some shot we did for a retrospective a few years back. The last one is of me. I'm sitting on Dad's lap with a red sweater on, and it's sliding up enough to see my little belly. I'm wearing some horrible quilted 1970s pants and no shoes. It looks like I was trying to talk, because my mouth is twisted, neither smiling nor still. Dad is in the very corner of the shot, and he's looking down at me. The look on his face is . . . the look. The caramel/molasses look. I stare at the picture, going deeper and deeper in.

"How do you like it?" Mom asks, coming up behind me. She takes in the picture I'm looking at.

"It's stunning. It's beyond stunning. The designer—when can I meet her?" I ask, hugging her.

"I did it, darling," Mom confesses, her hands folded in front of her. I look around again at the kitchen. No brass plaques. No "aged" armoires. No textbook, uninspired Zen gardens. I look at the pictures, so lovingly chosen. Not one misstep. Mom's true style.

"Oh, Mom, it's gorgeous. How did you? *When* did you?" I say, still standing with my mouth agape.

Mom smiles. "Rascal called from New York, and I just thought, why not?"

"This is just . . . it's . . . I'm speechless," I say, hugging her tightly.

"I think I wore poor Paul out with all of my questions," Mom says, looking back at the bank of computers. He flashes her a genuine smile. Mom blushes slightly.

"Whatever it is you did, Mom, it's . . . I just can't imagine a place more perfect," I say.

"I'm glad you like it, darling," Mom says, patting my back. I inhale deeply. Her scent. A slight hint of rose.

"You are going to make it to the charity event this week, aren't you, darling? It's at the Mayers' in Beverly Hills. I was also wondering if Daniel might donate a couple of tickets to one of those basketball games. I'm sure it'd be quite popular. Nevertheless, I'd love it if both of you could make it," Mom says, her organizer flipped open on the butcher-block countertop. She's more at home here than I am right now. I wonder if she's heard from Dad. Do I ask? Do I ruin the moment? Would she tell me if she had?

"Absolutely," I say.

"What are you going to donate?" Mom asks, her pen at the ready.

"Hmmm. What about a backstage pass? A tour . . . a seat at the picnic table for one of the shots . . . something like that?" I ask as I take in the rest of the house. I can hear the fountain from here. The flora and fauna framing the house is lush and calming.

"Are you thinking of moving in here, darling?" Mom asks, her face slightly giving away her desire for me to do just that.

"I've already hired movers," I answer, knowing I've done the right thing. Why would Daniel and I spend our nights in that slaughterhouse when we could have this refuge waiting for us? I know he feels like he should have been in the loop on this house, but I wonder if he can get past that long enough to appreciate it as much as I do. I wonder if I'm not the only one in this relationship with a bit of an ego problem.

"Are you bringing a guest? To the Mayers', I mean," Mom clarifies, inadvertently setting the wheels in motion on another invitation altogether.

"Daniel. I'll invite Daniel Sullivan," I say. Samuel comes across the kitchen.

"Oh, Samuel, lovely to see you. How's Margot?" Mom asks.

"She's— Well, she's . . ." Samuel trails off.

"She's miserable, right?" Mom finishes.

"Yes, I believe she is. Which brings me to— Elisabeth, Margot wanted me to ask if you and Daniel would like to come over for a Christmas Eve/housewarming/'get this baby out' dinner," Samuel says.

"Sounds great," I say.

"I'll tell her to deal you guys in, then. Look at us, hanging out on a school night," Samuel says, and laughs.

chapter thirty-nine

The pilot for my brand-new television show is airing right now. I'm not watching.

I'm at the Hollywood Christmas Parade.

That's right. Freezing my ass off to watch B-list celebrities drive by in vintage cars while we listen to marching bands perform the one song they all know: a cross between "The Battle Hymn of the Republic" and the theme from *Star Wars*.

"You know I'm Tivoing it, right?" Daniel says as he rubs his hands together, trying to get warm. Marilyn has a blanket over her; she's sitting comfortably in one of those soccer-field chairs everyone goes on about. After sitting in one tonight, I want to decorate my entire living room with them. They're so damn comfortable and convenient. Cup holders in the chairs! Truly inspired.

"I know. Maybe we can even watch it later. You know, after we watch your dad fly down Hollywood Boulevard in a giant sleigh," I say. Where did that sentence even come from? And said from a soccer-field chair while getting loaded on hot toddies, no less. Life is good.

"When do you find out how you did?" Marilyn asks.

"We'll know by tomorrow what the numbers are," I say. Meaning, by tomorrow I'll know that the show has tanked and

I'm going to be burdened with the deed to Rascal's house and no job to pay for it. Awesome.

◆

I couldn't sleep last night at all. Paul and Donna both called, letting me know that everything was looking great. They didn't have any numbers yet but promised to get them to me as soon as possible. Paul assures me everything is fine. Daniel and I dropped his parents off at the airport early this morning. Aside from worrying about how the pilot fared, this charity event has been weighing on us all day. Daniel has changed his shirt three times already, each one looking identical to the last. He's settled on a crisp white shirt, the silvery tie I bought him, and an impeccably cut suit that the UCLA head coach urged him to buy. Of course his mom noticed his need for a new suit first. The last time Daniel met the majority of my family, he was dressed in jeans and a T-shirt. Not quite the first impression he wanted to make. I'm also not completely over my fear of a replay of that night with Avery. I know Daniel is a good man, but since I've prized wit above all else, it's nights like these that test the very foundation of my supposed metamorphosis.

We pull up in Daniel's SUV to the monstrous McMansion just off of Sunset Boulevard in Beverly Hills. I am hit with the irony of the venue: Children of the Homeless and the biggest house I've ever seen. The sight of red-vested valets, Mercedes after Bentley pulling up in front of a house that could be used in a reality show to house all of the *Bachelor* hopefuls, has made Daniel especially tense. The Grecian gown I've chosen is stunning. A dark silvery-gray one-shoulder affair with beaded details at the waist and neckline. My hair is in a messy updo that took an hour to look windswept. My teeth are quietly chattering as I try to look effortlessly gorgeous. I'll be fine once I get inside, but for now I make do with the warmth of how Daniel looks at me while we make our way up the grand staircase into the mansion.

"You look dashing, Mr. Sullivan," I say, kissing him.

"Why, thank you," he says, grinning. Holding him, I can feel that he's tense.

"Now, if you turn your back, they'll shoot you with a tranquilizer dart, drag you off to some back room, and proceed to eat you," I say, linking my arm with his as we stand before the front door, which is decked in garlands of magnolia wrapped in copper-colored ribbon.

"So look out for tranquilizer darts," he says. He holds my hand tightly as we open the door and step onto the marble floor of the foyer.

The Mayers are a husband-and-wife producing team whose projects usually feature car chases, fiery explosions, and huge box office. Big money. Big *new* money. The foyer is anchored by a twenty-foot Christmas tree that is decorated in what must be a designer-themed color scheme of copper and the deepest of reds. More garlands of magnolia run up and down the sweeping double staircase, forcing me to stare at the huge Baccarat chandelier that hangs above. I watch as Daniel takes it all in. I squeeze his hand tightly as we approach a small blond woman at a table right in front.

"Elisabeth Page and Daniel Sullivan," Daniel says. The woman looks up. Her age-defying pulled-tight skin holds up better from afar: up close, she is terrifying. Her perfectly matched red and green outfit is absolutely adorable. Her blond bob shimmers in the glow of the twinkle lights. Her desperation to stay young is palpable.

"Oh my God! Elisabeth Page? I just loved your show last night! Barbara? Barbara? It's Elisabeth Page! From the Food Network!" Now the little blond woman is causing a scene. Daniel tucks his arm around my waist, bringing me in closer. He beams down at me. So proud. I soften and take a deep breath. Barbara comes over, and they ogle me just long enough to make me completely uncomfortable. I say "thank you" over and over again. They tell me all of their stories about the Hollywood Bowl and how they are *totally* going to make those red velvet cupcakes for the upcoming charity bake sale next week benefiting Music in the Classrooms. The line grows behind us.

"Thank you so much. May we?" I motion toward the inner sanctum of the gaudy foyer filled with the Hollywood elite and the waiters who look like runway models.

"Oh, of course! Of course! Please say hello to your mother for me, honey," the blond woman says as she hands us two tiny Santas. A door prize of sorts. Daniel and I walk past her, holding our Santas awkwardly. His eyes dart around the foyer as he pockets his Santa.

"Is that a Santa in your pocket, or are you just happy to see me?" I joke nervously, looking around the room in search of my family. I love that Daniel is here with me in theory, but I can't help feeling awkward about his presence. I guess I'm just globally worried right now.

"You probably want to wait until people have had a few drinks to start with those kinds of jokes." Daniel rests his hand on the small of my back as we wind our way through the crowded room. I scan the room for Mom. No doubt, she's positioned herself in some omniscient perch that only a World War II sniper could sniff out.

"The food is back through there. The liquor is probably back there, too," I say.

"Darling!" I hear the hounds. I stand up straight and look at Daniel. There is terror in his eyes.

"Mom, you look ravishing," I trill. She is wearing a black floor-length dress, simple and flowing. She leans in and kisses me, wiping off her lipstick, as she always does. She pulls back and takes Daniel in.

"Daniel, so nice to see you again," Mom says, giving him the most polite of hugs.

"And you, Mrs. Page. Always a pleasure," Daniel says, his voice tight and formal. I'm not breathing.

"Oh, please. Call me Ballard," she says.

"Ballard, then. It's a pleasure. I brought those tickets you asked about," Daniel says, passing her an envelope with two front-row seats to the UCLA season opener.

"Oh, how wonderful. Thank you so much," Mom says, taking the envelope and kissing him on the cheek. Her smudge of lipstick is visible, and she looks to me, then to Daniel. Daniel leans down a touch. She gracefully raises her hand and wipes the smudge from his cheek.

"Thank you again for inviting me," Daniel says, straightening back up to full height.

"My pleasure," Mom says.

"Mom, would you like us to get you some champagne while we're back there?" I ask. There's an edge to her tonight, a hollowness. Her eyes are darting across the room. In my mind, I replay the several thousand phone messages that Rascal and I have gotten from Dad and wonder what his path to redemption looks like with Mom. I would think that there is no forgiveness for Dad without Rascal allowing the first steps. And rightfully so.

"Oh, no, dear. Thank you, though. I'm going to find your brother—he's here somewhere. He's brought that unfortunately named girl . . . Dinah." Mom gives me the most subtle of raised eyebrows. The fact that she remembered Dinah's name at all is a huge vote of confidence for the girl. I take this opportunity to pull Daniel away and inch closer to the bar.

"Your mom is nice," Daniel says.

"Don't let her fool you. She's loading the tranquilizer dart as we speak," I say. Daniel and I squeeze through the bevy of Hollywood types milling around the room, staring at us that two seconds longer than normal, making sure we're not "somebody."

My heart begins racing. My one hope for the evening is to somehow be genuine through all of this. I watch as Daniel looks people up and down, at the clothing right out of a comic strip of what wealthy people dress like. Am I simply used to all of it? I feel as if I'm seeing it all for the first time through his eyes. What must he think of me? For all of my posturing that I'm not part of this world, here I am, air-kissing with the best of them. He's straightened his tie approximately fifty-seven times since we first entered. I take his hand and hold it in mine.

"Elisabeth?" Rascal is standing next to the long buffet table. He's holding a tiny plate filled to the brim with appetizers I'm at a loss to identify. My eyes fall on The Girl. Rascal spears a crab something from a serving tray and finds a spot for it on the last corner of his plate. His black eye is now a shade of purple-y yellow. Daniel doesn't react at all to the eye. He extends his hand to Rascal, who shifts his plate to shake Daniel's hand back. We all wait for Rascal to introduce us to The Girl.

"For fuck's sake, Rascal. Hi, I'm Dinah." The Girl extends her hand to me. Rascal turns to her with a full mouth, seeming more than a little indignant. Ohhh, I like this one. Her hair is jet black and cuts across her forehead à la Bettie Page. She's wearing a lavender shift dress with an ill-fitting shoulder-padded blazer. Dinah looks like she's been dressed for the prom by her parents—in the 1980s.

"Hi, I'm Rascal's sister, Elisabeth, and this is Daniel Sullivan," I say, trying to be the good one.

"Nice to meet you," Dinah says, tugging at her blazer.

Rascal melodramatically swallows his crab appetizer. "Jesus, give a guy a break," he announces. We all drop into an awkward silence. "You talk to Mom yet?" he says, leading us over to one of the small cocktail tables set up in the main room. There are copper and deep red silk tablecloths on the tables, finished off with centerpieces of hurricane lamps with copper glass ornaments and threaded red ribbons.

"Yeah, she tagged us first thing," I say.

"Son?" Dad approaches our table. He looks like a wreck—his hair is unkempt; he has the beginnings of a beard and mustache. He's tried to dress up for the event, but the clothes are wrinkled. Rascal whips around, nearly dropping his plate. Daniel and I stand back, trying to blend in, disappear. Dinah looks to me and Daniel and, taking our cue, stands back.

"Hey, Pop." Rascal barely gets the words out as he sets his plate carefully on the table.

"You didn't return my phone calls." Dad steps forward. He takes a quick glance at me; I immediately look to Rascal. Dad takes in the black eye. His whole body deflates.

"I didn't know . . . I don't know what you could say, Dad, that would make . . . could make this go away," Rascal says, motioning at his eye.

"I need to tell you," Dad begins, holding Rascal's novel out in front of him. The novel is worn with reading, rereading, analyzing, dog-earing, highlighting, and annotating. Rascal looks at the novel in its present state. I can see the magnitude of what Dad is saying hit him.

"I need to ask you some questions," Dad begins, opening up Rascal's novel to an already designated page.

"Okay." Rascal's voice is quiet.

"I . . . You talk here about greatness. I just wanted to ask if you could understand what it was we were going for. That there is greatness in the attempt—something in the trying. That in trying, we set up a certain scaffolding that a new generation can use to climb to heights we only dreamed of. I . . . I can't take back what I did, son. I needed . . . I fucked up. Shit, I've been fucking up for decades. I just . . . I needed to see you again. Needed to . . . I'm . . . I'm so sorry." Dad looks at Rascal. My entire body is still. I never thought I'd see the day. The day when Dad finally saw Rascal as a man.

Rascal's face reddens, and he turns away, obviously searching for something, anything, to say. He opens his mouth to speak, but nothing—he is silent. Dad pulls him in for a hug, not letting him go, stroking the mop of curls. I blink back tears, willing them to evaporate. I look up at Daniel, and he's doing the same thing. Dinah wipes her nose on the shoulder of the lavender blazer. Rascal and Dad hug until Dad breaks it and holds Rascal at arm's length in front of him. Dad takes the book and holds it out to Rascal with a pen. "Will you sign it, son?"

Rascal's face loses all color, and I hear him take a small gasp. He takes the book and the pen and signs his name, clearly in a haze. Dad watches him. Then, as if he can't help it, Dad raises his hand to Rascal's eye and just breaks down. I see Mom approach the table. Rascal and Dad stand face-to-face. Rascal is focused, but his nose is red, and there is definite moisture in his eyes. He wipes at them as if they're stinging wasps. I notice a few people glancing in our direction. Daniel is still, just taking it all in. His arm tightly wound around my waist.

"Okay, Dad . . . okay . . ." Rascal manages, nodding and nodding. Mom takes a few more steps forward. Dad notices her. They have a deep, seemingly hour-long moment of eye contact.

Just them, in a world by themselves. The first step has been taken to forgiveness, and in that moment it's as if Mom conveyed the hope to Dad that there could be more. Dad turns to me. My mouth is curling and shaking; I'm biting my lip so much I can taste blood. I'm wringing my hands as Dad approaches. Daniel stands at my side.

"Hi, my sweet girl. Come here," Dad says, pulling me to him. His arms envelop every bit of me, and I tuck myself in to the crook of his neck, smelling that same smell—the forest that's steeped in pipe smoke. "You made a lunch box, just like when you were little," Dad says softly. It's one of those moments that stabs at my throat, my heart, and that pantheon of old photographs playing in my mind. The man I thought I knew just said something I would have staked my life on his never uttering. My mind is officially blown, and the embarrassing need to intellectualize what's happening pulls me in to a schizophrenic seizure of trying to understand the gravity of it all instead of letting my dad hug me. I feel a sting of agonizing joy and raw emotion. I tighten my arms around Dad. I can feel him convulsing, mumbling that he's sorry, repeating that he'll work to earn my trust back. He doesn't let go, and I have to be in it—force myself to get lost in him, settle in to him, *let* him hug me. Let him love me. He breaks away and stands back, taking us all in. Then he slowly turns to Daniel. "Ben Page," he says, extending his hand to Daniel.

"Daniel Sullivan," Daniel says.

"You're . . ." Dad trails off, his voice still a bit raspy.

"Here with Elisabeth," Daniel finishes. Dad turns to Mom, then to Rascal—a look that says, "Just how long have I been gone?" Please don't ask what happened to Will. Please don't ask what happened to Will. Wait. Why? Why not? Where is all this coming from?

"And you're . . ." Dad says, turning to Dinah.

"Dinah Larter. I'm here with Rascal," she says, following Daniel's cue.

"Nice meeting you both," Dad says.

In the silence that follows, we all become a tad embarrassed about our little love fest. I'm sure some aspiring actor/waiter can't wait to get home and blog about it. The flood of emotion was way over the top, and none of us knows how to deal with the aftermath. Do we keep hugging? Do we talk about the changes and the future? Do we frolic arm in arm up and down the magnolia-draped sweeping staircases? Dad excuses himself in search of a tissue and probably a Scotch. Rascal takes Dinah's hand and walks toward the auction tables. Mom greets another well-wisher. I stand there feeling like the wind has been knocked out of me, and more than a little exposed.

"Do you want to see how the silent-auction item is going?" Daniel asks.

"I sure got lucky the last time I did," I say, squeezing Daniel's hand, looking at him to see how he fared through the whole family drama. He looks a bit dazed, but his demeanor has softened. He asks if he can get us some drinks. I tell him I'd love a glass of champagne and that I'll meet him back by the silent-auction tables.

* Baskets filled with exotic lotions and a gift certificate for a stay at the Golden Door in Escondido, CA: eleven bidders
* Two tickets to the UCLA season opener: twelve bidders
* An autographed football along with a weekend in San Francisco and fifty-yard-line tickets to a 49ers game: two bidders

* An exalted bottle of wine paired with a five-day
  jaunt through the Napa Valley: nine bidders
* Signed first-edition Ben Page: nineteen bidders
* Signed first-edition Rascal Page: sixteen bidders
* A day on the set of *Life Is Sweet with Elisabeth Page:*
  thirteen bidders

I snatch up my clipboard, skimming the names. I don't
know *any* of these people. The writing is all different. Is this
some kind of scam? If it is, it's quite an elaborate one.

"You're not bidding on that one, are you, dear?" A woman in
a low-cut white silk gown sidles over to me, cradling her bubbling flute of champagne.

"Oh, no. I was just . . ." I set the clipboard down. Why
wouldn't I bid on this, you pruney old bat?

"Good. I just put in a bid I hoped would knock out all
the competition," she says, sipping her champagne. I pick up
my clipboard again and look at the last name on the list. This
woman has bid a thousand dollars. For a day with me.

"I think it's lovely," I say.

"It seems to be a hot ticket tonight," she says. I'm a hot
ticket tonight? I'm a hot ticket? And yet she had no idea who I
was. Interesting.

"Always the height of efficiency, I see."

I whip around, almost dropping the clipboard. Will. His
gray dress shirt is open at the collar; no tie. We are a perfect
matching pair—little salt-and-pepper-shaker outfits. I smooth
my gown and wish I could magically change it to any other
color besides the exact color of Will's shirt.

"No one told me you were coming," I say.

"Is Finn MacCool here?" Will says, sipping easily at his
drink.

"The mythical Irish character? Uh, noooo, he's sadly still entrenched in folklore," I parry.

"You know who I'm talking about," Will presses.

"Of course he's here," I say. Will's eyes flare, just as they did when he was eight years old. I'm positive he's going to call me a stupid fuck-it any minute.

I look past Will and see his mom, Anne. She's wearing a bright red gown that accentuates her supermodelian height. Her blond hair is cut short, and her alabaster skin is as flawless as ever. She looks healthy and glowing.

"Elisabeth! Oh, sweetheart, you look beautiful," Anne says, kissing me on the cheek and wiping away the lipstick.

"It's so good to see you. How was Aspen?" I ask, not knowing what to say, feeling the heat of Will and the deafening pendulum swing, not knowing when Daniel is going to round that corner with a glass of champagne and a confused look on his face about why I'm standing here chatting with my ex-lover.

"Boring, darling. Utterly boring," Anne says, raising her mineral water in a mocking toast.

"It was only boring because you refused to take on the Scrabble master," Will says, back on his best behavior.

"Do you listen to yourself sometimes?" I say easily. Anne barks with laughter as she pulls Will in close, ruffling his hair. I melt a little in that moment. Beautiful. Just beautiful. Will is rocking back and forth. Over his shoulder, I see Daniel and Dad walking toward us. Daniel is carrying a flute of bubbling champagne and a bottle of Heineken. Dad has his usual—Scotch neat. They're talking about something. Daniel is gesticulating with his beer-holding hand—over there . . . over there. Dad is nodding and agreeing. Daniel hands me my champagne and takes a long swig from his beer, easing his other arm around my waist. Will, quite out of character, stares as Daniel's arm slides around my body. Dad eases in beside me. Daniel stares at Will, taking another long swig of his beer. Dad is checking the clipboards. Mine catches his eye.

"Will Houghton," Will says, extending his hand slowly to Daniel.

"Yes, W-I-L-L. We've met," Daniel says, shaking Will's hand. I see Will wince.

"Oh, that's right. I didn't recognize you in a suit," Will says, taking his hand back, shaking it out a bit.

"Yes, that would be confusing," Daniel says, wrapping his arm tightly back around my waist, languidly sipping his beer. Will tilts his head just enough, and a wide smile breaks across his face—the polite, upper-class equivalent of slapping an expensive glove across Daniel's cheek.

"Daniel Sullivan, this is my mom, Anne Houghton," Will introduces, easily remembering Daniel's full name. Daniel extends his hand to Anne.

"Nice to meet you, Daniel," she says politely. I watch them try to figure out exactly who the other one is. We all stand in awkward silence. I know that Will is behaving like a jealous brat, but I can't help feeling exhausted by all of this change. I know that things are better than I ever could have imagined. I guess I just thought that "better" would feel like home right away. Instead, I find myself in this odd purgatory, much like a goldfish having to assimilate to a new aquarium by spending time in the safety of a plastic bag from the pet store. It's unnerving how much I seem to like my plastic bag; I'm in no rush, apparently, to fully dive into the new aquarium, despite the beautiful waters just beyond.

Will breaks the silence. "Mom, can I get you anything?"

"No, sweetheart. I'm perfect," she says, pulling him close.

The introductions and well wishes continue as Dinah, Rascal, and Mom join our circle. Will and I make eye contact in the stir of it all. Something has changed in us. There's a quick moment when I know that what's changed is what's missing. It's funny, but we were each the worst and the most beautiful thing about the other. We stumbled through life together as two cripples would, leaning on each other and grasping for something to steady ourselves. But we've come to find out that we weren't holding each other up; we were dragging each other down with our own emotional handicaps. Will looks at me once more, and I look away, curling in to Daniel. Daniel pulls me close. Time to think about moving into that aquarium.

The next week Anne will move into Will's Hollywood Hills home. The next morning Rascal will leave for Montana. Dad will see him off, patting the trunk of his car as he drives away.

chapter forty

Our numbers were huge.

We got a nice slot on Tuesday nights at eight P.M. The last few days have been a frenzy of trying to fit in to this new life. I don't miss the restaurant as much as I thought I would. I also don't miss Will as much as I thought I would. Funny how you can get used to not having things you thought you couldn't live without.

By the time I walk down Slaughterhouse Hallway, I'm already getting excited about the holidays, beginning with Samuel and Margot's housewarming/Christmas Eve/get this baby out dinner party tonight. Before I get to Daniel's door, I scroll through my e-mails and see the confirmation that the movers have successfully completed the job of moving me into the Santa Monica house and have left the extra key under the mat. I'm excited to tell Daniel, but then I have a slight twinge. He's never fully warmed to the idea of the house. I slide my key into the lock and let myself into Daniel's apartment.

"Surprise!" Daniel pops out from behind a six-foot-tall Christmas tree wearing a Santa hat.

"Oh, sweetie, it's gorgeous!" I say, running over and hugging him. The tree is bare, save for the white twinkle lights Daniel has carefully woven in and out of the lush green branches.

"What do you think?" he asks, fluffing it up a bit with his hands.

"It's just lovely," I say, kissing him. Again and again.

"But wait, there's more!" Daniel says, running into the kitchen. He comes out with a washed Gatorade bottle with a bent paper clip speared through it, and hangs it on the tree.

"Awwww, our first ornament," I say. Daniel hustles back into the kitchen and emerges with a pitcher of water. He pops and creaks into a kneeling position, busying himself with pruning and twisting off stray branches, finally pouring the water into the tree stand. I just watch. The curve of his body. That snippet of bare skin from his belt to where his shirt has fallen forward on his back. The mountain range of muscle on his long arms as he pours the water. I put out my hand and smooth that patch of forbidden skin exposed to the light. Mine to touch. Daniel turns his head from underneath the tree branches and smiles. He takes the pitcher back into the kitchen, emerging once more with it filled.

"Thirsty little sucker," Daniel says. He bends back down and pours the water in. Something seems off about him tonight.

"What's going on? You're . . ." I trail off.

"Nothing. Well, nothing big," Daniel says, leaning on his good knee to get himself into a standing position.

"Nothing *big*?" I repeat, getting a bit nervous.

"I know it's last-minute, it being Christmas Eve and all." Daniel hesitates. "I've decided to go home for Christmas," he says, almost into the pitcher.

Aaand *kerplop*. The other shoe has officially dropped.

"What? Wait . . . why? I thought you were going to stay here—didn't we . . . You said the basketball schedule was too tight. You were going to celebrate with us at my parents' house. Did something happen? Oh, God, my family's too weird. They're too weird, aren't they? When did you decide? God, it could have been . . ." I'm babbling. The flickering lights on the tree are shadowing Daniel's face—on . . . off . . . on . . . off.

"No, they're not too weird." Daniel lets his hands drop to his sides, his head bowing slightly.

"What, then? Did I do something?" I ask, gently taking his hand.

"I was . . . That party was just overwhelming, that's all," Daniel admits.

"Where is this coming from? You didn't say anything—you never said anything," I stutter.

"I know. It wasn't the time, and I didn't know how I felt, but it got me thinking." Daniel pauses, carefully choosing his words. "I just wouldn't fit in at your parents' house at Christmas. I'm sorry, I know they're your family, but . . ."

"They *are* too crazy for you? You can tell me. God, I knew it. It was just—" Daniel cuts in. "They're not too crazy. I thought it was awesome how your dad and Rascal—I mean, that's not it."

"Then what is it?" I ask.

"My parents took you to Islands, Elisabeth. *Islands*. You ate chicken soft tacos, and my dad drank Budweiser. Shit, I drink Budweiser. Your parents' friends have valets and servers. My dad is Santa Claus. That was his goal. To *be* Santa Claus. Those people at that event—I've never even been around . . . I couldn't even open my mouth." Daniel pauses again, fighting with himself. "You know, I could have handled all that. It was the fact that—" He breaks off, his eyes darting around, connecting with mine and then darting away again.

"The fact that—" I press.

"Will," Daniel says, his eyes connecting with mine.

"What about him?" I say, the hairs on the back of my neck standing on end. Daniel crosses and recrosses his arms across his wide chest, searching for the words. All the while, I grow angrier and angrier. We're back here again? With the Will stuff? "Why are we even talking about Will?"

"It's not . . . I know you've come to some resolution about Will, and I know you love me. It's not that. You have to understand that Will would no sooner welcome me into your world voluntarily than he would lie down in front of oncoming traffic," Daniel explains. Will actually did that back in high school. I won't mention this.

"He doesn't have to welcome you into my world," I say.

"No, I know that. But he does have to take his cue from you. The fact is, you're still tolerating his bullshit. And I know that he's part of your family's history and all that, but . . ."

"But?" I say.

"But he's an asshole to me. And that should matter to you," Daniel finishes.

"It *does* matter to me," I say, mixing defensiveness with anger—a wonderful mix, by the way.

"Then where were you when he was talking about not recognizing me because I was wearing a suit?" Daniel says, his voice strong but heartbreakingly trying to soldier on.

"I thought you wanted to handle it. You *did* handle it. You were perfect," I say.

"I shouldn't have had to handle it on my own. I guess I just felt separate—distanced from you by that much more," Daniel says.

"But how does this lead to you going home for Christmas?" I ask, beginning to panic.

Daniel's face reddens, and he looks like he wants to say a thousand things all at one time. "You buy houses on a whim, Elisabeth! Rascal doesn't need the house anymore? Need the *house* anymore? My parents have been paying off their mortgage for twenty-seven years. I just don't understand sometimes.

I felt like I was . . . like not even my posture was good enough. I know you hate this—I know you think you're not part of it—but you are. Maybe more than you think." I feel like my legs are going to give way. I know what he's saying is true; I know it. I feared that once we got past all the smoke and mirrors that surround me, he would arrive at the juicy center of the Real Me and be met with a hollow void instead of the surprise bubble-gum treat. I knew being seen naked meant being exposed as imperfect. I knew I should have played it safer.

"I don't want you to feel uncomfortable—I mean, holidays are about family," I say, looking at the tree, the Gatorade bottle hanging askew. I grind my teeth and feel myself shutting down emotionally.

"Elisabeth . . ." Daniel steps closer to me.

"When do you leave?" I ask, not wanting to know the answer. Originally, I hadn't expected to spend Christmas with Daniel, figuring he had family of his own. But when he said he was staying, I allowed myself. I hoped. I didn't have to believe it to see it. Funny.

"I leave tomorrow morning. Seven A.M.," Daniel says.

"Tomorrow morning," I say.

"You've got to give me time," Daniel says.

"Give you time?" I say.

"I love you," Daniel says, kissing me gently.

I stand back from him. I don't understand. You've seen parts of me that are not perfect, and you still love me? "What?" I ask.

"I love you," Daniel repeats.

"Then why are you leaving?" I ask.

Daniel searches for an answer. "This is just not how we do things in Kansas," he says, almost to himself.

"So, the 'what's important' speech only works if you're from Kansas?" I ask, my voice rising.

"What?" Daniel asks.

"I love you," I say, as if it just occurred to me. This is what it feels like to do something completely unsafe and spur-of-the-moment because you want to be near the one you love. When I committed to buying Rascal's house, I didn't think. I didn't calculate. In that moment, I knew I had to do whatever I could, out of love. It was a gut reaction I couldn't control. "I bought a house. I bought a fucking house, Daniel. I don't just buy houses like I buy shoes, despite what you may think. I never thought I'd buy a house at all. I certainly never wanted one. All I knew in that moment was I couldn't stand being away from you," I say.

"Elisabeth—" Daniel tries.

"I fucked up at the charity auction. It's not the first time, and it won't be the last. I'm so sorry I hurt you by not defending you in front of Will, but I didn't want to emasculate you by coming to your rescue. Shit, I'll stab him in the neck next time I see him if that'll prove it to you," I say. Daniel barks out a laugh, and it breaks the tension in the room. I stand there, exhausted and smiling. "This is scary and overwhelming for both of us— for *both* of us. I'm not asking you to move in with me, Daniel. I'm just asking you to love me as big and messy as I love you."

"I should have been in on it. We're a team," Daniel presses.

"I thought you could put up a basketball hoop in the driveway," I say.

"I need to know that I can take care of you."

"That's what all this is about?" I ask.

"I don't know if I could put up a basketball hoop at a house I didn't buy," Daniel whispers.

"You have a lot to learn about being a team, then," I say. Daniel is silent. I continue, "I want to go to Samuel and Margot's dinner party/housewarming thing. It will give you some time.

Give *me* some time," I say, finding my purse and fishing my keys out.

"I'll go with you," Daniel offers.

"No, please. I'll go by myself," I say, kissing him gently. Daniel holds me close, his eyes imploring, sad and frustrated. He kisses me once more. I open the door and then close it tightly behind me.

chapter forty-one

My BlackBerry rings from the pocket of the jeans I'm wearing. I can't feel my face. I dig in my pocket as I walk back out to my car on my way to Samuel and Margot's.

"Merry Christmas Eve, darling!" Mom says. "I've planned an impromptu Christmas Eve at our house. I hope you don't mind. Rascal's driven in from Montana." Rascal lives and dies by the open road. Any normal person would have flown here for the holiday festivities, but the highway is like therapy for Rascal.

"Remember Samuel and Margot invited me over to their house for Christmas Eve?" I say. Usually, our family saves the festivities for Christmas Day.

"Your father and Rascal have spoken, darling," Mom begins.

"And?" I ask.

"It seems your father will be joining us for Christmas dinner." Mom's voice is tentative. She's obviously testing the waters.

"That sounds lovely," I say. I relax a little, trusting Rascal's decision completely.

"So you'll be in Montecito on Christmas, correct?"

"Bright and early," I say.

"Will Daniel be joining us for dinner?" Mom asks.

"Oh . . . he decided to celebrate Christmas at home. He's flying out tomorrow morning," I say.

"I never got a chance to speak with him properly, darling. We'll set up a lunch with him soon. Is that all right?" she asks.

"He'd love it," I say, aching and fearing that my big, messy love is too much for the boy from Kansas.

I sign off with Mom and head over to the local 7-Eleven, the only store open on Christmas Eve. I buy a bottle of white wine.

"Welcome! Welcome!" Margot opens the door or, should I say, her stomach opens the door.

"My God, woman," I say, contorting around her belly to give her a big hug. I hand the wine to Samuel as Oberon wags his tail, hoping to be next in line for some attention; he looks healthy. I kiss Samuel on both cheeks and take in their new home.

"Where's Daniel?" Margot asks.

"He decided to go home for Christmas. He sends his regards," I say, smiling. My voice is smooth and mechanical. I don't add that I fear our relationship is over and that while I sit here enjoying wine and good conversation, my boyfriend is packing up and getting as far away from my crazy ass as possible.

"I wish you'd seen the place before," Margot says, handing me a glass of wine. The large living room is decorated with over-stuffed couches in beautiful shades of red and brown. At present, however, the entire room revolves around a giant birthing pool set up in the dead center. Quite the icebreaker at parties, I expect.

Samuel brings out a cheese plate and sets it on the leather ottoman to the left of the birthing pool. He offers me a place on the couch. I walk around the birthing pool and sit. I can't help but take it in. It looks like a grown-up kiddie pool. Put some jets in this puppy, and you've got yourself an indoor Jacuzzi.

"We gutted the kitchen. Samuel's little sandbox, I call it," Margot says later on as we finish a beautiful Sierra apple tarte tatin with crème fraîche. Samuel is quiet, cradling a mug of yogi tea, taking in his wife.

"Do you need anything? More wine?" Margot lifts herself from her chair and doubles over. "Aaaaaaaarghhhhhh!" She holds her belly, and Samuel leaps up from the couch.

"What? What is it?" His voice cracks.

"I think my water broke, baby. My water broke. Call Joanne! Call the midwife! Oh my God." Margot looks up at Samuel. The purest expression. Love in all of its big, messy glory. Samuel leads her to the bathroom.

◆

I start to disentangle myself from what's going to be a pretty intimate affair, but Margot implores me to stay. She says she'll need the company because giving birth is probably going to take most of the night. She takes my hand and says, "Please?" I realize I have nowhere else to go. All of my belongings are in boxes at Rascal's house—I should probably stop referring to it as Rascal's. I'm not quite ready to go back to Daniel's. I could drive up the coast to Montecito, but I wouldn't have anything along. I accept this most outlandish of invitations: dinner party turned birthing party.

Watching a woman give birth doesn't seem real. It's like a dream. Margot in her polka-dotted bikini being helped into the birth pool. The midwife is calm and I don't catch her name. I also don't know if her role is any different from Joanne's. I keep this realization to myself, certain my ignorance in this matter would be the object of much derision. Joanne and her assistant calmly and serenely walk around, timing contractions and asking Margot how she's feeling. Samuel paces, paces, paces. I take on the role of court jester, busily yammering on about anything I can think of. Margot laughs in her haze. After a while, Oberon and I stand back and watch. The blur of life is beginning all around us. Music is playing throughout the house. Fresh-cut flowers are everywhere. There is laughter, there are phone calls to be made. Life is coming. Life is pushing its way into this little house in the hills.

"Okay, Margot, sweetheart, you're fully dilated," the midwife says, Joanne right at her side. As the sun comes up, there is not one anecdote or joke left at the bottom of my bag of tricks. I've been a one-woman all-night telethon where the only calls have been from Daniel. He's been calling me all night. I've let the calls go straight to voice mail.

"I'm ready," Margot says. Samuel has changed into his swim shorts with no shirt. I've gotten used to a half-naked Margot being escorted around the house for bathroom breaks and leg stretches. Samuel's family is on the way from New Orleans, and Margot's family is taking the red-eye in from Wisconsin. They should all be arriving shortly.

"Okay, Margot, go ahead and focus for me," the midwife says. The sloshing water and the scent of candles will be forever burned in my brain. Jasmine, I think. I sit in the chair and hold my mug of steaming yogi tea. I made up a batch somewhere around four in the morning. I also baked off a batch of scones, and I laid them out on a tray sometime around five-thirty. When in doubt—bake.

With every quiet moment, I'm haunted by Daniel's absence. There's something bigger happening here this morning. No squeaky hospital floors. No heart monitors and tubes every-where. That scared me at first. I thought it would be gross or hard to look at. But all I've seen this morning is family. Life. Soothing water and soft music. Its very simplicity is stunningly beautiful. I remember again how I've tried to complicate everything over the years. Each dessert the carefully measured set of cabalistic ingredients. Each relationship a complex maze of fear and no trust. That perfection is somehow an attainable goal. I think of my new approach to food. "Simple and pure" is not ordinary or pedestrian. Having someone see me naked, warts and all, and love me anyway is by far the sweetest delicacy of all.

There is more water sloshing. Samuel sits behind Margot in the pool. Her full weight is leaning on him. Her hair is wet and braided tightly. That was one thing I could do for her.

Margot's face contorts in pain, and Samuel holds her.

"Here he is! Okay, sweetheart, the baby's here!" The midwife reaches below the water, and Margot's face relaxes. She immediately wells up with tears. Samuel is crying. We're all crying.

"It's a boy! It's a boy!" Even Oberon gets up for that minute and walks toward the birthing pool. Samuel curls over Margot's exhausted body as the midwife brings the baby up to Margot's polka-dotted bikini, and there. Right there.

Flash.

That indelible image of Margot, Samuel, and their tiny son is the most beautiful thing I've ever seen. Everyone is looking at everyone else. Are you seeing this? they must be thinking. His tiny, tiny hands. His little eyes blinking and blinking. He cries and sniffles. Margot and Samuel are gazing at the boy. They kiss. Samuel smoothes her hair. She can't stop crying and touching the baby all over. Is he real? Is he okay? Samuel quietly wipes away tear after tear.

"What will you name him, dear?" Joanne says, offering Samuel the tools to cut the umbilical cord. He does so with precision and confidence. Margot and Samuel look at the boy.

"Julian," Samuel says.

Margot looks up at Samuel and kisses him right on the jaw-line. It's so impromptu and, oddly enough, private. Joanne begins the cleanup as the midwife climbs out of the birthing pool. Margot tries to get Julian to breast-feed, but there's far too much commotion. At last Margot looks at me. Her eyes are gleaming and full of life. I can't get myself under control.

"Isn't he beautiful, Elisabeth?" Margot asks.

"He's unimaginable. He's gorgeous," I say. As I look at Julian, I allow tear after tear to fall. Thank God I'm in a room where everyone is crying, even Julian.

Oh, God. It's happening. Do I just walk around like this? How do people walk around like this? Am I going to start crying at movies now? I thought it was an aberration when I got teary watching an ad for Toys for Tots the other day. Did that start to open the floodgates? Is this the Big Bang I've been waiting for? Not the moment my two worlds collided but the moment I col-lided with myself?

"Do you want to hold him?" Samuel walks over to me with his brand-new baby boy. His face looks so calm, like he's been fulfilled somehow.

I look right in Samuel's deep brown eyes and hold out my arms. "Yes, I'd love to," I answer. Samuel adjusts Julian's silk cowboy blankie and passes him to me. Julian is cooing and simultaneously sucking on his entire tiny hand. His eyes are calm, and he looks up at me with an unblinking wisdom. His little fingernails. His tiny nose. His dimpled chin. He's perfect.

"You are quite the Christmas gift," I coo. I am swaying back and forth, cradling Julian.

Samuel looks on. "You're putting him to sleep," he says. The phone rings. It's been ringing all morning. Samuel asks if I'll hold Julian while he gets the phone. I nod. I hear Samuel in the distance. The proud papa. He's giving directions to the new house. He says to bring food and drink. There's laughter, and Samuel says his son's name. His voice catches.

"Julian," he says.

"They almost named you Lot," I whisper, swaying back and forth. Julian's eyes close. If he only knew.

I slip out when Margot and Samuel's families converge upon the house. Samuel asks me to do him a quick favor—he thinks he might have left his cell phone at the Santa Monica house. Could I stop by and see on my way to Montecito? I have to drop in and get some clothes for my trip up the coast anyway, so I tell him I will, and I hop in my car. It's barely six in the morning. There's no traffic as I head down onto Sunset Boulevard. Daniel's probably at the airport already. I check the time once more. He probably hasn't boarded yet. I dial his cell phone. Please pick up. Please pick up.

"Hello?" His voice is urgent.

"Hey," I say.

"Where are you? Where have you been?" Daniel asks.

"Margot had the baby. He's just lovely. They named him Julian."

"Where are you?" Daniel asks again.

"I'm driving from Silver Lake over to the Santa Monica house before I head on up to Montecito. Samuel thinks he left his cell phone there, and I've got to grab some extra clothes. But I just—"

"Elisabeth, I'm so sorry about last night," Daniel begins.

"You don't have to be. It's the holidays. They make people do crazy things—like buy houses. You can't get rid of me that easily," I add, weaving through the empty streets of Los Angeles.

"I can't?" Daniel softens. I can hear the smile in his voice. I have to take this leap of faith. Loving someone and letting him know how important he is won't automatically trigger his inevitable exodus from my life. With Daniel, I'm home. It's pure and simple. Not because of who he is but because of who I am when I allow myself to be trusted and loved.

"No, you can't," I say, finally acclimating to this big, new aquarium.

"Okay, well, merry Christmas. Merry Christmas to your family," Daniel says.

"Merry Christmas," I say. Daniel signs off. I'm glad I caught him but wish we had more time before he flew home.

After another half an hour on the road, I turn the final corner and pull up to the Santa Monica house. I grab my purse, slam the door, and beep my car locked, then run up the walkway to the front door. I'm anxious to get up to Montecito and see my family. Anxious to see Rascal. Mom. Dad.

There is Daniel, sitting on the front porch. "Hey," he says, creaking and popping to a standing position. His Jayhawk overnight bag is at his feet. He's leaning on a huge cardboard box with a red ribbon stuck to the side.

"I thought—" I let out a faint sob.

"I couldn't. I just—" Daniel stops. I put my hand over my mouth. The tears are rolling down my face. Daniel waits. He fiddles with the ribbon on the present. "I thought I could put it up—maybe—when we got back," he says, turning the box to reveal that it's a basketball hoop. "You won't believe how many stores I had to go to—Christmas Eve and all."

"You stayed," I blubber.

Daniel steps down off the front porch. "So, this is it, huh?" he soothes, focusing in on me, trying to get as close as he can.

"This is it," I say, running my hand all the way down his arm and grasping his hand. I lean in to him, and we kiss. My lips are wet and salty with tears. Daniel laces his fingers in mine.

My eyes close; I let him stroke the side of my face. I open my eyes and smile. We turn around. We're facing the front facade now. It couldn't look more divine. We walk forward and Daniel bends down, hooks his gym bag over his shoulder, and leans the cardboard box against the porch railing.

"Home," I say, turning the key in the lock and running quickly inside to punch in the code while the beeping blasts throughout the house. Daniel stands on the porch. The beeping stops, and I hold my hand out over the threshold. My hand is wide open. My eyes are unflinching.

"Needs a lot of work," Daniel says, smiling, taking my hand, and leading me inside.

about the author

I was born and bred in Pasadena, California. I've held every degrading job one could think of, until I finally realized my only talent lies in writing. Thank God, someone else thought so, too. *Seeing Me Naked* is my second novel.

Five Recipes You'll Find in
Seeing Me Naked

1. Poppa Don's Chicken and Dumplings

2- to 3-pound whole chicken, cleaned

2 1-quart containers chicken broth

½ teaspoon each: sage, thyme, marjoram, and summer savory

1 teaspoon Hungarian sweet paprika

1 clove fresh garlic, crushed

12 to 16 ounces red potatoes, skins on, halved

8 ounces baby carrots, peeled and cut in 1-inch chunks

8 ounces fresh sweet corn, cut off the cob

8 ounces petite green peas

1 cup heavy cream

3 tablespoons butter

3 tablespoons Bisquick

Salt and pepper to taste

Dumplings

2 cups Bisquick mix

⅔ cup whole milk

To a large 8-quart Dutch oven, add chicken, breast side down, stock and all seasonings. Bring to a full, rapid boil. Reduce to a simmer and cover. Cook for 45 minutes.

(continued)

Remove chicken from stock and set aside to cool. Add potatoes and carrots to chicken stock and cook for 15 minutes. Add corn and peas and cook another 10 minutes.

Debone cooked chicken, tear into bite-size pieces, and add to stock.

Add heavy cream and return to a boil.

Melt butter in a small saucepan and add Bisquick. Whip into a roux. Slowly add this roux to the stock, stirring until the mixture is the consistency of a medium gravy. Add salt and pepper to taste.

Dumplings

In a mixing bowl, add Bisquick to milk, mixing with a heavy spoon into a soft, doughy consistency.

Bring chicken back to a low boil and spoon heaping table-spoons of the dumpling mixture on top. They should look like little white pillows floating on the stew. Cook uncovered for 10 minutes on low heat, then cook an additional 10 minutes covered.

Serve dumplings into the bottom of a bowl, and spoon the chicken mixture on top.

2. Harry's Bar French 75s

Created by Harry MacElhone of Harry's Bar in Paris, 1925. Named after the 75 field gun used by the French army during World War I.

³⁄₄ jigger gin
½ jigger freshly squeezed lemon juice
½ jigger simple syrup
Champagne

Combine all ingredients except champagne.

Shake and strain into a champagne flute. Top off with
champagne.

3. Sandra Pelaez's Silky, Roasted Pumpkin Flan

1 cup sugar for caramelo
1 cup roasted pumpkin puree (fresh or canned)
1 14-ounce can condensed milk
14 ounces half-and-half
1 teaspoon vanilla
6 eggs
2 tablespoons cornstarch
1 tablespoon pumpkin pie spice

Preheat oven to 350°.

*(Skip the next few steps if you use canned pumpkin for the
puree.)*

Deseed one basketball-sized pumpkin. Cut pumpkin into
eighths.

Roast for 1 hour or until tender.

Remove skin. Puree the meat of the pumpkin with a hand mixer.
It's best to use the softest part of the pumpkin.

Use the cup of sugar to make the caramelo in a small heavy-
duty saucepan.

Melt on low heat until golden-brown. Don't stir, swirl—no
metal utensil can touch the caramel, or it will crystallize.

Pour a swirl in each ramekin or the pan you'll use for the flan.
Set aside.

(continued)

In a large bowl, mix the pumpkin puree and all the other
remaining ingredients.
Pour mixture into ramekins or baking dish. Set in a water bath.
Bake at 350° for 1½ hours or until a knife comes out clean.
Remove from water bath, let cool, and chill for 3 to 6 hours
(6 is better; overnight is best).
To unmold: dip bottom of pan in a warm-water bath. Run a
knife around the side of the pan to loosen. Invert platter.

4. Cherry Clafouti

Fresh cherries highly recommended. This is a super, simple
dish, and it relies on the taste of the cherries!

2 pounds* fresh cherries, pitted, or one 16-ounce package frozen unsweetened pitted dark sweet cherries,
thawed and drained.
1 tablespoon plus ½ cup sugar
1 teaspoon cornstarch
4 large eggs
Pinch salt (ha!)
⅓ cup all-purpose flour
1 cup whole milk
¼ cup (½ stick) unsalted butter, melted
1 teaspoon grated lemon peel
1 teaspoon vanilla extract
Powdered sugar

Preheat oven to 325°.
Butter shallow baking dish. Combine cherries, 1 tablespoon
sugar, and cornstarch in medium bowl; toss to coat.

*Enough so that the cherries will blanket whatever baking dish you're
using.

Arrange cherries in bottom of prepared dish. Whisk eggs, salt, and remaining ½ cup sugar in large bowl to blend. Whisk in flour. Add milk, butter, lemon peel, and vanilla extract; whisk until smooth. Pour custard over cherries.

Bake clafouti until set in center and golden on top, about 55 minutes. Cool slightly. Sprinkle powdered sugar over and serve warm.

The only thing to watch for is overcooking, which will cause a rubbery batter, so make sure to watch the dish and gauge how it's cooking.

5. Yogi Tea

3 quarts water
20 cloves
20 whole green cardamom pods, crushed
20 whole black peppercorns
5 whole sticks of cinnamon
3 to 5 slices of fresh gingerroot
milk
honey

Combine all ingredients, bring to a boil, and then simmer for an hour. (Optional: Steep one black tea bag in the mixture for some caffeine. Remove tea bag.) Let sit for 2 to 3 hours or overnight, depending on how strong you like the taste.

Strain the tea and discard the used spices.

Add about ¼ cup milk for every ¾ cup of tea and bring to a boil again.

Add honey to taste.

Before you add the milk, store the tea in a glass container in the refrigerator for later use.